Praise for The Consequences

"*The Consequences* attempts something that's not easy, and succeeds. A person thinks about herself exhaustively, yet doesn't become a bore. She writes about what she's doing and you want to know all about it because it's so vividly told. The temptation not to exist, to disappear from the world you're walking around in, the art you come upon and live with—when you write it down it sounds like heavy going; When you read it it's light. So read it."

—Cees Nooteboom, Award-winning author of *The Following Story* and *Rituals*

"In this novel, tingling with ambition and fascinating ideas, the life and art of the main character revolve around loss, existence and disappearance. A determined tone characterizes this crazy book."

—NRC Handelsblad — 5 stars

"A surprisingly mature debut, shaped by deep knowledge of human nature."

—Holger Heimann, WDR 3

"An impressive novel on the art of creative living or the creative and destructive vital force of being an artist."

—Maarten Asscher

"How is it that some people aren't able to tell that their own lives are a highly gripping story? Minnie can't do that. Weijers fortunately can."

—Vogue (Germany)

"This sharp and luminous debut novel, of which Beckett is the real mentor, also gives pride of place to a "neonatalist," in other words a specialist in newborns, which will not astonish anyone in a history that speaks of art, that is to say, also, of the search for origins."

—Le Point

"Birth. Floating identity. Who we are in the eyes of others—these themes are at the heart of *The Consequences*. At first, however, the book resembles a series of brilliant variations on the contemporary artistic scene. [...] The tone is created in the first pages. Ironic and sharp. Weijers mocks the extreme narcissism prevalent in these circles. She spares us the boring question "What is art?" but questions the boundaries between artwork and life, between the visible and the interior self. [...] An amazing game of mirrors. [...] Original and promising. Other books are sure to follow."

—Le Monde

"A smart and wry view of the art business, referencing real artists and told by Minnie with a great deal of irony. At the same time, [the novel] is an in-depth biography of an artist who experiments with vanishing into her own art."

—Augsburger Allgemeine

"*The Consequences* is a text replete with truths about grief, love and failed opportunities. Existing is a difficult task, as each character testifies."

—Libération

"A multifaceted portrait of a female artist ... full of astute observations."

—BÜCHERmagazin

"A bit of mystery, some philosophy, a lot of art and some existentialism—out pops a sparkling, surprising, refreshing story."

—EMOTION (Germany)

Niña Weijers

The Consequences

The Consequences

By Niña Weijers
Translated by Hester Velmans

DoppelHouse Press gratefully acknowledges the support of
the Dutch Foundation for Literature.

Nederlands
Nletterenfonds
dutch foundation
for literature

Publisher's Cataloging-in-Publication data

Names: Weijers, Niña, author. | Velmans, Hester, translator
Title: The Consequences / by Niña Weijers ; [translated from the Dutch by
Hester Velmans.]
Description: Los Angeles, CA: Dopplehouse Press, 2017.
Identifiers: ISBN 978-0-9978184-3-7 (pbk.) | 978-0-9978184-2-0 (Hardcover) |
978-0-9978184-4-4 (ebook) | LCCN 2017945533
Subjects: LCSH Art--Fiction. | Conceptual art--Fiction. | Women artists--Fiction. |
Amsterdam (Netherlands)--Fiction | BISAC FICTION / General
Classification: LCC PT8177.33 E33 C66 2017 | DDC 839.3--dc23

PRINTED IN THE UNITED STATES

DoppelHouse Presss
Los Angeles, California

“I really like that moment when the performance becomes life itself.”

—Marina Abramović

PROLOGUE

THE DAY Minnie Panis vanished from her own life for the third time, the sun hung low in the sky and the moon was high. It was February 11, 2012, the day was bright and cold, but not cold enough: even early that morning she had felt the warmth of the sun on the pale, chapped skin on her face. It was Saturday.

For several days in a row there had been a hard freeze. The sluices of Amsterdam's inner city were closed, and for the first time in years there was skating on the canals. Long-distance skating tours were organized and called off, people speculated there might even be an *Elfstedentocht*, the famous Eleven-Cities marathon, yes, and then again no; a winter's dance keeping the country on its toes, like the gyrations of a stock market in which everyone owned shares. Then, abruptly, the freeze was over. The sky grew grey and moist, appearing not gentler, but harder, emptier. Yellow ice floes canted up out of the Herengracht, beer cans and empty chips bags came bobbing up to the surface, and it was as if everyone had only just begun to be aware of the cold, and the weight of winter.

The human brain is remarkably shortsighted when it comes to both love and the weather: it believes the current conditions will last forever, and it learns nothing, not one thing, from the past, which may be trying to make itself heard, but shouts it helplessly into the wind. So when the sun broke through on that Saturday in February, no one had taken that possibility into account. Thousands of eyes blinked in surprise upon beholding the splendid, improbable light that had suddenly spread across the world, turning every molecule in the atmosphere blue. On days like that you have little choice. You can keep the curtains closed, but outside the world stretches itself out, and everything out there is stretched with it, onward and upward, toward the sun.

You may wonder why Minnie deliberately stepped out onto the thin ice at around two o'clock that afternoon, and stood there as it gave way, only slightly startled when this started happening beneath her feet, this transformation of solid into liquid. Or why she wasn't just seeing the trees but was really *staring at* them and was certain they were sycamores. Or why she didn't instinctively throw out her arms as in a parody of a tightrope walker, or why the hell none of it made any sound at all.

2012

MINNIE SAT ACROSS from her mother in a big lunch café along the water. It was a noisy place with a predictable and expensive menu, a tastefully restrained interior and servers who entered the orders on touch screens that made eye contact a thing of the past. It was their usual meeting place.

That morning her mother had called her at the crack of dawn. A rare occurrence, not only for the early hour, but also because their communication was mainly by email, meant to schedule, without too many sidetracks, their thrice-a-month lunch dates at which they'd update each other in broad strokes on the latest developments in their lives. Her mother understood very little about Minnie's life, and Minnie knew just as little about hers. How two people could be so different and yet related by blood had astonished her even when she was a little girl, gazing at the cheesy glow-in-the-dark stars on her ceiling and wondering if it was possible to wind up in someone's belly by accident.

"Thank God," her mother had blurted out when Minnie answered the phone that morning. "You're still alive."

"Of course I'm still alive," said Minnie. "Why wouldn't I be?"

There was a brief silence.

"I had a dream about you just now," said her mother. "In my dream I walked into your bedroom, it was your childhood room, but you were grown up. You were lying on the floor next to the bed, tightly wrapped up in a sheet, like a mummy. I rushed up to you to pull the sheet off your face, but it was already too late, your lips and eyelids were blue and your skin was stretched white and taut over your bones. Even though I really didn't want to, I touched your face with the tip of my finger. It was hard and cold, like, I don't know, a package of fish sticks in the freezer. It was so, so terribly... realistic."

Minnie had listened to her mother's story open-mouthed. There was no one she knew who was as down-to-earth as her mother, so averse to anything that did not fit within the most concrete, obvious reality. Her mother was also utterly unsentimental. Minnie had never seen her laugh uncontrollably, or weep, or scream in fury; her emotions were doled out in minute doses that were never amplified. The life of her mother, Minnie sometimes thought, followed the lines of a painting by Mondrian: horizontal and vertical, without even the slightest deviation. She was, in short, the last person in the world you'd expect to attach any significance to something as irrational as a *dream*.

"I really don't know why I'm calling you," said her mother, clearly getting a hold of herself. "Now that I've said it out loud it sounds quite silly, and not at all realistic."

"Oh well," Minnie had said. In an impulse, perhaps to help her mother get over her unease, she'd suggested they have lunch together that day, and now here they were. It was quite poignant, really, she thought—a dream breaking through her mother's body-armor of rationality just like that.

It was the first of February and extremely cold even for the time of year. A tumble on the ice the day before had left Minnie with a bruise on her hip that was changing color by the hour and that she couldn't help touching to see if it still hurt—which it did.

"Sorry about ranting and raving at you like that on the phone," her mother said before she'd even taken off her coat. She sounded like herself again, bright and businesslike. "I had just woken up, I wasn't thinking."

Minnie observed the deliberate way her mother extricated herself from her coat, pulling her scarf neatly through the sleeve, smoothing her skirt, and sitting down. She was beautiful, her mother, in an unostentatious but well-preserved way. A professional. Minnie remembered her mother waiting for her when she got out of school, how different she was from the other mothers, who simply seemed born for that role, blending in with the schoolyard, their children, the other mothers, in an utterly natural way. Her own mother always looked surprised to find herself standing there, as if she had gone for a stroll and ended up at the school by accident.

For the past thirty years her mother had been working at the Cancer Society, where she'd made herself indispensable as the right-hand person of every director who came along. She talked about the war on cancer with something bordering on real passion, although it was never very clear to Minnie if that passion was fueled by the idea of battling a disease, or because she was so good at raking in large sums of money for the fund.

Once properly installed, she peered at her daughter narrowly for a moment. "You look different. Not worse, but different," she said. "Have you gained weight?"

Minnie understood she ought to take this as a compliment. She had been too small for her age from the time she was born, and had never had a true growth spurt. As an adult her build was still childishly petite, which made her infinitely attractive to a certain type of male. That, combined with an asymmetrical face in which everything was just a touch off kilter. People, men, liked to read something wild and untamable in that face. Perhaps they weren't wrong. Maybe your life lived up to the face you were given.

"How's the cancer biz?" she asked, pressing hard on the bruise. Everything was just a replay of the same old; the same old questions, the same old answers.

"Not great," said her mother. "People keep getting sick. They smoke too much and they eat garbage, that's what it comes down to. Meanwhile there's one therapeutic breakthrough after another, but sure, what do you expect if people keep on courting death with their bad habits... I sometimes think there must be a direct connection between the economic downturn and the growing incidence of the disease. A society that's running out of money all over the place, you know... ah, well. A colleague of mine saw you in a magazine recently, I don't remember which."

A waitress with a tablet took their order, wildly stabbing at the screen. "Sorry," she muttered, not looking up, and then again, walking away, "sorry."

Now her mother would ask her how *her* work was going. Minnie would throw out something vague, her mother would mutter inattentively and then start talking about something else. Then they would eat their soup and fall silent, each in her own way.

As a teen Minnie had for a long time been obsessed with speculating what her father was like. She could stare in the mirror for minutes on end, trying to discover a face behind her own face, an explanation her mother wouldn't give her and which she wasn't going to insist on, either. It had been a passing phase.

"Are you still with, what's his name, that artist?"

"No, Mother," said Minnie. "It's been six months." I cheated on him, she would have liked to add, I cheated on him without the least bit of guilt, apparently I am the kind of person who is good at doing that. She thought about the photographer. To be exact, he was constantly in her thoughts, like a buzzing undercurrent, for several reasons, none of which were all that important. The thing was to think about him for the time being in terms of a project, she decided, if such a thing existed.

Minnie never asked about her mother's love life. As far as she knew her mother hadn't had a boyfriend in decades, and she could not foresee that changing any time soon. Her mother was carrying something hard inside her, as if she had a pebble sewn into her body. It may at one time have been soft and gentle, but had petrified with the passing of time. Maybe love was something you could just tuck away in a drawer at some point, together with other remnants of the past you no longer needed.

"And how's your work?" her mother asked.

"Nothing new," said Minnie. "A time for reflection."

"I read something recently about an American artist who swallows colored liquids and vomits them onto a canvas. The canvases sell for a lot of money. I don't understand how something like that can be called art. That people are willing to pay thousands of dollars for that."

"No," said Minnie, "that doesn't sound like real art to me."

She remembered how her mother had just silently nodded when at the age of eighteen Minnie had announced she wanted to go to art school. She hadn't brought it up in the following weeks either, which had made Minnie furious, and more determined than ever. One evening a few days before the start of term, when Minnie was about to move into a tiny attic room in Amsterdam-West, she found her mother sitting at the kitchen table with a glass of wine. She pushed an envelope across the table at her with five hundred euros in it, a strange, novel currency that looked like toy money. "For your art supplies," she had said, and that had been that. In the years since, she had faithfully come to every opening, and although Minnie had never hear her say one word about the art itself, she did seem, in her own inscrutable way, proud, or at the very least not overly critical.

They parted on the sidewalk in front of the café. As always, Minnie couldn't wait for the moment right afterward, when they would both turn and walk away in opposite directions, back to their own lives. Just as she was about to turn, her mother put a hand on her shoulder.

"Minnie," she said, with that same scrutinizing gaze. "I want you to know that I always wanted to do my best for you. You were so tiny, back then... sometimes I was afraid the world would just swallow you whole, and never spit you back out. I wanted to make you able to defend yourself. That dream, last night, was nonsense, of course, but... well, Ok, you just—take care of yourself." She seemed to be about to say something else too, but then changed her mind.

Minnie gave her mother a quick peck on the cheek, the limp skin of a woman no longer young. As she walked away, she could feel her mother standing there watching her daughter striding down the street, wincing, cringing, until she turned the corner and was no more.

IT WAS A PRECARIOUS undertaking, a project that could fail in countless ways, and that was probably exactly the reason she had taken it on. Minnie might hardly know the guy, but she had a strong and perhaps empirically-based suspicion that they were made of the same cloth, she and the photographer.

They had been introduced to each other a year earlier at the art opening of a mutual acquaintance who had won a major prize with his canvases, which were submerged in chemical baths. Weird paintings, they were, with oily patches that changed shape as you walked past. "A horizon, a window," the gallery owner, holding a glass of white wine, said to Minnie, "and at the same time they cast a disquieting light on the interior of the soul."

The next few times they met, it was at the photographer's place, an apartment whose walls were bare of any photos. This was an oddity much to Minnie's taste, as was the fact that he was seventeen years older, never married, and had no children, mortgage, household insurance or food in his refrigerator.

A man without a shadow.

Their trysts followed a set pattern, more or less: Minnie would call him, she'd arrive at his apartment at a set time, they'd have sex, and then they'd order take-out Thai or finish a pint of Ben & Jerry's Chunky Monkey between them, depending on the time of day and what they were in the mood for.

Their conversations weren't significant or very arresting in themselves, but they were part of the rhythm, and that's why they mattered. Later, when the affair was over, Minnie had to conclude that the exchanges they'd had were in fact the most concrete memory she had of those months with the photographer. As if that had been the real reason for getting together: idle chat, saying nothing in a way that's possible only in very particular circumstances, words that mean something because they don't mean anything and so, free of substance, remain rooted in the area between the chest and the belly, where the body stores human touch.

They had an unspoken agreement: she never slept over. Minnie knew that for the photographer, as for herself, these hook-ups were mere interludes in their lives, and not meant for the long-term. Commercial breaks set on mute, letting the excesses of our consumer society silently scroll by.

The photographer was an interesting bed partner; he'd growl softly as he bit Minnie's neck, and grew very excited if she stuck her fingertip in his anus. "I can't think of anything I'd like better than to be a Doberman," he once sighed, flopping onto his stomach beside her. "To pad around all day with your tail in the air and your butt in the wind." She loved his unerring intuition in figuring out the needs of his own body and hers. She loved the brazen greediness of the way he kissed her armpits, her back, the insides of her thighs. The way he buried his nose between her labia and tongued her crack as if it was an envelope he was carefully licking shut. Some men remained totally human when they fucked, because they did it mostly in their heads. This one did not fall into that category.

"You have rare and phenomenal animal traits," she told him one afternoon as she lay on her stomach and he grabbed her hips from behind not all too gently, although not exactly roughly, either.

"Oh yeah?" he said, making a growling sound, then bit into her shoulder, quite hard.

She was only too aware how very clichéd the situation was, and there were moments when she'd suddenly be overcome with shame for the ludicrous biting and panting, the fingers, the tongues, to say nothing about the gallons of ice creams afterward. Still, she never had a moment's guilt, and to her own astonishment, was finding it so simple to lie (or omit to tell the truth) that it was easy to tell herself there was nothing to hide anyway. It was an addiction. That was the conclusion that was fairly indisputable for now.

The entire affair would probably have limped on quietly for a while longer, petering out slowly the way most such things peter out, had Minnie strictly kept to her own rules. The problem with rules is that people like to kid themselves they are elastic. This applies most of all to self-imposed rules, in which the impulse to call the shots finds itself hopelessly at loggerheads with the one who is supposed to comply. No good can come of that—even if it is only a matter of perception.

Minnie broke her own rule on one of those days between the middle and end of summer, that last gasp of hot weather, so bloated with heat that the contrast between sun and shade was the only thing that mattered. It had seemed even hotter in the nighttime, or maybe not hotter but more oppressive, the darkness heavier than the light.

Minnie and the photographer had sweated themselves into a stupor, their sodden bodies absorbing each other's humidity, leaving their skin mottled red and white, wrung out like wet rags, stretched to their carnal essence. There they lay. Perhaps, thought Minnie, it was these few minutes between sex and getting up that justified the lust, that made it all worthwhile. Those few minutes of consummate exhaustion, during which the body and the world are in perfect harmony and you're certain that gravity will be strong enough to hold everything in place.

When a little later she emerged dripping wet from a cold shower, he asked her if she would stay the night, then tossed a gossamer silk nightgown at her.

"Present for you, kid. No big deal."

She knew he was lying. He had broken the old rules, and this was the opening move of some new game. But what game?

"Know why I'm so crazy about you?" he said, not waiting for an answer. "That look, there, that exact look. I can almost *hear* the little cogs spinning inside that head."

Why had she stayed? Maybe it was the way the slippery silk felt between her fingers, the incredible lightness of the thing, the cool cyan blue. Or maybe it was the heat smothering everything and drawing all the oxygen from the air, the way you can suck all the flavor out of an ice pop, or maybe it was the time of day, grown so sluggish and listless that even the clanging of the streetcars down below existed only as a faint echo of impatience that's long lost its urgency. Or perhaps it was simply that word, *present*, which tends to come with ramifications, because every word can have a secret agenda, and some more so than others.

Naturally, there are times when saying yes isn't a way of getting out of saying no. Times when it has something to do with courage, and not with cowardice, with confirmation, with determination, a grand self-affirmation, but this was not one of those rare times. Especially not if you take into account that what Minnie said was "OK," and OK is, as everyone knows, only another way of saying nothing.

She immediately knew it wasn't a good idea. The photographer's place wasn't meant for sleeping, or for having breakfast, or for anything to do with living. The photographer's home was a place for leaving.

The problem with making a wrong decision is that, once you've taken it, it becomes irreversible at the very moment it might still be undone. So there was Minnie, prone like a dog in the tropics, incapable of moving. The air, heavy and still, was pressing her into the mattress, and the open windows let nothing in or out. I'm getting flattened, she thought to herself, I'm getting crushed and it's my own fault.

The next morning she awoke unusually late from a deep slumber. She found a note next to her pillow. *Just gone to the studio. Back soon. Stay.* She snatched together her clothes, stuffing the silk night dress—Lanvin, she saw on the label—in her handbag. Crossing the street, she looked back once, thinking, I'll just look back once. The building shimmered in the heat as if conceding that it had been a mirage all along.

What did she know about the photographer on that last, sweltering morning of August 2011, as she turned to look at the hologram of his home and realized she would never go back? Practically nothing. Yes, that he was a fashion photographer. That he smoked

Gauloises, and that in that he reminded her of her very first boyfriend, who also smoked Gauloises, which he pronounced *Gollywas*, "and a pack of Gollywas, please." That he opened his mouth wide when he came, making no sound, a silent movie scream. That he had tricked her into something, she didn't know what, and that she would never be strong enough to resist him. That he was a man who bought Lanvin for his lovers, for Christ's sake.

She rode her bike straight to the home of her boyfriend, a rather tortured artist who had been trying for ten years to market himself as a promising newcomer, told him about the affair, had a paintbrush hurled at her head, and that was the end of that. For three days she didn't get out of bed. She had lost something, and she knew that it wasn't the tortured artist.

IN 2006, NOT LONG after finishing her studies, Minnie had said in a magazine interview that she was an artist because that was what people called her. *"Artist against her own will,"* was the headline, with underneath a grainy portrait in which her face showed as a black-and-white sketch, a head like a rock, rough, proud, plain and utterly unadorned. It struck her as a bit exaggerated, she hadn't meant it that categorically, but her agent had been jubilant on the phone.

"This is it, baby! This is going to be your breakthrough. An artist who doesn't want to be an artist, that's fucking brilliant."

She had met the agent a few months before at the opening of a group exhibition titled *Shared History: Decolonizing the Image* in the former post office building on Oosterdocks wharf. The exhibition's curator had seen her final art school project, *Does Minnie Panis Exist?* and thought it fit the theme perfectly. Minnie wondered what the theme meant in the first place, and suspected her work would have fit in just as perfectly if the theme had been "Chickens and Other Barnyard Animals." Five minutes before the doors opened, the agent made a beeline for Minnie's work. He shook her hand, then spent several minutes staring at her work, deep in thought, as if considering his next move in a chess game. A thin man with fine, sharp features, glistening black hair and a faint hue to the skin. Some kind of mixed-race, although Minnie couldn't tell which. The most salient feature were the eyes, which were set extremely wide apart, almost untidily, as if they'd been stuck on his face haphazardly.

"It's not bad," he said. "But your attitude is lousy. You're standing there as if you're feeling contrite. Are you apologetic about your work?"

He never took his eyes off her work as he said it. Not that it was necessary, thought Minnie; those eyes of his, she was sure, must give him three hundred and sixty degree vision.

"No," she answered, mortified, "not really." As she said it she knew it wasn't true. In her eyes, her own finished work always had something bizarre about it, as if it was too little and at the same time too much, and she, the "artist," should be adding something to it and erasing it all at the same time.

"Does Minnie Panis exist?"

"I'm not sure about that yet."

"That's what I mean. Listen. You need me. This could be something. The imagery is interesting, and I appreciate the chutzpah. Now all you have to do is stand up straight as *act* as if you've created, what is it, 'a *decolonized image*', OK?"

Three years later her work had been shown in Leipzig's Museum der Bildenden Kunst, Barcelona's MACBA, the Kusthalle Fridericianum in Kassel, and the Louisiana Museum of Modern Art in Humlebaek, Denmark. For her next work, *Nothing Personal*, she was awarded the 2008 Prix de Rome, upon which she was declared to be "one of the most promising Dutch artists of her generation" by a correspondent in *Art Review,* which led more or less directly to her first international solo show, at Arndt & Partner in Berlin. There, in Berlin, she had lunch one rainy afternoon with Sophie Calle, who (by coincidence, or perhaps not) had seen the show and called Matthias Arndt to ask if the artist was still around. It was Calle who'd asked her, in French-accented English, if she considered herself an artist, upon which Minnie had replied, *"Je ne sais pas, je ne sais vraiment pas,"* a pathetic answer, but the only one that didn't sound like an outright lie.

The truth was that Minnie did not identify so much as an artist, as with her art—the things she made, the things that came to exist as art because they would not have any reason to exist otherwise. Being an artist was Minnie's passport, an identity card that gave her a place in a world where everything had to be legitimized. It had been bestowed on her by an art teacher in high school, followed by the instructors at art school, the collectors, the journalists, the curators, the gallery owners. They had seen an artist in Minnie because they had identity papers of their own that endowed them with the license, nay, the obligation to be the gatekeepers of the academies, the institutes, the foundations, the funds, the art grants, the talk shows, the museums, the galleries, the openings, the journals, and the corporate collections.

In the beginning Minnie had listened in amazement to what was being said about her work (the fact that her work was even being talked about), but little by little she came to understand that every form of identification, of legitimization, had its own vocabulary, and that the language of art consisted of words like *identity, engagement, vision* and *malaise.* Without the words, the entire edifice would collapse, and the artist would be a stateless person, illegitimate, unsanctioned and unhinged.

Minnie had met two artists at an art expo once, twin sisters, both of them so emaciated that their skin was grey. The sisters made video installations of the eating disorder they nurtured in each other. They had become world-famous and wealthy with these installations, which showed the dire consequences of the female beauty ideal, lambasted the consumer society, questioned both individualism and collectivism, etcetera. Truly, Minnie thought to herself, for some lunacies you couldn't come up with any word other than "art."

The fact that the way she'd acquired her artist's passport was by rejecting it, or, indeed, that every rejection on her part seemed to lead to renewed confirmation of her status as artist, was a paradox that continued to fascinate her. Often, on seeing her own work on the walls of a gallery or accepting another prize, she had the sensation of leaning over herself like a coroner leaning over his own corpse: the white noise of cause and effect reduced to nothing more than the banality of a bone fracture here or a bruise there. Art as death, but hey, who would go there in this day and age?

IT WAS A FLUKE, the year before she graduated from art school, that put Minnie on to the mammoth senior project that would later be shown in the Post Office-building show, the first and only one to sell without gallery representation, purchased for a ludicrously low price by a partly deaf collector who had made a status symbol of his antique hearing-aid trumpet.

The fluke was a rundown storefront in Kinkerstreet, the take-out joint Hiroshima Sushi. Minnie must have cycled past it a hundred times without noticing, but one fine afternoon she found herself sprawled on the sidewalk out front—she'd been trying to pry her buzzing cellphone out of her backpack while riding, and her front wheel had got stuck in the tram rails. The fall itself wasn't that spectacular, but since the backpack was zipped open, dozens of loose drawings were sent flying, a striking image that for a few frozen seconds bore a remarkable resemblance to Jeff Wall's *A Sudden Gust of Wind*, though it's doubtful anyone noticed.

A little Japanese man in a white cap had come darting out of the tiny store, and, nimbly weaving his way through the traffic not without risk to his own safety, started picking up Minnie's drawings. She'd wanted to stop him, it was just some unremarkable sketches from a live model class earlier that day. (A plump model sitting nearly motionless for almost an hour on a wooden folding chair, right arm dangling over the backrest. Minnie had imagined the wood digging deeper and deeper into the flesh, leaving harsh red grooves where it blocked the bloodstream. When the time was up, the woman had hastily thrown on a bathrobe, her naked body all of a sudden strangely vulnerable now that it no longer served a purpose.)

Minnie, seeing the little man vaguely bustling to save her worthless drawings from oblivion, was overcome by a stab of sadness somewhere in the region of her breastbone. Ever since she could remember, other people's kindness had generated in her a special kind of distress. As a child she had once burst into tears because her teacher had tried to explain to her with infinite patience why 1/4 + 1/5 did not equal 2/9. The teacher had thought she was crying out of frustration at not getting it, and Minnie hadn't been able to explain that her tears were meant for the teacher, for the fact that her patience was disproportionate to the purpose she was using it for. When at eighteen she read Camus' *Myth of Sisyphus*, about the whacky hero Sisyphus, condemned for all eternity to haul a heavy rock up a mountain only to have it roll down again of its own accord, it was as if she had finally found a rationale for the deep, wordless sadness she so often experienced as a child.

She wanted to shout that it wasn't necessary, but it was already too late, and suddenly it occurred to her that maybe it *was* necessary, not because those drawings needed to be saved, but for another reason. She watched the calm efficiency with which the man carried out his mission, and wished she had it in her to work on something with the same dedication, when the goal, to all intents and purposes, was quite banal. Maybe this, Minnie thought, is what they call enlightenment. She blushed. She had been to a guest lecture on Orientalism just last week; was she projecting that purportedly profound Eastern wisdom onto some random sushi vendor on Kinkerstreet? She picked up her bike and stared sheepishly at the scraped skin on her palms. Shreds of white pellicle spotted with myriad dots of red, the hands of a child. It wasn't until the little Japanese man handed her the sheets of drawing paper that she looked up, hearing herself say to her own surprise that she'd like to order some sushi. Articulating something out loud can awaken an unanticipated desire. Which was the case now: she was suddenly convinced that that was what she wanted, an order of sushi, the future making itself known, clear as water.

Edward Saïd can just go fuck himself, she thought, and, cradling the bundle of drawings in her arms like a baby, followed the man inside.

Hiroshima Sushi's interior was plastered with aerial photographs of the 1945 atomic disaster, black-and-white images of the flattened ghost city and, behind the counter, one of a young Emmanuelle Riva, infinitely mournful in her Japanese kimono. Not waiting for further instructions, the little man disappeared into the back, returning ten minutes later with a plastic box containing a selection of sushi glistening with almost obscene freshness.

"Thanks again, you know, for the drawings."

Minnie handed him a ten-euro bill.

"Yes," said the man. He looked at her impassively, as if he weren't really looking at her but at something that existed only in his own mind.

"You really shouldn't have. I mean, it was very nice of you."

"Yes," said the man.

Minnie wondered if he knew any Dutch besides "yes." She felt vaguely uncomfortable with their eyes on her, the man's and Emmanuelle Riva's, like the blind eyes of dead fish.

"All right then," she said. "Thanks again."

"Yes."

Minnie smiled and was about to turn around when the man pointed at the box. "I've given you an extra portion of ginger. To help you concentrate. I have cars, bikes and trams racing past my window all day long, and they've all got one of them phones clamped to their ears."

"Yes," said Minnie. She felt the blood rising to her face.

"People are so addicted to talking, they no longer see what's happening right under their noses. *Where you now?* they ask whoever's on the other end of the line. Over and over, where you now, where you now, where you now. While no one's anywhere but *on the phone* these days. At least, that's how *I* see it. You ought to be more careful, because a broken neck's still a broken neck. Are you an artist?" The man nodded at the drawings.

"Not really," said Minnie.

"Well, anyway, you should still be more careful," said the man. "We must learn to defend ourselves."

Upon which he gazed pensively at the door over Minnie's shoulder, as if at any moment something might appear there that couldn't tolerate the light of day.

When she got home Minnie put the sushi box down on the table before her, and what happened next was unexpected and yet made complete sense: the thought of sticking those blobs of raw fish in her mouth suddenly made her gag. The revulsion she felt was greater than her earlier hunger for it, and it startled her, the total reversal that had taken place, with the gleaming pieces of sushi now lying in the bottom of the garbage bin. Later that evening she carefully fished the sushi pieces back out of the trash bag, arranged them on a white sheet of paper, and photographed them from above with her Canon 450D. In an empty notebook she wrote:

January 25, 2005. Does Minnie Panis exist?

It was the start of a project that was to consume her for a year and a half, generating exactly 2,095 photos of her own trash, which came out to an average of 3.8 photos a day. In the beginning she tried to tell herself she was working on a project about the consumer society, overproduction, surpluses, limited shelf life; but soon she had to concede that these subjects really did not interest her, at least, not at the meta-level at which the artist is expected to take a socio-political stance.

No, her real motive was much simpler: she grew so fond of the simplicity of the ritual that its daily repetition gained an almost religious urgency. When, a few weeks into it, she had to skip three days because she forgot to bring her camera on a study trip to the Ruhr region, she'd felt such a sharp physical withdrawal that she had been ready to cut her trip short. It had taken her totally by surprise. Even more so because she had been laboring under the illusion that the project wouldn't keep her interest for much longer (it wasn't particularly original or provocative, after all), but she did cherish the feeling of missing it, and the extreme sense of relief when she came home, opened the garbage bin, took out a three-day-old sandwich, arranged it on a white piece of paper and opened the camera's aperture so wide that the photo turned out a bit overexposed, just enough to blur the contrast between object and background.

The more pictures she took, the more she grew convinced that it had very little to do with 'making art'. For the first time in her adult life she was doing something that had absolutely no purpose other than the act itself. The thought of doing something more with it faded into the background and then vanished into thin air. The photos weren't beautiful, they weren't deliberately ugly either, the only thing they had going for them was that they kept multiplying. But that could be said of so many other things.

The other projects Minnie worked on during this time period—the more or less compulsory curriculum of the art academy—were jumbled together in her memory as a vague mishmash of both semi-successful and utterly failed attempts to keep her teachers happy. When at the start of the last semester she saw her fellow students stressing out about the approaching finals, she realized all she had to show for herself was a lot of completely interchangeable crap that meant nothing and was ripe for being tossed straight onto the ever-growing mountain of art school trash. With a shock, she realized she wasn't an artist, and would never be one, either. The second shock was that she really couldn't care less. What's more, seldom had she felt as liberated.

And so she told the dean that she was quitting.

"That's the dumbest thing I've heard in a long time," he made no bones telling her. "That piece of paper may be meaningless, but if you quit now you'll never know what it is. I assume you know the myth of Sisyphus? *You*"—here he prodded his forefinger into Minnie's chest with undisguised scorn—"have now made it to somewhere halfway up the mountain with that heavy rock, and you don't feel like taking another step. Like some whiny little kid, you just want to give up, don't you, but the fact is: you don't have the right. You are responsible for that damn rock and it *has* to get to the top. The fact that it'll roll back down again in the end, doesn't matter. That's life. If you walk away now, you might as well lie down and bite the dust."

Over the next few weeks Minnie began sorting through all the trash photos she had taken in the past year and a half. Great amounts of empty plastic packaging were considered, apple cores, wilted flowers, milk cartons, postcards, rotting vegetables, putrid meat, fish bones, noodles, tomato sauce, bottles, tubes, boxes, cans, razors, underpants, menstruation pads, condoms, hairballs, CDs, flowerpots, paperclips, Band-aids, matches, cigarettes, suntan lotion, orange peel, umbrellas, broken glass, magazines, a television. The sheer quantity of it overwhelmed her: without her having any real awareness of it, a parallel trash-universe had come into being. It was both fantastic and horrifying, and, beyond that, irresistible.

She started working on it feverishly, obsessively. She slept when her eyes fell shut of their own accord and started working again the moment they flew open. Entire days went by when she'd forget to eat. The hunger that was making her lightheaded seemed a thing that was happening outside her body. When the work was finished, she could feel her bones under the surface of her skin, sharp and hard, the underpinnings of a building that is otherwise stripped bare.

She was exhausted and at the same time radically alive. She

hadn't the faintest idea what it was that she had created, even less what it *meant*, but for one long, heady moment she felt herself teetering on top of that mountain with her rock.

Then she discovered that gravity is the ultimate deciding principle.

A few years later a reporter for *De Groene Amsterdammer* would argue in an article about Minnie's early work that *Nothing Personal* (2008), crowned with the Prix de Rome, was in fact the diapositive of her final art school project of two years earlier. He used the term "self portrait in negative" for both works, a description that would later crop up again in a retrospective at Hamburg's Deichtorhallen, titled *Minnie Panis: Negative Selves.*

> In *Does Minnie Panis Exist?* we see the first contours of Panis' fascination with what I like to call the "self-portrait in negative." The seventeen-minute silent film consists of 2,095 images of trash scrolling by in fast and slow tempo. The grand finale happens in the last few minutes, when the images tumble after one another at such speed that the effect is almost stroboscopic. Every so often an image (an empty pill-strip, a sandwich) freezes for a few seconds, only to be swept up again in the great whirlpool of waste.
>
> Trying to find out if you exist by scrutinizing the stuff you throw out is of course ambiguous in more than one sense. If here it's "You are what you throw out," that "being" is far from unproblematic; it is in essence disposable; rather, it doesn't even really exist any more. Every confirmation of identity is also a denial, each discovery also a loss. This effect is strengthened by the flatness of the images, in which

the contrast between background and the photographed object is blurred.

Since the hallucinatory film starts off inviting the viewer to lose himself in the images, that finding/losing of the "self" becomes a theme relating not only to the artist—does Minnie Panis exist?—but also to anyone who identifies with the piece. The images may be personal (underwear, scraps of private notes), but they are also generic, imparting the sense that they hide more than they reveal.

Like a sorcerer, Panis makes herself vanish from the stage, only to pop up again in unexpected places, yet never for very long.

Minnie had been quite taken with that "sorcerer" label; there's nothing that enhances an artist's reputation as much as a bit of mystery. She had once come across the work of the Cuban-American Ana Mendieta, who in the seventies and eighties created a minor furor with her ritualistic blood- and mud-pieces. Not only did this Mendieta possess a great fascination for the occult; she was also fond of subversive self-portraits in which she would disfigure herself, pasting on moustaches and beards, distorting her face by pressing it onto plate glass, or rolling naked through chicken blood and feathers, leaving life-sized prints on a variety of surfaces—lugubrious riffs on the Shroud of Turin. Just when Mendieta, thirty-seven years old, was beginning to break through, she fell to her death from her New York apartment window. Her body slammed with such force into the roof of the delicatessen thirty-four floors below that it left an imprint. To this day nobody knows for sure if it was an accident, suicide, or murder, but that uncanny silhouette tied her life forever to her death, and her death to her art.

There were many others like Mendieta, naturally. Not only had Banksy gotten away with his concealed, enigmatic identity for years now, but his fame was in fact based on that carefully maintained mystery. There were writers who were never seen in photographs, but nevertheless sold millions of copies of their books; dandies who organized masked balls in French chateaux, with invitations in reverse-lettering and exclusive guest lists as lofty as the summit of Mt. Everest. Or geniuses who dwelled forever in the limbo of their early promise, because they died too young, or went insane, or became religious.

No, there was nothing wrong with a bit of mystery. As long as she herself didn't start believing in her oracular role, she'd be on the safe side.

IN NOVEMBER 2011, three months after Minnie lost both her official boyfriend and her lover in the space of an hour, and when she was just past the phase of thinking she recognized the photographer whenever she saw a dark haired man in the street, things took an unexpected turn. It began with a phone call from an acquaintance with a fashion label and a coke problem.

"Darling!' he screamed. "What the fuck!"

Minnie held the receiver a few inches from her ear.

"What the fuck what?"

"*Vogue*. Vee-oh-gee-you-ee."

"Vogue?"

"British *Vogue*, baby! Hysterical!"

Minnie wondered if he was referring to the fashion magazine or his own state of mind. It was shocking how little trouble people had telling you exactly how they felt. "In writing, one principle trumps all other principles," she had once heard a relatively famous author tell a group of young disciples. "Three words: *show, don't tell*. If someone's depressed, you don't write 'He's depressed'. You *show* that he is." A principle, Minnie thought, that must apply specifically to literature, since in real life people were depressed, sad, angry or hysterical because they *said* they were.

"Photos... really... new direction... no, really!"

"I can barely hear you," Minnie yelled back. "Where are you, for fuck's sake?"

She heard a pulsing drone, as if he were standing inside a gigantic heart pumping out gallons of blood.

"Wait. Can you hear me now? Can you hear me? Do you hear me?"

Something slammed shut somewhere. Then it was quiet.

"Berlin, baby, I'm in Berlin. Crazy shit."

"It's eleven a.m.," said Minnie. "On a Tuesday."

"If you say so. I stepped outside a couple hours ago, to get some Vitamin B into me, know what I'm saying? Sunlight on my skin."

"D," said Minnie. "Vitamin D."

"It isn't until you come staggering out of a club in Berlin that you can see how grand and brilliant daylight really is. Even if it's cloudy, or, no, especially if it's cloudy. Because you're not expecting it. But that's not the point, that's not what this is about, not why I called."

She heard a loud sniff. White rims around his nostrils, a swipe of the finger.

"So I was basking in that sunlight like a newborn, or maybe I mean *re*born, but anyway, I needed a smoke, so I stepped into one of those German newsstands..."

"A German newsstand?"

"Yeah, well, I don't know, they're different from the ones in Holland. They're German. Anyhow, I step into that newsstand and stand there recovering from all that sunlight when my eye just happens to fall on British *Vogue*, and what do I see?"

Silence.

"What did you see?"

"Minnie. Panis."

"My name?" The conversation had suddenly taken an even weirder turn.

"Bingo!" She heard rustling on the other end of the line. A second voice. *"Nein,"* whispered the friend, *"nein, wart! Moment,"* and then loudly again, "Minnie? Are you still there, Minnie? Listen, I have to go, all right? I just wanted to congratulate you. That's all. So congrats, baby. And remember..."

The rest of the sentence was swallowed by the drone on the other side of the door, monotonous as waves crashing against a shoreline of concrete. How on earth did people dance to that?

Minnie pulled on her coat and rushed to the international newspaper and magazine stand in the center of town. Her name was her name. At least, she couldn't imagine there could be anyone else in the world who'd had the bright idea of giving their baby that name.

*

It was a downright bizarre experience to open *Vogue* and find herself featured in a fashion spread on pages 82-92. It wasn't only bizarre because she hadn't known about it beforehand, or because it was in *Vogue,* or because she was wearing hardly any clothes in the pictures. It was bizarre because of a superstition she'd never known she had, and wouldn't ever have admitted having either. And so she pushed it away as it started tapping at the fringes of her consciousness, emerging as a fully fledged thought: that the *click* of the shutter had dislodged a piece of her soul, a piece that was now gone forever. Someone was clutching the *Vogue* magazine, and someone was pictured in the pages of that *Vogue,* and somewhere in between something had been irrevocably lost.

MINNIE, SLEEPING was splashed in big letters across a two-page spread with, in the background, Minnie on her stomach on the photographer's bed, one leg bent, the curve of her buttocks visible through the stuff of her nightgown. She looked like something that had washed up on shore, a woman hammered by a storm at sea. The impression was strengthened by the picture's pitilessly harsh lighting, hiding nothing from view. Not the tiniest black hair between her shoulder blades, not the wrinkles in the sheet, not the dirty ashtray on the nightstand. All in all, it looked like a pretty powerful fashion shot: raw, concealing nothing, hyper-realistic and meticulously staged.

The ten photographs on the next pages had headings like "Minnie, 03:24 a.m." and "Minnie, 05:46 a.m.." The chronology showed her moving steadily closer to the edge of the mattress in the course of the night, until her right arm was dangling down, the fingers just hovering above the floor, *oh, the beauty of it.*

In the last photograph, "Minnie, 08:08 a.m.," the sheet covered only her left calf. The dress had ridden up to her armpits, just about. She was lying there naked and vulnerable in the morning light, white body against white sheet. The shapes were incontrovertibly hers: the way one leg was raised, the spine twisted just slightly to the left, the small buttocks. That's my body, she thought, and at the same time she knew the opposite was also true: that is not my body.

*

You can imagine the kind of feelings someone has when confronted with pictures of herself three months after the fact on the kind of thick, glossy paper evoking champagne and Chanel and caviar galas on the Côte d'Azur *(Je ne fais pas la mode, je suis la mode).*

Anger, first of all, at the crass invasion of privacy, the opportunism, the shamelessness of it, the despicable manner in which—. Anger, secondly, at your own oblivion, your deep, dreamless sleep, your weakness, *click*, the photographer's finger on your nipple, *clack,* on the button of his reflex camera: *Just gone to the studio.*

Minnie thought all these things, exclaimed *motherfucker* when she read (white letters on dark background) how much the Lanvin dress cost, but at the same time knew that the fury was ebbing and making room for something else, bigger and more stubborn than any theoretical resistance.

Admiration.

For the plan's simplicity, the nonchalance with which he had tossed that purported "nightie" at her, his unscrupulous violation of every standard of decency. He knew she wouldn't pose for him. He knew it because he had asked her once, a few weeks after they'd first met. "I wouldn't dream of it," had been her answer. "Never! I'd be the mother of your *child* before I'd ever be your model."

He had laughed, wiping a blob of Chunky Monkey from the corner of her mouth with his finger. The dark hair on his forearm, his fingers in her mouth. Two strangers playing at intimacy.

*

That afternoon Minnie had a call from her agent.

"My phone is ringing off the hook, damn you," he said. "Why

the hell didn't you tell me about this project? Aren't I supposed to be representing you?"

"I'm sorry," said Minnie. Why did every phone call have to be so hysterical?

"Jesus Christ."

"I'm sorry."

"Never mind. Tomorrow we'll do a few interviews for the papers. *NRC Handelsblad* wants a piece for the Cultural Supplement, or whatever it's called these days. I fobbed off Radio 1 for tonight, I'm still hoping for some TV talk show to come through."

"I want Radio 1," said Minnie, to her own astonishment.

She heard her agent sigh on the other end of the line.

"OK," he said. "Never mind."

When she was shown into the recording studio that evening, she had no idea what she was going to say. What was there to say, anyway? Still. In spite of everything she felt a rare sense of calm come over her, one that she recognized from the way she felt just before starting on a new project, when everything was still possible and her ideas were still sitting unrealized inside her head, only in her head, before reality stepped in and started whittling away at it.

As Minnie climbed out of the taxi, announced herself at the reception desk and took a sip of the lukewarm automatic-brew coffee she was offered by a blushing production assistant, she still didn't know what she was doing there. She didn't know, but she did know it would come to her, something programmed into her somewhere beneath the surface of her consciousness. *Project*, she thought, running her tongue around the sharp edge of the plastic cup, *why the hell didn't you tell me about this project.*

MINNIE HAD JUST climbed into a taxi on her way home from the broadcast studio when the photographer rang. She was expecting his call, and yet it was startling to see his name on the screen of her cellphone. She suddenly realized that he had never called her before. For a brief second she tried imagining what it would be like if he called her every day, if they lived together in that empty house of his, if he held her tight whenever she asked him to.

"I'm impressed," he said. She could hear that he was trying to sound nonchalant. "Bravo."

A few minutes before the broadcast she had suddenly known what to say, and when she'd started talking it had all sounded just right—pieces of a puzzle that could not have fit together any other way.

How had she come up with the idea for this project? Well, she and the photographer, a close friend of hers, were sitting around one evening over a bottle of wine trying to think of a project they might tackle together. She was a great admirer of his work, and had been wanting for a long time to work with him on something. The way he staged his photographs so painstakingly in order to create an effect of spontaneity, was truly amazing. Really, she considered him to be in the same league as photographers like Erwin Olaf, Gregory Crewdson, Jeff Wall.

Anyway, when a few months later the photographer was approached to do a fashion spread for British *Vogue*, he had immediately called Minnie. To her surprise he was prepared to leave the concept to her, giving her carte blanche. *Vogue*'s only condition was that the silk Lanvin dress had to play a central role.

It hadn't originally been the intention to have Minnie model it herself. Sure, her work was often described as "a struggle with the self-portrait," but she had never literally posed for a portrait before. The turnabout came, she told the interviewer animatedly, when she'd started pondering the role of the model in fashion photography. The model was essentially subservient: to the clothes, to the photographer, even in some way to her own body. To say nothing about the huge sums of money that body was supposed to milk, the mirror it was supposed to hold up to all the different lives a person could live. Might it be possible, she'd thought, to radically undermine that role, and do it within the discourse of the fashion world itself? That is how she came up with the idea for a fashion shoot in which not only the clothes faded into the background, but the whole idea of posing too. Her first choice would have been to have the photographer take pictures of empty rooms, totally empty: no model, no clothes, none of the things you'd expect to see in a room. No products. But with the obligatory caption, of course, *model such-and-such wearing Lanvin.* That was *her* idea of carte blanche, anyway, a radical attempt to breach the boundaries of the imagination, to topple the pillars of fashion photography, to create the very antithesis of an illusion—or the ultimate illusion, if you will. However, *Vogue* was and still is "the world's leading fashion magazine," naturally; it was not, in the words of the art director, "some obscure outlet for conceptual art."

Minnie had given in, and agreed that a model would be used in the series, but insisted that it should be a reluctant model. Since she didn't know anyone who was as good as not-posing as she was herself (ha ha), and since the idea of the "artist as muse" was appealing to both the photographer and herself, it soon grew clear that Minnie was the only possible model for this shoot.

Sleep—Minnie had found her stride now—was the ultimate form of not-posing, of course. As you could see in the photos, there's tension between on the one hand the carefully staged setting and, on the other, the curious abandon of the poses. Yes, absolutely, she had been asleep during the shoot, that had been a must for ensuring success. She had taken a sleeping pill as a precaution, and she'd been out like a light until the next morning.

Would she say it was one of her most intimate, personal works? No, she wouldn't say so. To have yourself photographed asleep did in a sense make you vulnerable, true, but on the other hand, this was, after all, a commercial assignment. They had simply made an ad for a fashion label, and were paid a pretty penny for it too.

"An ad," said Minnie, the words now flowing freely, "succeeds if it creates the illusion of intimacy." Why? Well, that's simple: most of our desires can be boiled down to the longing to be close to another person. If people wanted to believe they were seeing her naked and vulnerable here, and it made them feel closer to her, or feel they now knew her better in some way, then in that sense the pictures had done what they'd set out to do.

Wasn't that a bit cynical? No, not at all. All she meant to say was that illusion and artificiality are fundamental to our existence. Wasn't this interview a manipulation of reality too? A private conversation between the two of them would have been quite another kettle of fish. Here they had to follow a certain set of rules, with the goal of persuading the listeners they were learning something "real" about Minnie.

"We spend our whole lives looking for something real," she concluded, no longer afraid of making grand generalizations, "but we tend to forget that even the earth beneath our feet is an illusion."

Just as she started worrying she might be taking it a bit far, the interview was over. The jingle of the news came on, Italy was pinning its hopes on Mario Monti, and Damascus was turning into a living hell.

"'An interview is a manipulation of reality too'? Jesus, Minnie. If bullshit was soft-serve, you'd be Dairy Queen."

"Dairy Queen?"

"The soft-serve ice cream, at Dairy Queen."

"How much did they pay you, in fact?"

It was quiet for a moment on the other end.

"Listen, kid," said the photographer.

"I'm not your kid."

"OK, but listen. Maybe it wasn't cool of me, to get it done that way, but I couldn't resist. I knew it was going to be very good, and I also knew you wouldn't let yourself be photographed. You of all people should understand that."

"*How much did they pay you?*"

"Do you really care about the money?"

"All right," said Minnie, "different question: did you drug me that night?”

She heard him sigh, or maybe she was imagining it.

“We’ll share the money, OK? Half for you, half for me.”

He mentioned an amount that made the blood rush to her cheeks. She was glad there was a telephone between the photographer and herself. Stay cool, she told herself. Stay cool.

“Fine,” she said. “In that case I’d like to use my half of the earnings to hire you for three weeks, starting early next year, some time between February first and the twenty-first of March 2012, does that work for you?”

Half an hour later they had come to an agreement. From a February date to be determined by him, the photographer would shadow Minnie for three weeks and photograph her. He was to work from a distance, with the utmost discretion, and under no circumstances would he ever interfere, no matter what. There was to be no contact between them during this time. If they did happen to bump into each other by accident, there would be no interaction whatsoever, not even the slightest sign of recognition. The photographer was to drop off his pictures between March 20 and 21 at the law offices of Specht & Vink, Prinsengracht 997, where Minnie would pick them up the night of March 21. Minnie would have an official contract drawn up, to be signed by both parties in early January.

The photographer had demurred at first (the proposal was ludicrous, he didn’t have time for it, it wasn’t his line of work) but his resistance wobbled considerably when Minnie dropped the words “adventure,” “spying” and “private detective.”

“So you’re asking me to play private eye for three weeks?”

“You could look at it that way, sure.”

“And I’m supposed to spy on the person who’s hired me?”

"Correct."

"You're a funny thing."

"That's beside the point," said Minnie.

"What *is* the point, then?"

"A two-way commitment. Over the fact that we're responsible for B when we say A. Implications."

"Implications?"

"Do you know the story of the Tacoma Narrows Bridge?" she asked without waiting for an answer. She loved that anecdote. The analogy was easy to grasp, and it worked on all kinds of levels, depending on where you put the emphasis. "The Tacoma-Narrows Bridge was the third-longest bridge in the world in 1940, but four months after it opened, it collapsed. An engineering error caused it to sway up and down whenever it was windy. One day a gale-force wind set the entire roadbed undulating like the sea. The event was caught on film. You see the bridge span billowing more and more wildly, galvanized by its own momentum. Imagine that: asphalt and concrete, fluid as water. In the end, of course, the bridge crashes into the sea. That kind of thrust can't keep going forever."

"Aero-elasticity," said the photographer. "I studied mechanical engineering once, briefly."

"My point is," said Minnie, "that from the moment the engineer made an error in his calculations, that bridge was doomed, don't you see? The consequences were embedded in the design. It was set in stone before the first contractor even started pouring the cement."

Her thoughts strayed to the night she'd met the photographer for the first time, at an art opening. They had stood in front of a large abstract painting graduating horizontally from dark red to blue-black. The photographer had asked her what she saw in it, and she'd answered that she could see the artist's physical labor in it, the effort required to spread the color across the canvas. They had stood there a while longer without speaking. *"All is falling,"* Minnie had then said, though she couldn't remember where that expression came from, or exactly why it was applicable to that painting. But the photographer had nodded and then gazed at her as if he understood something about her that few people could see. Something she didn't really understand herself.

"That seems a bit fatalistic to me," he now said.

"But the downfall of that bridge was glorious!" said Minnie. "Dancing its way to its own destruction. It's a choice, and not just that. You could call it a proposition to reality. Was anything like this even conceivable before this happened? Billowing asphalt? Never."

"And now you want to make your own proposition to reality."

"Basically, yes."

"The artist as muse."

"Nicely put."

"Sounds... interesting." There was something in this voice that sounded as if he actually meant it.

The taxi turned into Minnie's street.

"Why are you asking *me*, besides the all-too-clear revenge motive of wanting to get back at me for this *Vogue* business?"

"I have been wanting to work with you on something for a long time," she said as she got out of the taxi and slammed the door shut behind her. "As you know, I am a great admirer of your work."

"Funny ha-ha, kid."

Minnie tried to picture the photographer as he was now, holding the phone and leaning against one of his apartment's bare walls. Doing this project with anyone else was out of the question.

"You're the stealthiest person I know."

He laughed: *Ha*, just once, short and hard, like a punctured tire.

"How *are* you, anyway? I suddenly stopped hearing from you, and I thought... I spoke to Cleo recently and she said that you and... well, that the two of you had broken up, and I thought... well, anyway. Perhaps we could..."

"I'm fine," said Minnie. "Not too bad. I'll see you in January at the notary's office. Happy holidays and all that."

Her hand shook as she stuck the key in the door, but it didn't matter. It was a game, and she was the one who'd just written the rules.

MINNIE HAD THE CONTRACT drawn up by the Specht & Vink law office just before the end of the year.

Specht means "woodpecker" in Dutch, a bird to whom the notary bore little resemblance. If there was any animal he could be likened to, thought Minnie, it was a dachshund, not a bird. His limbs were unusually short, and his trunk relatively long. Notwithstanding the long torso, his height was considerably below average.

Minnie, having never herself experienced a growth spurt that would have taken her from pint-sized to average, had felt immediate sympathy for this little dog-man and the formal mannerisms his profession seemed to require of him. He referred to himself in the third person, underscoring the artificiality of the whole business.

"This agreement will be executed by the notary," Specht said once she had taken a seat at a heavy oak table in a small office crammed to the rafters with filing cabinets. "It is to be drawn up as a covenant, written in the first person singular therefore. What exactly did you wish to stipulate?"

If Specht was at all surprised at the terms Minnie requested, he did not show it. Once the rules of the game were set down in black and white, he shook her hand as if they were now business partners.

"Excellent," he said. "The notary will execute the deed, then, on January 3, 2012, at three p.m., in the presence of all parties concerned. He will ascertain that all parties have understood the conditions before signing the deed. The evidential value resides in the original document the notary will keep in his safe in perpetuity."

"In perpetuity," said Minnie. "Well, at least that's a start."

*

It had been over four months since that hot August morning when she'd woken up in the photographer's bed and almost two months since the photo spread in *Vogue* (*"Vogue-gate,"* was how her agent referred to the affair. Minnie had called him after the radio interview, slightly tipsy and somewhat euphoric, to tell him the true version of the story. He had burst out laughing. "Those guys should take that as a warning," he hiccupped, "better think twice before you screw an artist!").

The photos quickly went viral, spread around the world by art and fashion bloggers. Aside from the Dutch papers, there were articles in *The Guardian*, *The New York Times* and *Le Monde.* Opinions ran the gamut from the lyrical ("Panis reveals herself to be quite an intransigent *anti*-artist, rising above the whole notion of subversion to discover there, in the very heart of commerce, a 'third space' of resistance") to the downright disparaging ("The fashion world is by definition superficial and transient. Art, *true* art, must transcend, and must therefore never get bogged down in the need to peddle handbags or dresses").

She turned down interview requests that came in by the dozen, except one: a sixteen-year-old girl who was writing her final "art appreciation" essay on Minnie's work. The request had flattered her more than any of the others, but it wasn't just that. The girl had written something in her email that was more insightful than anything else she had read on the subject of *Minnie, Sleeping* up to then: that it wasn't anything like Minnie's previous work, and that she thought that was a bit odd.

The girl had come to her studio one afternoon armed with pen and notepad, and a body like some unfamiliar piece of clothing she needed at least two more years to grow into before everything fell into place. Minnie remembered her own relief when she'd turned twenty and realized she would never be a teenager again, and she'd had this vague urge to put her arms around the girl, squeeze the limbs firmly together, pat the face to smooth out the features. The girl—watery grey eyes and wavy orange hair (henna?) brushed into a fluffy halo—had asked some smart questions, and for the first time in ages Minnie had managed to talk about her work without resorting to the rote answers that always made her so disgusted with herself; not because the answers were untrue as such, but because ex post facto they turned her work into something untrue. She could never shake the feeling afterwards that those automatic answers diminished her work somehow; as if every word made it crumble a bit more, and some day all she'd have to show for herself would be a pile of rubble.

Normally Minnie wasn't very good at relating to children, let alone teenagers. She wasn't sure if you were supposed to talk to them in a different voice than with adults, and tended to wind up somewhere hopelessly in between. Whenever she was confronted with a young person, she'd try to recall what it was like to be a seven-year-old, a ten-year-old, a fifteen-year-old; but it was impossible to tell one age from another. Were other people able to? Maybe it was just an inherent aspect of childhood—that all that was left of it in its wake was a swampy puddle of sludge occasionally belching out a bubble or two, leading you to suspect there was something going on down there, but divulging little else.

Minnie had no idea why she didn't feel her usual discomfort with this girl. The girl herself seemed uncomfortable enough. She was perched so rigidly on the edge of her chair that a mere nudge would have sent her tumbling. She was plucking at the pages of her notepad, and every ten seconds a hand would go up to her head, not to scratch or arrange her hair, but just to touch, a gesture—like the plucking—to reassure herself that her unease reached this far, but no farther. And yet there was something fearless about her that seemed to win out over her bashfulness every time. Maybe that was it, thought Minnie, maybe she wanted to let the girl win out over herself, and the only way to do that was to answer her questions seriously and thoughtfully.

So she spoke about the fine balance between accident and necessity, the constant doubt and flashes of certainty, the never-abating terror of starting something new, art as cultural bullshit (the rest was just a by-product); the sporadic desire to vanish, dissolve into nothingness, whatever that might be. The girl had sucked it all up like a sponge, her lips following the movements of her pen. Then, suddenly, she looked up. With a frown so forthright and so completely unselfconscious that it was almost shocking to behold, she asked: "Are you happy?"

No reporter had ever asked Minnie that question. Perhaps no one ever had. She wondered if it was the most irrelevant thing anyone could ask, or the only one that really mattered.

"I once met an old artist," she was surprised to hear herself say. It had been years since she'd thought about the man, and until a few seconds ago hadn't even realized that the memory was still stored inside her, clear as a bell even, untouched by time. "According to this artist, he had been happy just two times in his life: both times while sitting on some bench along Route 66. It was in the middle of nowhere, and in the middle of nowhere he'd suddenly felt joy. Other than that he had never been happy, although not in a particularly *un*happy way."

The girl wrote something down, crossed it out again and then stared at the pad as if it held some complicated mathematical formula she was unable to solve.

"I mean," said Minnie, who wasn't sure what she *did* mean, "for him, happiness was simply not the point. His art was a physical need, you see; he created his works because he *had* to. One day his studio burned to the ground, with hundreds of paintings in it. It was all over the national and international TV news, but he didn't really care."

"Gee," said the girl, "that sucks."

It wasn't clear what she meant by "that sucks," the destroyed paintings or the artist's indifference, but her face flushed bright red, she couldn't help it, her body was merciless.

"He wasn't sentimental," Minnie said quickly. "Least of all about his own work. Over the years, he probably destroyed more canvases on purpose than the number torched in that unfortunate fire. He was happy to be rid of them, he felt free again, happy to regain the emptiness, the void where everything's possible again."

The girl nodded her head slowly a few times, as if to realign the cogs spinning inside her brain.

"Same as *Nothing Personal*, then," she said.

"Right," said Minnie, startled, what was this girl, some kind of shrink? "Exactly, in fact."

She'd finished *Nothing Personal* almost five years ago. The project that had put her on the map. Everything she'd hoped for had come to pass: doors flew open for her, museums around the world wanted to exhibit her works, she was accosted at parties by art dealers and wannabes. For the first few months she had been sure that sooner or later she would be unmasked, and had been a bit disappointed when that didn't happen. The more the acclaim grew for her as an artist, the more she began to mistrust it. It wasn't *real*, she sometimes thought, or at least not in a way that corresponded to what she had once imagined when she'd just been starting out, incapable of conceiving of anything more desirable or fair than recognition. The sum was, simply, less than the parts. More banal, shallower. And less interesting too.

Maybe it was self-indulgent to say it, or even think it, but ever since the success of *Nothing Personal,* she knew that the thing she had always taken for granted until then was much more meaningful, basically, than any amount of accolades for her work. So she began to treasure the actual *work*, the process itself, the moments when it seemed to just pour out of her, the madness, the days she couldn't even think of sleep, of food, or of any physical needs at all. Yes, to work without fear or longing for anything else: *that* was the highest attainment. Even though the doubts and paralysis did always come back, there was one piece that was never affected, a tiny island barely jutting up above the surface of the ocean. She kept rediscovering it, and each time she knew *this* was it, this minuscule piece of soil where life and art intersected and seamlessly merged.

"*Nothing Personal* was the first time I really took a risk," she told the girl, who was still making those slow head-bobbing movements. A bobble-head, thought Minnie, one of those bobble-head doggies for your dashboard. "It felt as if everyone could peer right through me. As if I had given a piece of myself to the world, literally. After the opening I was sick for a week. Vomiting, fever, everything. I remember wondering, shivering, between bouts of delirium, if it had taken too much out of me. The thought was heartening, strangely enough. Maybe this state of utter exhaustion is actually the closest thing to pure happiness, I thought. And then I threw up again in the bucket by my bed. A little less sublime."

The girl looked at her with an expression registering both confusion and disbelief. God, what was she *saying*? She hadn't even been sick for a week, really, a few days at most, and bouts of delirium, as far as she knew, were for nineteenth-century novels inhabited by hysterical women with repressed sexual rage. Wasn't she laying it on a bit thick? "Putting on the artist," was what she called it when she saw others do it. She hated that, all the misery-flaunting, and now she heard herself talking exactly the same way.

"So you're only happy, really, when you're not feeling well."

"Uh—well," said Minnie. Now it was her turn to blush, not just because she had managed to back herself into a corner, but because she wondered if there wasn't a kernel of truth there. If she was honest, she had to admit she understood the old artist and his incinerated paintings. The unhappiest people she knew, and there were quite a few, were (as far as she could tell) unhappy because they were tyrannized by rather superficial ideas of happiness and, especially, success. They wanted love, a career, a home, a child, but forgot that all of these were abstractions—vague notions of perfection that would never correspond to unpredictable reality.

One of the things she remembered most clearly about her childhood was the way school teachers, babysitters and the men who dated her mother always asked her what she wanted to be when she grew up. She would get all flustered, and even though she could easily have made something up to get out of it, a blank sheet of paper would come drifting across her mind's eye, so dazzling white that it almost hurt her eyes, as if it let a light through that obliterated all clearly defined shapes. As a child this had worried her quite a bit. It was linked to all the other things she thought weren't normal about herself—the kink in her spine, which made her list slightly to the left, the sticky stuff between her legs that smelled of cheese crackers, her left-handedness, the inhaler she used in the morning to huff a fine powder into her lungs, how she'd been slow to learn to tell time, to learn arithmetic, to tie her shoelaces, and, when she was a bit older, the masochistic urge to sniff a shoe smeared with dog poop, or suck on a lemon—which was why as a child she was often beset with a great terror of turning out to be *nobody at all* when she grew up, leaving behind only a hole in the shape of her body, she imagined, like a cutout of the *Looney Tunes'* Coyote as he plunges into a ravine for the umpteenth time. It wasn't until she was much older that she realized that most people were in fact empty holes like that, neatly cut out in their own shape, not filled in with any intimation of the future, but left blank.

"People make themselves unhappy by constantly wishing to be different versions of themselves," she said, "more successful versions. They forget they can't take themselves out of the picture they create in their heads. They forget about their own shortcomings. And so"—she was astonished at the conviction of the words issuing from her mouth, as if it had really been like that, as if a life could be built around a handful of significant moments when you consciously choose which way to go: left over here, right over there, no detours—"I decided not to chase after that kind of happiness. I'll just keep on working, and if it ends up making me sick, then maybe it was worth it."

She pointed at the 2006 magazine photo, which was still hanging above her desk.

"Artist against her own will," the girl read aloud.

"Yes," said Minnie. "'*All that matters is work.*' That's what Andy Warhol said to Lou Reed and John Cale when they were hanging around the Factory not doing anything. Warhol couldn't stand idleness. He may have been a narcissist, but he was a hardworking narcissist."

Once the words were out, she realized it was unlikely a sixteen-year-old in 2011 would know who Lou Reed or John Cale were, and suddenly she felt old and a bore, her voice just as overbearing as that of her art school theory professor, who preached revolution and never stopped talking about Slavoj Žižek and Zygmunt Bauman.

In silence she watched the girl earnestly writing down the Warhol quote in her notebook, Andy Warhol, words that became words of wisdom only because people kept writing them down. She suddenly felt exhausted, everything appeared sharply outlined and yet hazy, the girl's serious expression a harsh spotlight that was making black spots dance before her eyes.

"Sorry," she said, "My time is up."

She spent the rest of the afternoon asleep on the sofa in her studio. When she woke up with a start toward evening, for one terrible moment she couldn't remember who she was, where she was, what she was doing there. For the next few hours, some residue of loss was left inside her, as if she might as well never have existed, or at least existed in very different ways.

IN LATE 2007 Minnie decided on the spur of the moment to sell all her belongings. It had started with her imitation Versace sofa, a ghastly thing—blue satin printed French lilies—of mammoth proportions, which she had impulsively bought on eBay. She had adored it, the gaudy decadence of it, its downright ugliness a reflection of the tastes of a certain class of nouveau-riche climbers, to whom newly acquired wealth was synchronous with anything that was big, shiny and soft—or fast, of course, in the case of cars and other vehicles. The sofa was, all things considered, a thoroughly ironic object. It made people chuckle; they understood that its ugliness was cancelled out by the context, so that it even attained a certain allure, even if it was only the unpretentious allure of a lumbering old dog.

Getting rid of the sofa had come in the immediate wake of a heartbreak that may have been banal, but no less painful; a broken heart of the sort that most people may experience once in their lives, twice at most, and hardly in proportion to the actual loss—although that's something that can only be grasped once the grief has shrunk to a compact memory that has lost all semblance to the grief itself—just as a book's synopsis can never evoke the book's actual mood.

The lost lover in question was a documentary filmmaker who liked to call himself and his peers "makers," and the film school he had graduated from "The Academy," as if filmmaking were the only thing in the world worth doing. He had developed a fascination with "vanishing cultures," and would therefore often disappear off the radar for months at a time in search of authentic tribes with leathery faces tanned by sun or cold, who in spite of a life of poverty and losses, and in defiance of the inexorable encroachment of the modern world, stubbornly clung to their way of life, or at least made a brave attempt at it. One winter he'd been snowed in with ten villagers and a herd of sheep in the mountains of Bosnia; on the tundra above the polar circle, he had found a handful of Siberian Chukchi whose native language was on its way to becoming extinct; and in the Belgian Ardennes he'd come across a village of such phenomenal *tristesse* that when he got home he almost drowned himself in the hundreds of hours of film he had shot there. He modeled himself after Victor Kossakovsky and the Dardenne brothers (the early work, not the later kitsch), and besides that he was a romantic who could fall head over heels in love with a woman in less than a minute, but quickly lost interest once his love was reciprocated and the woman was foolish enough to assume she was the one he would come back to. All of this happened to Minnie just as she was having her first modest success as a solo artist, laboring under the delusion that she possessed a self-image that was more or less intact, or at least intact enough to be able to judge what she could or could not put up with. Oh, how wrong she'd been!

The ecstasy could, at the drop of a hat, turn into fear, a terror feeding on even more fear—until the next moment of ecstasy. She floated on air, knowing that gravity could yank her down at any moment; knowing, too, that it wouldn't be a soft landing. Fucking hell, she thought, pressing her nose deep into the mattress to smell what was left of his scent: all the clichés were so disappointingly *real*! When he was away she missed him so much that her life was split into two: an outer shell that kept going, while inside all she could do was wait for his return. The tragic thing, of course, was that his return was never enough; his presence simply did not outweigh the agony of missing him, and when they were in bed, he asleep next to her, she wide awake, she longed to be alone again, so that the missing could begin again, and she could at least keep up the illusion that the *idea* of love corresponded with something real.

What she'd been so afraid of all that time finally came to pass: there came a point when the affair just fizzled out, just as even if you keep ladling something out in small portions there still won't be anything left in the end. They were sitting in a vast, airy restaurant in Amsterdam—one of the many revamped industrial spaces the city now abounded in, pitching a fresh respect for man, beast and the seasons—and Minnie hadn't been able to swallow a single bite, listening to him gushing about his latest film's wildly enthusiastic reception at various festivals, as he ate his Cornish hen with gusto, then helped himself to the practically untouched pork tenderloin on her plate. (He was a true gourmand, just a bit on the heavy side too, which had charmed Minnie to no end at first, at least until now, when it suddenly became a big turnoff.)

The more he talked, the more Minnie vanished. She might just as well be a chair, she thought—not without a sense of melodrama—, or the exposed pipes running across the brick wall.

After he was finished eating, he'd stepped outside to call his producer. If he stayed away more than ten minutes, she promised herself, she was out of there. She stared at the hands of the huge railway clock on the wall and thought about leaving money on the table, just her half, or maybe even the entire bill, and calmly walking away, the drama residing in the very lack of it. When after seven minutes he came back to the table, ordered an espresso and proposed they go back to her place, she hated him, but herself even more, because she could see right through him (which was shockingly simple to do) and *still* wasn't able to resist as if she were Stephen Hawking, damn it, or that man in *My Left Foot*, or any other lame jerk you might think of.

Two days later he rang her doorbell to inform her he was leaving her, he didn't love her enough, he'd decided, it was nothing personal, he just didn't love people very much in general, in fact, or at least not in the sense of their expecting too much of him. He was planning to set off soon for Point Hope in Alaska, a peninsula actually, home to a tribe of Inuit that once a year went out and killed a whale that provided them with, well, everything, really. Interestingly enough, the island was sinking into the sea, the entire Arctic coastline was eroding thanks to the melting ice caps at the North Pole, so that the natives kept having to move to a different part of the island. Since all the young Eskimos were leaving for college in the lower forty-eight, the tribe was also dealing with a rapidly aging population. Taking into account the fact that this whole whale hunting business was now taboo, it was clear that if he didn't go now he'd probably never get the chance again. It was at this point that Minnie told him to get out. Maybe she'd see him around sometime, or then again maybe not, should that sinking island disappear off the face of the earth sooner rather than later.

She'd watched him disappear down the stairwell. Legs,

shoulders, head. Only then did she notice the clear plastic bag in his hand. Swimming trunks and a towel. He had planned to go swimming after this, he'd just have time to get in a few laps before the adult swimming hour was over. That simple fact was so mortifying that she remained frozen in the doorway for several more minutes, unable to even think of moving. Fifty laps, she thought, half an hour. That was all he needed to rid himself of her, to rinse her off. It was nothing personal.

The next morning she put the sofa up for sale. The broken heart tolerated neither irony nor moderation; it was an unequivocal and rather humorless condition that wanted to see itself projected onto the whole wide world.

Within a day the thing was sold to a pair of middle-aged gays from Amstelveen, who came to pick it up in an old Mercedes van that clearly didn't belong to them. They not only looked alike but also both looked like Woody Allen, thought Minnie, and in an impulse she snapped a picture of the couple with her sofa. When the men drove it away she felt, for the first time in days, absolutely nothing, and for the next several hours managed to breathe normally, and not as if she'd swallowed something large and sharp that had got stuck in her gullet.

The cash the men had paid for it was stowed in neat twenties and fifties in her billfold. It occurred to Minnie that the sofa had in some mysterious way transformed itself into these bills, a small miracle that made her think of the very first time she'd earned money of her own, in the cramped kitchen of a tapas restaurant. She was fifteen, but since her skinny five-foot-two frame could still pass for that of a twelve-year-old, they wouldn't take her on as a waitress. She was offered the dishwashing job instead. Two evenings a week, right after school, she'd scraped plates clean of baked-on aioli crusts, fished soggy calamari rings out of the fryer and listened to a Buena Vista Social Club CD on a loop that kept getting stuck at the same place, so that the waitresses in their red sweatshirts had to rush over to the CD player every hour to get it going again. Every week they handed her a thick envelope with her name on it, and riding her bike home smelling of shrimp and cooking oil, she'd feel the envelope in her pants pocket pressing almost obscenely into her thigh.

It had been her first introduction to the world of adults, and the mysteries of work, money and sex attracted her like a powerful magnet. Even though it would be another year at least before she'd make her first halfhearted stab at sex—and then another considerable while before she understood that it might entail more than some jittery foreplay resulting in a boy's shaky hands tearing open a condom wrapper—that first paycheck taught her that the game of the adults was an economic one, in which everything was measured in terms of quantifiable commodities that were compared, traded, copied, or transformed into something more valuable.

In the days after she'd sold the sofa, she put several other things up for sale: a standing lamp, a glass coffee table, the two Pastoe chairs she'd bought with the income of *Does Minnie Panis Exist?* She didn't realize she had "started" something until a friend of hers, a video artist, looked around her living room in surprise and asked what had happened to her furniture. She'd tried to look at the living room through his eyes. A table without any chairs, an empty space where the couch used to be. More than just the furniture, something else was missing, something that had less to do with the things themselves than with an absence of logic, a missing link in the chain of cause and effect. *What the fuck is the matter with her?* His dismay pleased her, and the thought that came to her was so urgent that she felt her heart start racing in her chest. Would she be able to sell all her possessions? Had anyone ever tried to do that?

The project took months to complete. She advertised her stuff on different websites, exchanged emails with the most unlikely characters, and documented the whole exercise with the thoroughness of a detective conducting a murder investigation. Some things were practically impossible to sell—underwear, books, CDs, half empty tubes or jars of day or night cream, foot lotion, shampoo, hairspray—but in the end she sold everything except her bed, one blanket, a few items of clothing and a toothbrush. She was astounded at how little effort it took to detach herself from the most personal objects she possessed. The signed Ger van Elk print, rare art books, a silver cup containing her first tooth: everything went out the door with no regret, all that coerced nostalgia exchanged for plain, straightforward cash. It seemed an excellent deal to her. When, as her last act of severance, she sold her passport to a Romanian migrant in a trailer park on the outskirts of the city (with a grey dog chained to his car and a gold canine glistening in his mouth, because reality is more often modeled on fiction than the other way around), the broken heart was finally a thing of the past. It was as if she had tossed her whole life into a big hole, and all that was left for her to do was close it up and rake it over.

The illusion didn't last very long; it isn't that easy to get rid of yourself, but she did catch a glimpse of the complete freedom that unfolds before those who have nothing more to lose or to wish for.

She started sorting through the hundreds of photos she'd taken over those months of her belongings, emails and notes. Over the short stop-motion film of her ever emptier house, she ran a voice-over about the vanishing coastline of southern Louisiana and the consequences of Hurricane Katrina. ("Southern Louisiana is one of the fastest disappearing landmasses on the globe. A football field-sized area of land disappears every forty-five minutes. Since the 1930s an expanse the size of Delaware has been eroded...") The result was a cross between a diary, an indictment, a nature documentary and an auction catalog. This could be something, she thought, although as usual she had no idea what that "something" might specifically entail.

"I DON'T KNOW what this is," said her agent, pointing at the items spread out before him on the floor of her studio.

It was one of the first days of April, 2008, when from one day to the next you suddenly smelled it in the air, subtle but unmistakable: spring. Three nights before, Minnie had woken from a nightmare she was sure she'd had before, when she was little, maybe; the fear had felt childish, anyway, overblown and overwhelming. In the dream she'd been a fish-like creature swimming under water, with glistening scales and fins and black eyes on either side of her head. She realized suddenly that she didn't have gills. How long had she been without oxygen? Swimming up to the surface in a panic for a gulp of air, her fish-head crashed into a thick layer of ice. Again and again she rammed her skull against the slab, which didn't budge but kept getting thicker, enveloping her, no, infiltrating her, so that all the liquid in her body began to freeze, making her grow as stiff and as hard as a salmon fillet in the freezer. Just before she woke up something had flashed through her hard fish-being, the onset of a thought, something that seemed important but vanished when she tried to get hold of it. She had drops of sweat prickling between her breasts, the sour smell of saliva on her pillow. She got out of bed, disoriented. In the bathroom she splashed water on her face. If she'd still had a mirror, she'd probably have stared at herself for a while, but the point was that she no longer owned anything, everything was gone, sold, finished. Her apartment was as hollow as a three hundred square-foot whale carcass. The bare windows had become black holes allowing the night to intrude mercilessly, blank eyes staring at her from all sides. *What the hell are you doing?*

She'd jumped on her bike and raced to her studio, shutting herself up in there for two days straight without even showing her face in the courtyard. She ran around like a mad dog at first, zigzagging from one piece to the next. Next she sat huddled in a chair in a corner for several hours, head buried in her hands, too scared to look up. She'd been sure the whole thing had been for nothing, that it was nonsense, incoherent and—*the horror!*—pathetic, amateurish crap. Burn the lot, she thought to herself, and at first she'd really thought herself capable of doing that.

That's when her agent had called her, as if he'd sensed something was up. The first two times the phone rang Minnie didn't pick up, but the third time she answered it, as he knew she would. She calmly told him that the whole thing was a complete fiasco, and that being the case, not to expect anything from her for the foreseeable future, upon which he'd said he'd be there in fifteen minutes. Half an hour later he was pounding on her door.

Now he took a sip of the Sancerre he had brought along, already iced. He swirled the wine carefully around inside his mouth, sucking air through his teeth.

"Damn fine little wine. Drove to that French grower myself and picked up ten boxes, scandalously cheap of course. He even gave me an extra bottle to go, plenty to spare. Looked like some dirt-poor fart, with a wino's nose and a beer belly, but he lived in a beautiful villa, had a wife twenty years younger and the cutest three-year-old granddaughter. That fucker lives like a god over there in France, ha! As for this,"—he circled his hand in the air—"this is absolutely fabulous. Your best work yet. No kidding."

He took another big gulp of the wine, eyes closed in ecstasy, partly genuine but mostly feigned. Opening them again, he gave a loud "Aaah."

"Everyone knows the art world is sick," he went on, the wine in his glass whirling ever wilder. "Artists shut themselves up in musty, windowless cellars stinking of their own stale recycled sweat. Sweat from what? From hard work? You must be kidding. They're just plain feverish. They're sweating out a fever of their own irrelevance, for which they have only themselves to blame. What's the public supposed to do with the umpteenth overpriced rip-off of Beuys, Hirst, Koons, Ofili, or Andres fucking Serrano? What's the public supposed to think of the Vienna Biennale snooze-fest? What are people who aren't called Jay-Z or Beyoncé expected to do at Art Basel Miami? Spare me your mutant Virgin Mary, your blood, your piss, your elephant shit, your dead cat and your dried sperm! It's a fucking disgrace, it's just too embarrassing having to explain to the hard-working middle class that their precious tax euros are going to *that*, to that bunch of mediocre jokesters who dare to pretend their tired old offerings are actually exercises in provocation. Art is the new capital, an investment for Russian oligarchs, hip-hop millionaires and child stars. Look at Charles Saatchi watching from the sidelines, laughing all the way to the bank! It's too tragic for words, Panis, but this here, *this*,"—he picked up a piece from the floor at random, a snapshot of a fat woman from North Amsterdam who had bought

Minnie's entire DVD collection, "isn't another gassy fart to add to the fetid air in that cellar, no, this, at least, is a good gust of wind to make the shutters squeak on their hinges. Breath of fresh air!"

He flung the picture in the air, and it drifted down slowly, like a feather. He burst out laughing. Minnie had never seen him like this. She hadn't the foggiest idea if he was pulling her leg, with his "gust of wind," but she didn't have time to think about it, because he had already started railing again. He didn't have steam coming out of his ears, but it was close.

"I mean it, Panis. This here is irony of a higher order, and don't you go fucking confusing it with cynicism. Cynicism is the leukemia of art, the putrid cadaver fumes steaming from the pores of an organism that tells itself it's still alive. It makes me sick!"

From fetid cellar air to cadavers, things kept going from bad to worse for art. He had shoved the glass into Minnie's hands and was now pacing up and down the room, gesticulating wildly, as if making a sculpture out of the air itself.

"And of course I don't mean sarcasm, the lame-ass sarcasm that some people can't help wrapping their tongue around like some porn star's dick" (a startlingly detailed picture of a porn actress being banged by two men at once while almost gagging on a third penis being shoved down her throat flashed through Minnie's mind. Porn as factory-farm, human beings as battery hens) "whereas irony should be the beating heart, or rather, the beating member of all the arts. Have you ever heard of the expression 'truthful pretense'?"

Minnie understood that the question was a rhetorical one, and did not reply.

"It's by some dead writer. 'We pretend to know what we're talking about and we don't for a moment forget that it's only make-believe.'

Clever dick. The ignorance has to be honest and true, that's what it's all about. Then you can make up anything you want, but the glass does have to get foggy, don't you see?"

He snatched his wineglass out of Minnie's hand again, drained it to the last drop and began panting like a maniac. He raised his trophy in the air, out of breath.

"The glass?"

"The glass, the window, whatever. Art has to *show* that it's art. It has to turn itself inside out. Get rid of what's behind the scenes, the voyeurism, the method acting. The sewers must be dug up and laid bare."

"But I thought you just said it was too stinky already," Minnie said, knowing it would annoy him. Of course she knew what he meant, she knew exactly what he meant. The faux-naïf act was a bit of fun she often allowed herself with people—men—when they started fulminating against the world as if they were the first in history ever to get upset about anything.

"Christ, Panis," he panted, "there's a difference between the meta-stench of art and the very necessary stench of the individual work of art. A turd is *supposed* to stink, a toilet isn't supposed to stink. Not even of air-freshener. Anyway, I was trying to give you a compliment, in case you hadn't noticed. People are constantly harping on about dangerous art, but what *is* dangerous art?"

Another rhetorical question. Gripping her theatrically by the shoulders, he brought his face up to hers. She could see the individual pores on his nose, a greasy moonscape in close-up. She had an urge to press them with her fingers. Thin little squiggles of fat spilling out like maggots from a corpse.

"*This* is dangerous art! Not because it's posing a danger to anyone, but because the goddamn artist is a danger to herself. Because the work is vulnerable and not untouchable, like a piss-Christ or, I don't know, a platinum skull made of eight-thousand-six hundred diamonds."

"It created quite a stir at the time, I seem to remember."

"A stir! What does that have to do with vulnerability? *Nada!* That's the greatest misconception-scam of the twentieth century, and the twenty-first so far, actually, that art is supposed to unmask everything. A religious icon submerged in urine reveals faith to be kitsch, and a fifteen million dollar skull proves we are all trying to buy our way out of our own mortality. Do you think that's interesting? Oh give me a *break*, if art can be reduced to one corny buzzword, then it can't be dangerous art, can it? All that so-called unmasking is nothing more than the perfunctory ambition they teach you at art schools full of teachers who have raised cynicism to a religion and peddle deconstruction as if they're the apostles of a new world, without for one second realizing they're not only standing in a sinking ship, but also that they're they ones making it sink. My god, it's lucky there's still someone out there making good wine."

He pulled open the fridge and poured himself another glass to the brim. This was a man who did not believe in moderation, Minnie thought to herself. She watched his Adam's apple bob up and down as he swallowed, as if trying to gulp down life itself. Something about that throat movement touched her, maybe the involuntary nature of the bodily function.

"The same goes for all that post-9/11 art, by the way," he went on, calmer now, leaning against the fridge door. "Other than a few exceptions, political engagement has become so terribly *tedious*. A multiple-choice test for political-science majors, sometimes even more hokey than that, because the meaning is plastered all over the art piece in red letters, with sirens blaring. A wall of gas cans titled *Israel and Palestine*? Give me a break. I recently heard someone talking in all seriousness about 'feel-good idealism'. Museum shows featuring artists going bat-shit over 'the other', that sort of thing. It wouldn't surprise me if I'd see them knitting condoms for Ethiopia or, I don't know, creating an island installation in the North Sea for all the asylum seekers who've been refused entry. Nice work! Anyway, my point is: art should go back to being a masquerade. Mysterious, obscure, and by definition impossible to reduce to some elevator pitch, or whatever other infantile term for it has blown over from the advertising world these days. I don't want to be made to feel uneasy because the world is being unmasked, but because I have to do something with my own unease. Because now I'm looking at a work of art that doesn't exactly know what it is either, and so it's a work of art that relates to the world *honestly* for a change. The art I want to look at is *your* art, Panis. This here"—he made a sweeping gesture with his glass, the wine spilling in all directions, dribbling a trail all across the floor and over his own shoes—"...is a weird fucking collision between crazy personal junk and images as stale as three-day-old bread, in other words, it makes no sense, yet it all adds up. What are we going to call it?"

Nothing Personal became a solo show at the Gemeentemuseum in The Hague, and a coffee table book. Minnie, who had never understood why conceptual art always had to come with reams of illegible jargon, kept the accompanying text short.

> On November 3, 2007, Minnie Panis' lover left her. He departed for an island sinking into the sea somewhere near the North Pole and she put her sofa up for sale. Five months later all she had left was a bed, a few items of clothing and a toothbrush. As far as she knows her ex is still on that island, perhaps with water up to his ankles, or perhaps not.

"This kid is a genius," her agent told anyone at the opening who would listen, "a fucking genius."

The success was unanticipated, but—as can always be said about such things in hindsight—also completely predictable. Everyone seemed to discover something personally relevant in the work, which according to visitors and art critics alike went beyond the particulars of her love life and carried in it "a universal message of human freedom from bondage."

In an interview with a trendsetting arts magazine, Minnie said that this project's true revelation hadn't been about freedom, but rather about bondage, or the lack of freedom anchored deep within ourselves. When the journalist asked her what that bondage consisted of, her reply was short, terse and in hindsight a bit pompous, winding up as the article's headline in a big fat letters: *Life and Gravity.*

"*Nothing Personal* intrigues on a number of levels," an elderly museum director remarked in his rather chaotic weekly newspaper column on art:

> It is in the first instance an extremely intimate and raw self-portrait of a woman in search of the ultimate consequences of her broken heart. Ever since her lover's departure she wonders if she can manage to "put her entire life up for

sale," in order to "dispose of the whole damn mess reflected in the resultant void." The reader of these diary-like jottings feels he is a voyeur peeking into another person's life, a peeping Tom, until he (m/f) starts getting the uneasy feeling that he is just as exposed as the artist herself, and, moreover, reluctantly has to admit that he is likewise taking a hard, uncensored look into himself.

Through the agency of her belongings, Panis reconstructs and deconstructs her life. Visiting the show and leafing through the accompanying book feels a bit like wading through a pathologist's forensic report: exhibits that are there more or less by chance, but nevertheless worthy of being documented with the utmost care and objectivity. That is where Panis shows herself to be masterful: her art appears to be personal, verging on exhibitionism, but in the end you have to conclude you have not learned anything truly real about her. What's left is an empty home, a few baby teeth that could have been anyone's. The artist has vanished, erased against the white background of her stripped-bare home.

ROUGHLY SPEAKING, MINNIE thought to herself, you could divide humanity into two categories, the first being the ones that always arrive fifteen minutes after the appointed time, and the second who will leave themselves half an hour for a trip that can't possibly take more than ten minutes. She had always felt there was something tragic about this universal inability to estimate time, not because she thought punctuality was such an important asset, but because of humankind's complete inability to synchronize perceived time with real time. She'd once read about a Frenchman who had spent several months-long periods living in caves deep beneath the earth's surface. As a scientific experiment, with support from NASA, he wanted to see if his biological clock corresponded to actual time but he'd sadly misjudged it every time. Toward the end of a six-month-long experiment in a cave in Texas, his "days" varied in length from eighteen to fifty-two hours, and when in an attempt to make a pet of his only friend, a little mouse that occasionally came sniffing around, and he accidentally squashed it to death, he thought of taking his own life.

So when Minnie arrived that January third at the Specht & Vink offices, glanced at her phone and saw that she had more than ten minutes to spare, she came to a somewhat unhappy realization: after almost thirty years, she still hadn't mastered something that ought to be elementary, a failure of all humankind.

She stopped and lit up a cigarette under the gold-lettered sign over the door, then another one, staring at the other side of the canal, where the pavement was dug up and people were hobbling slowly across an improvised path of wooden planks laid over the sand. The city had been struck by gale force winds the day before. Bicycles with twisted frames listed out of bike racks, branches almost as big as half a tree blocked the way and every street corner was littered with trash from toppled garbage cans and dumpsters. Someone—or some*thing*? how did these things work?—had forgotten to turn off the streetlamps stretched on cables high above the tram tracks, which were getting buffeted from side to side by the wind. The light cast by the lamps left the sky looking heavy and grey, as if they, having sucked up all the daylight, were now trying to emit it again. She couldn't tell if it was a good omen for the New Year or a bad one, but decided that it could easily go either way.

She thought about lighting a third cigarette, now that she was standing there anyway, staring into the water of a canal in a city in disarray, a world in disarray, people sleeping in tent camps on Wall Street and Amsterdam's Beursplein, dreaming of democracy and free Ben & Jerry's. *We are the 99%.*

January 3, three cigarettes. If you looked for symmetry you'd always find some.

She was nervous.

She hadn't seen the photographer since that evening in August. Anything that had had to be discussed had been done by phone.

Last week, in the early hours of New Year's Eve, he had called her to announce that he'd changed his mind. He couldn't do it, it was going take a ridiculous amount of time, how could he possibly stay on top of where she was day and night, if that was something he wanted to do, he'd have joined the paparazzi. She'd let him talk, had not tried to dissuade him, and when his monologue was over she'd heard him sigh deeply. "OK," he'd said, "I'll do it, but don't ask me why. Don't for fuck's sake ask me why."

She'd called him back the next day. There was an empty studio down the street from her, a neighbor who made tons of money writing books on management, and who divided his time between Amsterdam and Bali. She could rent his studio for the months of February and March. "That way you won't have to sleep in your car," she said. "From his window you can see my window. In theory you could shoot me, like one of those snipers bringing down a terrorist, or the president. It all depends on what you consider to be justice."

"A sniper," said the photographer. "Snipers operate in groups. Did you know those guys use guns that have to be loaded manually, one cartridge at a time? It makes for a steadier shot when you pull the trigger."

"Then you'll just have to take good aim," said Minnie.

"In my opinion, kid, you're just as lethal as Lyudmila Pavlichenko. Who says you won't shoot me first?"

For the past few days she'd been certain that he'd show up at the notary's, but now that there were five minutes to go before the appointed time, it suddenly appeared most unlikely. Not for any specific reason (although there were reasons enough), but because she could not imagine that he existed as anything but a number of remembered impressions, and a voice on the phone.

She lit a third cigarette and tried her best to take long, calm puffs. She wasn't used to smoking so many cigarettes at once, and the carbon monoxide made her wheeze. Even though she had officially grown out of her asthma at a fairly young age, her lungs still seemed to have trouble sometimes filtering enough oxygen from the air. Breathe, she'd often think to herself, breathe, breathe, breathe. Why was this so automatic in other people?

"Minnie."

A hand on her shoulder, his face close to hers.

So he really did still exist. A living person who eats and poops and swallows and sleeps. She could smell him, the odor of his skin and something else, something dark, that made her think of his profession. He was wearing a black felt jacket, pants that were too thin for the season, All Stars. Minnie remembered the toenails of his big toes, which he painted gold to hide a fungal infection. Everyone had their own private war to wage.

He gazed at her long and intently, as if he would find some truth about her in her facial features. She never could tell if it was a photographer's gaze or a pose. Perhaps it was both, maybe he was both: a real person and the parody of a real person. He had a several-day-old stubble and the profoundly dark eyes of someone who is able to vanish in the night. His hand felt heavy on her shoulder. She could feel, through his hand, the shapes making up the rest of his body, and all of a sudden she remembered what it was about this man. She couldn't help shaking her head. To compensate.

"Are you ready to sign our Faustian contract?" she asked him in a voice she hoped sounded nonchalant.

She flicked the half-smoked cigarette onto the stoop, stubbing it out with the tip of her shoe. Just before turning round, she saw something gold shimmering in the water. She looked up to see the gold letters on the building's façade. *The reflection of gold letters in the water.* She had seen this once before. Not something similar, but exactly *this*. She looked down at the water again, but the glint was gone, and by the time they were following Specht up the narrow stairwell it had already slipped her mind.

Specht wasn't the type to waste any time on small-talk about the weather or the current affairs, and within quarter of an hour the deed was read, signed and locked away in the safe.

"Where's Vink, anyway?" Minnie blurted out.

"Vink, alas, has left us," said Specht. "He was in that airplane crash a year and half ago at Tripoli. An unimaginably tragic accident. His daughter is right now training to be a notary. She used to be a flight attendant."

Upon which he opened his office door with a sweeping bow.

"The notary wishes you all the best happiness," were his parting words, as if they had just drawn up a prenuptial agreement. Which in a sense was true. The prenuptial conditions of a rather short and definitely strange marriage. For better and for worse, indeed.

That night, after a cocktail, dinner and two bottles of Pouilly-Fumé, they wandered over to a dark dive in Rembrandt Square, where they sat down on two red velvet bar stools.

The photographer, without consulting her, ordered two shots of chartreuse from a barmaid wearing red lipstick and a neckline deep enough to make a whole school bus disappear. As if she'd done this hundreds of times before, she slapped two small glasses down on the bar, wheeled around and blindly grabbed the right bottle from the shelf. As she poured, her torso leaned forward across the bar. There was something intimate about it because of those breasts, but also in her movements. And in her eyes. Good barmaids always look as if they're about to tell you a secret.

"Chartreuse," she confided, as she put the bottle back on the shelf. *"The only liquor so good they named a color after it."*

"Tarantino," said the photographer. He drummed his fingers on the counter. *"From Dusk till Dawn."*

The barmaid smiled. She was in her thirties, Minnie guessed. Great face, especially on account of the squinty left eye.

"With a pint of green chartreuse ain't nothing seems right," the photographer crooned in a hard-to-define imitation growl. The barmaid listened, amused. Did those two know each other? Was this a kind of ritual, scoring points by quotation? *"...You buy the Sunday paper on a Saturday night."*

The barmaid winked at Minnie with the squinty eye and then without saying another word walked over the far side of the bar, where two men in business suits were silently sipping at gigantic mugs of beer. For a brief moment, as she winked, her face had looked different. Ordinary. As if the act of closing that squinty eye dropped another curtain as well.

Minnie once met a woman artist from New York who as a performance piece had spent a year at a full-time job in a restaurant. She was definitely play-acting at first. She would take orders, pour drinks, serve the food, repeat the same standard lines. The strangest thing about it was that everyone just accepted it as normal. No one seemed surprised; on the contrary, the patrons, the chefs, her fellow servers, everyone spoke the same coded language, night after night, over and over, indefatigable human machines. After a few months the artist began to get used to it, and some months after that to her own astonishment realized that the role she was playing was more and more growing part and parcel of who she was. Her view of the world changed. She noticed people working at jobs she had never really noticed before. Traffic cops, cleaners, custodians, call center employees, subway clerks, you name it. All these people kept an awe-inspiring service industry going, one of which she was now for the first time part of. She had discovered an extra level of reality, she told Minnie, which was extremely artificial, but at the same time realer than real. Even outside the restaurant she now felt herself to be a waitress more than an artist, and she was starting to realize something she hadn't suspected when she'd started the performance: in order for the art piece to succeed, she had to erase the artist part. A waitress couldn't also be a meta-waitress, that would make it a gimmick. Fortunately she worked so hard, and for so little money, that she spent most of her time off in her studio apartment (30 square feet) in Brooklyn, watching sitcoms and sleeping. Every Friday night she'd have a beer with the cooks and a dishwasher everyone called Ali—more because it was easy than because it was his name—after which she had sex with the chef in the kitchen on the sous-chef's stainless steel work table. The table was cold and hard but the sex was great, possibly because the chef was such an unbelievable bastard during working hours. That too was new to her. The artist had always been a serious feminist, and still was, but in her waitress year, the coarsest, most sexist comments would turn her on. Even men who unabashedly slapped her on the bum in the presence of their wife and kids could count on a friendly smile from her. It had something to do with compassion, she thought. It was the first time she had truly realized that people are helpless sloggers, captive to their own urges and stupidity. Empathy was the only way to rise above it, the rest was bullshit, and yes, she knew she sounded like some Jehova's Witness but that was fine with her.

In the end she was barely keeping up with what was going on in the art world. She was still invited to all the gallery openings, but the truth was that she could no longer stand them. Those people were living in a bubble. They talked about making statements and anti-statements, spouting intellectual garbage that would have been at home in a PhD thesis. It made no difference to them that it was all insider talk, or, worse even, that that had become a goal in and of itself. And she ought to know, because she used to be just like them. A few months before she'd started working in the restaurant, she had had a handful of term papers in plastic binders framed, and hung them as a DIY installations in a gallery in the East Village. She had called the series "Science 1 through 15." The framed dissertations had sold like hotcakes. Since they were being used as objects and not as texts, she couldn't be accused of copyright infringement, either, and their authors had no right to compensation. "Can you believe it?" she'd asked Minnie, although it wasn't completely clear what she meant, or if it was a real question. Minnie had asked her what she was doing now that she was no longer waitressing. "Oh," the artist had replied, "now I'm just back to making sculptures. They're *huge*. Everyone wants one. My only other option was to wait tables for the rest of my life, trapped in a performance that's stopped being a performance. What would have been the point?"

The barmaid was now leaning over the bar toward the two men with their beer mugs. Maybe she had an appropriate quote for them as well, about beer this time. Maybe she too was in the middle of a performance piece. Maybe everyone in this bar was a performance artist.

Chartreuse. The drink's color made Minnie think of a picture book from her childhood, something to do with a frog, a gold ball and a murky pool filled with algae. She'd never drunk this before. The photographer raised his glass.

"Cheers," he said. "To our crazy contract."

The drink had a chameleon-like taste, the first sip changing from sweet to spicy, sharp and even salty. She tasted aniseed, cloves, fennel. Black pepper. The different flavors filtered into every corner of her mouth, quietly, but with the promise of danger. She liked it.

"They say this stuff can make you delirious," said the photographer, tapping a finger against his glass.

"You could say that about anything," Minnie answered. "As long as you drink enough of it."

"It's got a hundred and thirty different herbs," he went on imperturbably. "One of the most complex drinks ever made. The recipe was given to the Carthusian monks in 1605 by François Annibal d'Estrées, Marshall of France under King Henry the Fourth, who, in turn was given it by an alchemist, who told him it was a life-enhancing elixir. To this day there are only three monks alive who know the precise herbal formula, and even then, they each only know one part of it. The secret has been kept this way for over four hundred years."

"How lonely," said Minnie.

"Terribly lonely. Those monks are allowed to speak only once a week, on Sundays. The strictest religious order of the Western hemisphere. On the other hand: all that dedication and discipline must also create a close bond. Those monks are utterly dependent on one another for the preservation of their way of life. It applies even more in the case of that recipe, naturally. They have to be able to trust one another blindly."

"Imagine one of the monks dying before he's had a chance to entrust his part of the recipe to someone else," said Minnie. "That would be a catastrophe."

"Still, it's never happened, in all those centuries."

"That's no argument. Stuff can happen."

The photographer waved a hand at the barmaid and ordered two more shots. Minnie didn't know if it was his talk of deliriums and secret recipes, but the chartreuse seemed to be spinning her senses into a tunnel-like orbit. She had a sense of an extremely keen but limited focus, like some radio frequency at its sharpest: free of noise-interference but surrounded by it on all sides. She longed for an important confession, something emotional. The photographer was staring at the barmaid, who took out two clean glasses, leaned across the bar again to pour the bright green liquid into them. Could something be déjà vu if you had experienced it just ten minutes before? "I love you," that was it, the confession on her lips. To take his hand and say those words. Even if it wasn't true, or maybe it was, or could something like that only be true to a certain level? Instead she raised the little glass.

"To our immortality, then."

"And to those phenomenal tits," said the photographer, nodding in the barmaid's direction. "They always make me think of a snowfall, of fresh powder. That's the secret, see. They create the illusion of never having been touched. Anyone could still be the first. And yet there's also something maternal about them, which rules out the possibility of virginity, by definition."

"That's the secret?"

"The paradox, the mystery."

"If you ask me, that's what they just call a Madonna-whore complex," said Minnie.

At that the photographer had to laugh, the way he always laughed: a single, hard, *Ha!*

"Oh kiddo," he said. "I do believe I'm fonder of you than you suspect. In my way."

"Your way, what's your way?"

The photographer looked at her thoughtfully and then put his hand on her cheek. Transparent men, thought Minnie, what *is* it about transparent men?

"Come home with me, I've missed you."

This was the moment. She had to say it. Even if it was proved to be wrong later, it was true *now*, in this bar where it was hard to tell what was real, with its red velvet stools and a hundred and thirty different herbs tingling on her tongue.

"I wouldn't *think* of it," she said. "And anyway, it was *Death Proof.* Not *From Dusk till Dawn.*"

AT FIRST GLANCE the photographer's apartment looked exactly the same as before. It wasn't until she peered around more closely that she saw the subtle but real changes to the bare interior: the black leather Gispen chair had been replaced with a simpler mustard-color model; the square black rug was now a furry white; the modest bookcase had been moved from the left wall to the right, as had the standing lamp and the curious dwarf palm the photographer had received, she seemed to remember, as a gift from an ex who had called his home "alarmingly sterile."

Minnie tried to imagine the photographer pushing the furniture around with precision and purpose. But why? Her eye fell on two identical stone statuettes on the windowsill she had never noticed before. (From the same ex? A new girlfriend?) They looked like reproductions in miniature of those famous terracotta warriors. Maybe, thought Minnie, the whole redesign had to do with feng shui. Yin and yang, unity in duality, ancient wisdoms repurposed for magazines and TV. She remembered an American collector who had come to her studio and had started rearranging her things without warning, like a man possessed. "The energy in here is all wrong!" he'd exclaimed, "all wrong, all wrong!"

It wasn't until the photographer grabbed her by the shoulders and said her name that she realized she'd been staring at those statuettes for quite a while. It took an effort to tear her gaze away from the little soldiers, who appeared to have been carved out of stone with great precision, a pair of twins in perfect symmetry. She had a strange sense that this belonged to her, not the statuettes per se, but rather the act of gazing at them.

She was drunk.

The man without a shadow put an arm around her neck and then another arm under the backs of her knees. The next moment she had changed from an upright being into something that was being moved sideways. Why, she wondered, would you lift someone who hadn't fallen down? She let her head fall backward. A dead Christ in the arms of the Holy Virgin. She tried to think of the name of the sculptor, but it was extremely hard to think in this position. Was it true the earth's electro-magnetic field was getting weaker? All things considered there was a certain logic to it. Reversal of gravity, furniture dangling down from the floor. Maybe, she thought, it had something to do with feng shui.

The photographer lowered her gently onto the bed. She wondered if that was a good idea, and at the same time knew she was only wondering because that sort of thinking was required in situations like this. The mattress was pleasantly cold and hard, gusts of wind kept howling through a crack in the window. Eeei-ee-eeei-eeei-eeee-ee-ee-eeei.

It seemed to mean something, a code or a signal, something to do with symmetry, but with every moan it became clearer to Minnie that it didn't signify anything, that it was just a sound, a rhythm, and that there was nothing meaningful to say about it.

MINNIE KNEW SOMETHING was up. She'd known for a few weeks there was something in the offing, she had known it, to be precise, ever since January 3rd when the photographer and she had signed that contract, but that knowing was so close to not-knowing that she had done a great job hiding the information from herself. That is: until the letter came.

Most of her business mail was sent directly to the agency, where it was sorted, filtered, and then forwarded to her home address. The secretary at the office was big on sticking fluorescent pink post-its on the letters, marked with anything from a single exclamation point to a detailed commentary on the sender's logo or writing style. Thanks to the post-its, the mail became just a matter of perception, and this helped soothe Minnie's not unreasonable fear of unopened envelopes, although of course she understood that this was actually an agent's entire raison d'être: reassuring artists that they don't have to be afraid. That the world can be provided with a coat of protective pink varnish for a commission of twenty-five, oh, all right, thirty per cent.

The letter in question had been sent straight to her home address. Since the letter slot in her door served mainly to receive a never-ceasing cascade of junk mail, coupons and the curious leaflets (photocopied and cut by hand) of a *Professor Ganesh Kahn, clairvoyant and medium,* Minnie didn't notice the letter until she was carrying a bag of paper to the recycling bin. Her gaze happened to fall on her name, *Ms. M. Panis*—the slight shiver that reading your own name in another's handwriting gives you—, written in peculiar, upright fountain pen letters that were vaguely familiar to her. In the upper right-hand corner was a little blue fish, a simple loop whose ends formed the tail. Underneath, the letters CBTH.

Inside the envelope were two typewritten sheets of thick, expensive-looking stationery. The letterhead consisted of the same fish as the one on the envelope, with beside it, in watermark, so that Minnie had to hold the letter to the light to read it:

The only thing the fish has to do is to lose itself in the water

January 15, 2012

Dear Ms. Panis,

This letter is to inform you that next month it will be twenty years since your treatment with the CBTH ended.

The Center, founded in 1990, was, in the year of your treatment (1991–1992), still in its relative infancy. You belonged to our second group of "patients." Since then we have come many years further in experience and expertise, and we can state with authority that the methods we developed have turned out to be successful or extremely successful in 93% of cases.

CBTH's philosophy, in a word, is that every human life is

marked by a number of major shifts, both internal and external. These shifts are closely connected with various cyclical phases.

Anno 2012 has seen people become estranged, on the whole, from the cycles that run our lives. We live our lives according to a linear and extremely neoliberal understanding of time, in which progress seems the only feasible way. The big problem with this progress-mentality is that the moment inevitably comes when progress stagnates. People get sick, societies get sick, the whole system crashes. There is a clear connection between such "prosperity ailments" and our current extremely artificial experience of time.

Based on over two decades' thorough empirical research, the CBTH has been able to establish that being made aware of life's cycles is not only of considerable benefit, but can even make a crucial difference.

The longest cycle in a human life lasts roughly twenty years. Even the Long Count of the Mayan calendar took this cycle, the so-called k'atun, into account as an important unit of time. To mark the end of a k'atun, the Mayans built special "Twin pyramids" every twenty years in Tikal, Guatemala. These pyramids were identical and symbolized eternal duality.

As you are doubtlessly aware, there is widespread speculation about an Apocalypse on December 21 of this year. According to certain interpretations, that date is the last day of the thirteenth and last b'ak'tun: at 394 years (or, put another way, twenty k'atun) the greatest unit of time in the Long Count. The earth and sun will supposedly align at Hunab K'u, the heart of the Milky Way. There is no doubt that such predictions rest on a fundamental misapprehension of the Mayan calendar, which is by definition circular in character: the end of one cycle is always the start of a new one.

All this does not mean that 2012 doesn't mark anything significant. After exhaustive calculations, historians and scientists have been able to prove that in all probability this is indeed the year of the ending of the thirteenth b'ak'tun, and thus the twentieth k'atun of this b'ak'tun. To put it more simply: the k'atun 1992–2012 is ending, and a new twenty-year cycle begins.

The fact that your treatment in 1991–1992 coincided so exactly with the beginning of the current cycle, which is now about to end, is an exceedingly interesting circumstance. From the data the CBTH has at its disposal concerning your treatment (written reports, recordings, medical records and such) we may conclude that you are extremely sensitive to the cyclical nature of time. You will therefore in all probability come to experience a major transition in the upcoming period.

The nature of this transition cannot be foreseen; however, there are definite "symptoms" that have occurred in previously registered cases. Memories you did not know you had may return. A very strong sense of déjà vu can occur. Your pursuits may present themselves as arbitrary to you, or, on the contrary, uncommonly significant. Furthermore, you may notice a heightened state of alertness in yourself, although the opposite may also (and even simultaneously) happen: you feel dazed, confused, under water, so to speak.

It is quite understandable if this letter makes you feel rather bewildered. We realize that you probably remember very little of the treatment, not only because of how young you were when you underwent it, but also on account of the nature of the treatment itself. Nevertheless we request with some urgency that you make an appointment. There are things that must be discussed on a one-on-one basis, for which a correspondence simply is not adequate.

The undersigned is aware of your demanding profession and your doubtlessly busy agenda. He has followed your career with great interest from the very beginning. He is impressed with the way you deal with the consequences of the artistic vocation, although he suspects that in your case life and art are inseparable, and that the word "artist" is therefore either a very broad term or a purely linguistic construct, worn chiefly like an item of clothing, just as an evening gown is required for certain occasions.

Undersigned hopes that he will have the pleasure of receiving a reply from you (see self-addressed envelope). Please consider this letter as an invitation to the ultimate session of a treatment you began twenty years ago.

Yours truly,

Bob Martina, P.A., o/b/o
Dr. J. Johnstone, Director

It was by far the strangest letter Minnie had received in ages—not counting hate- or fan-mail, although even the letters that looked the most extreme often turned out to be a surprisingly straightforward and consistent line of thought, composed of either indignation working up to condemnation, or admiration bordering on obsession, and sometimes a combination of both.

Her first thought was that it must be a case of mistaken identity, but as she read on it became clear to her that this bizarre medley of social criticism, pseudo-scientific theory and shamelessly personal observation was well and truly meant for her.

But why? Who was this Dr. Johnstone, and what in heaven's name was the "CBTH"? She couldn't for the life of her imagine she'd undergone some sort of new-age treatment when she was little. Her mother was the last person on earth who would go for that kind of nonsense. She stared at the stylized little fish on the envelope. As far as she knew, it was a symbol for Christ, something to do with the ancient Greek word for fish, although it seemed to her most unlikely that this had anything to do with a Christian organization.

She read the letter again. Something about it got on her nerves. She didn't know if it was what it said, the tone, or the fact—assuming it wasn't a joke—that the letter had landed on her doormat without warning, and that she was now supposed to *do* something with this excess of information explaining nothing at all. She felt a childish longing for a pink post-it that would tell her in a few clear words that what the letter said was even more ridiculous than the silly stationery so forget it and just throw it out, exclamation mark, smiley-face. Still, she realized that beneath the pretentious crap—the tiresome denigration of belief in progress, the annoying "empiricism" that insists on viewing everything through a scientific lens, the inanely specific "93% of cases," the Mayas, for fuck's sake—there was something about the letter that was stopping her from tossing it in with the recyclables. Yes, that was what was getting on her nerves, she thought, on reading the letter (Christ!) for the third time: she wanted to find this ludicrous, it *was* ludicrous, but she couldn't bring herself to find it so. Something was up, something was definitely up, and the letter was a symptom of it.

The next few days Minnie kept working up the resolve to tear up the letter, but every time she was about to do so, she'd decide that no, that was the easy way out. It meant giving in, it meant making the letter something important enough to be destroyed. Even trying to find out who this Johnstone was, and what the letters CBTH stood for, would mean capitulating.

As a compromise, she had briefly toyed with the idea of writing RETURN TO SENDER on the envelope in big letters and putting it back in the mailbox, but she couldn't shake the thought that it would be cheating. So, she realized with a start, this was a game, apparently, and you were supposed to play fair, too. She was in the dark about what kind of game it was, the stakes, or the other players taking part, but she refused to do what would have been easiest: dial the number and demand an explanation. Obstinacy had taken hold of her, and she found herself feeding it with even more pig-headed stubbornness. Maybe it was a sign of fear rather than of strength of character, but isn't everyone entitled to the benefit of the doubt just once in a while?

And so the letter sat on her kitchen table as if left there inadvertently among the pile of psychics' and soothsayers' leaflets. Every day she had the vague hope that it would have suddenly, somehow, disappeared, which didn't seem that unreasonable to her, after all, all kinds of things are always disappearing without being lost on purpose. How many single socks didn't she have in her bureau drawers, how many incomplete sets of underwear? Still, every night it was a relief to find the letter still sitting in the exact same spot where she had left it that morning. Even the things you detest at some point begin to feel comfortably familiar. (Minnie had read somewhere that abused women felt relief when the beating started. When their husbands were in a good mood, kind and caring, cracking jokes, the women were more scared than when they were actually being slapped around. It was the latent presence of violence, not the violence itself, that did it.)

Sometimes Minnie could see the envelope clearly before her even when she wasn't home, and then she'd experience a yearning that was familiar to her from her art projects: a pressing, all-absorbing need to perform a certain act, which in this case boiled down to picking up that letter, holding the watermark up to the light—*the only thing a fish has to do is lose itself in the water*—and read it for the umpteenth time from beginning to end. In the middle of having lunch with a gallerist from Germany, the urge overcame her so strongly that she had trouble sitting still, until finally, between the mackerel sandwich and the coffee, she had a chance to slip away to the ladies' room, where she managed to talk herself down, like a dog owner talking to his puppy until the unruly animal lies down. Suddenly, in a wave of nausea, the mackerel came back up, and she found herself throwing up for the fourth time that week. For a while she stood there staring at the flecks of vomit swimming in the toilet bowl, reading them as if they were tea leaves, but the sour pieces of fish just smelled bad, and remained stubbornly mute.

IN 1991, "THE YEAR OF your treatment," Minnie was seven years old. Pictures of her at that age had been stuck into photo albums with plastic sleeves, which after years of heat, cold and humidity, had begun to stick together. The manufacturer hadn't given any thought to durability, Minnie thought to herself when for the first time in ages she took the albums off the shelf and peered at the photos under the bubbling plastic.

Her mother had given her the albums some years ago, after *Nothing Personal,* when Minnie was cautiously starting on refurnishing her home. On a rare visit home—they preferred to meet in public spaces, so that their attempts at communication would seem less doomed, less essential, a conversation that would be drowned out by the general din around them—her mother had let slip that Minnie's home made her think of "a head without a brain." A few days later Minnie had received a package with three photo albums she'd never seen before, leafed through them quickly and then stowed them away in a closet. She'd have preferred to send them back, but that would have been too mean, too much of a statement.

Not only were the cells that made up the Minnie in the photographs one hundred per cent different from the cells she was composed of today, but the old photographs reinforced the feeling she'd always vaguely had, which she suspected was not so much a universal principle as her own individual truth: there was a *then* and there was a *now*, but there was no such thing as a direct link between the two. Where in other people, life was a map with a gradually expanding road network, the coordinates on Minnie's map remained separate, isolated from one another. You might find the occasional dirt road there, but they were so narrow and twisty that you couldn't really characterize it as any kind of real infrastructure.

So she was always amazed to hear people giving their lives a more or less logical story. No matter how many the turns or detours, no matter how many steep slopes or dead-end paths, there was always some sort of clearly marked course. Even the worst decisions and the greatest coincidences fit into the overall plan. How did people *do* that? How did they manage to get every cause to flow seamlessly into an effect, as if it wasn't hard at all but the most normal thing in the world, a law of nature, like water in a river flowing in just one direction? And how in God's name were they able to view themselves as more or less the same person the whole time, a single person, notwithstanding decades of growth, change, and decline?

When she was twenty-one, around the time she was taking photographs of her own trash at an average rate of 3.8 a day, Minnie had had a half-hearted fling with a young artist who was working on a PhD because some government initiative had pumped a few million euros into the creative industry's "knowledge and innovation platforms," with the goal of turning the sector into an "international leader in excellence." (The subject of his research was the artist and cult figure Bas Jan Ader, who in 1975 drowned in the

Atlantic Ocean, a rewarding subject for thinkers like the young artist, theory-obsessed types determined to make the world fit their theory. As far as Minnie could make out, the object was to make his thesis, composed of semi-abstract articles, art installations and performances, be a dissertation and an art work at the same time. A terrible idea, naturally, and the young artist did in the end become hopelessly mired in it.)

The young artist was intelligent, clever and utterly predictable—from his remarks on Guy Debord's *Société du spectacle* and the films of Wes Anderson, to the way he cracked his knuckles before going to sleep. Yet *he* was the one who broke up with *her*, after Minnie had confessed that she had wound up in bed with a number of fellow students after a party.

"I am a man of consistency," he had said, "and I can't deal with these sorts of shenanigans," whereupon Minnie had wondered out loud how that "consistency" applied to his work, and why it was always cited as a good quality in a person. The young artist had just sighed, annoyed, and said she should grow up. "You're a good person on other levels, but when it comes to love you're completely schizo," he told her. When Minnie asked in what regard then, according to him, she was "a good person," he had not deigned to reply.

After peeling apart the plastic pages and forcing herself to look at the photographs, she started feeling like a peeping Tom.

The seven-year-old version of herself was a petite, scrawny little girl with wispy, straggly blond hair. Her spine was slightly twisted, so that everything listed to the left and just a bit forward, as if she were about to topple over in that direction.

When she was a baby she'd been in an incubator for a while.

Minnie had never asked for the details, but she knew that it was the reason for the scoliosis and small stature. When she was around eight years old, her mother told her about her stillborn sister, who would have been a year older than Minnie. It seemed that in the eighth month of pregnancy, the umbilical cord had wrapped itself around one of the little feet, choking off the food supply; the fetus had starved to death. That was just how her mother had said it: straightforward, businesslike, drained of any emotion.

At night in bed Minnie sometimes imagined she was her sister, her body a shell to contain the first baby's soul. But the thought soon grew too muddled, since if she was her sister, then there wouldn't *be* any sister, would there, they'd be the same person, who wasn't Minnie, but wasn't anyone else either.

The fact that she didn't have a father was conveyed by her mother as an irrevocable, matter-of-fact circumstance, and accepted by Minnie as such. Yes, she did sometimes go over to the homes of neighbor children growing up in big, warm families with tea-drinking mothers and fathers who seemed to be constantly lifting things—their children, their wives, plates of food—but it simply did not occur to her to compare their situation to her own. Her father had left when her mother was a few weeks pregnant, that was all she knew about it, or needed to know.

It wasn't until she was older and realized that two people could not be more different than her mother and her, that she started to wonder. Where did her love of church music come from, her disproportionate horror of the smell of hospitals or dentists, her unerring spatial perception? And why the heck was her name Minnie? There was nobody else with that name, except for Minnie Mouse, and, as she later discovered, the creepy old lady in

Rosemary's Baby. It was hard to imagine her mother, who strove for the utmost degree of normality and conformity, choosing that name. And so Minnie chose to assume that it had been her father. Her father, who lived his life free as a bird, and didn't give a damn about convention.

Her favorite fantasy had her bumping into him in the supermarket thanks to some singular twist of fate. She'd immediately recognize he was her father, and he that she was his daughter, because they were as alike as two peas in a pod. He'd have on cowboy boots and would take her to his ranch in America, where they'd spend the days riding wild horses, raising bison and listening to music by The Pogues, songs that made them weep because they were so sad and so beautiful.

Later, when she was at art school, a teacher—half drunk, in a pub in Huidenstraat where they'd bumped into each other by chance—had encouraged her to go look for her father and to turn the search into an art piece. "In the vein of a documentary about your roots," he said, "a quest on the knife-edge between the self and the other." Minnie had asked him how such a search would be any different than an episode of *Missing*, upon which the teacher had exclaimed, indignant, that TV shows were the opium of the people, gently lulling them to sleep to the rhythm of the bromides handed out to them, confirmation upon confirmation of their own narrow world view. Later that night the teacher had tried to persuade Minnie to go home with him, but that was another quest she had politely turned down.

She sometimes asked herself if she shouldn't be more curious about her father, but even more than her fear of a letdown (after all, the chances of his being a cowboy were nil), one thing was clear to her, anyway: he hadn't stuck around for her sake. That categorical rejection was both undeniable and terribly unfair. Without knowing what sort of person she would grow up to be, he had chosen *not* to choose her.

Whenever Minnie allowed herself to stop and think about it, she'd feel an icy chill inside, at the level of her midriff. For a long time she couldn't find a word for that coldness—she couldn't even tell you if it was the presence or absence of something—but when the documentary filmmaker left her for a handful of Eskimos in Alaska, and, watching him disappear down her stairwell with that swim bag, she stood there frozen in place for quite a while, it suddenly struck her that the cold, hard thing in her midriff was definitely something that could be defined. It was what you felt when you were wounded in the deepest part of your soul.

*

Especially in the photos where Minnie was surrounded by other kids, she was hard to detect at first, either because she was partially hidden by another child, or because she stood turned away from the camera, or blinked just when the shutter clicked, whereas now those eyes—dark brown, just a bit slanted—were her face's most striking feature. The photographs reminded Minnie of botched daguerreotypes from the nineteenth century, in which sitters who didn't stay still or blinked their eyes too much were turned into ghostly phantoms with hollow eye sockets and blurred figures.

Where the other kids were constantly all over each other—arms slung around another, hands covering someone else's face, V-signs held up behind another's head—she was usually on her own, off to the side, only just in the picture. It was strange, thought Minnie, because even though she couldn't remember many specific friends from that time, she was sure she hadn't been shunned either. They didn't tease her, like Dirty Eli in her class, one of the few she could still clearly see before her: Dirty Eli, with his pants just a bit too short, his Velcro-tie shoes and the smelly gap in his mouth, acquired after breaking a front tooth on the monkey bars. Instead of an implant, the dentist had given the poor kid a set of braces that were supposed to pull the remaining teeth together, so that the gap eventually disappeared, but left him with one incisor in the middle, instead of two on either side.

Minnie wasn't snubbed when there were birthday parties, unlike several other children in her class. She had always pitied those kids, including Dirty Eli, pity that could nevertheless, in no time at all, turn into equally fierce disdain for their helplessness, their inability to blend in even just a little bit, so that they wouldn't always be so ostentatiously ostracized.

No, she hadn't been one of the unpopular kids. And yet, examining the photos closely for the first time, she felt herself growing convinced that this was another girl, a different girl from the one she thought she remembered. More lonely, or, at least, more alone.

There was one photograph Minnie studied longer than the others: a picture of herself in a red and green Speedo at the edge of a swimming pool. It must have been taken just before she'd gone in, since her hair was still completely dry. She didn't smile for the camera, but was staring with a frown at whatever was going on behind it. Her arms were stretched out at a ninety-degree angle from her body, like the caricature of a sleepwalker. She may have been showing the photographer (her mother?) her diving stance. The camera lens was focused tightly on her face, the outstretched arms were blurry, which gave the photo an artistic quality. Unlike the other hopelessly bland, over- and under-exposed snapshots, this photo gave an impression of three-dimensionality, a glimpse of something that existed that way outside of the photo as well.

When she was little, she had been an accomplished swimmer. Between the ages of four and six she'd passed four swimming stage tests in quick succession; the four diplomas had hung, neatly framed, above her bed for a while. The smell of chlorine still stirred up a vivid memory of swimming pools with slippery tiles, yelling children and a special sort of excitement that later little else could evoke in her. Still, at some point, not long after collecting all those swim-diplomas, she'd lost all interest in swimming. For no particular reason, or so it seemed; she wasn't able to come up any logical explanation, anyway. When she'd brought up the subject with her mother one time, she had shrugged and said something about Minnie's volatile nature as a child, how she'd be obsessed with some activity one moment, only to shrug and give it up the next.

It wasn't until she came to live around the corner from the swimming pool, at age nineteen, that she took it up again; hesitant at first, afraid it might be a big mistake, but as soon as she'd swum a few laps she couldn't believe she had ever stopped. The water felt like a natural skin encasing her body, helping her along, like a stiff wind in your back. Since then she swam laps twice a week early in the morning, She loved the way the repetitive strokes lulled her into a kind of trance, the weightlessness, the emptiness; oh yes, all those quasi-philosophical platitudes pretty much covered it.

Carefully she peeled the photo out of its sticky sleeve. *May 1991* was written in ballpoint ink on the back, nothing else. She brought the photo up closer to her face. What was that little girl staring at? Looked at more closely, it didn't really seem as if her gaze was directed at anything concrete. The eyes seemed to be looking inward rather than out, somehow. It made Minnie think of Rodin's Balzac, in the garden of the Van Abbe Museum. The sculptor had given the writer a look of haughty irony. This Balzac gazed at the world with a scrutinizing stare, the head tilted sideways a bit, chin up. It was only when you looked at the sculpture from up close that you noticed the deep sockets didn't contain eyes as such. The gaze was made up of nothing but shadow and suggestion.

Minnie tried to push the photograph back in its sleeve, but the uncooperative plastic tore when it was halfway in. She stuffed the picture in her pocket and shut the album.

People were always kidding themselves about their own place in the world. In reality, thought Minnie, all you have is bits and pieces continually dying off and never coming back. You keep vanishing from your own life, over and over, without ever saying goodbye to yourself. She didn't know if she should consider that a tragic fact or a reassuring idea, but suspected it actually had nothing to do with either one. Time simply rolled on, as it had always done and presumably always would. No matter what that Johnstone guy might say in his letter about cycles and eternal calendars, a moment was gone when it was gone. Resolutely she pushed her chair back, walked to the kitchen and tore up the letter.

Sometimes you had to bend in order not to break—a piece of wisdom that the Maya or perhaps some other visionary race had probably written down eons ago in hieroglyphs that looked like childish scribbles.

ON THE NIGHT of January 30, Minnie awoke, startled, from a strange dream in which she found herself cycling through Amsterdam with Notary Specht perched on her bike's luggage rack. They were riding down Staalstraat, across Waterloo Square, past the botanical garden, on their way somewhere, looking for a building with a special type of column—Specht was trying to explain it to her, but his shouts were drowned out in the wind. He had shrunk to the size of a lapdog. He'd pause his incomprehensible jabbering only to cackle like a madman, clutching Minnie's hips with his paws. Just as they were about to be run over by a tram coming around the bend of Plantage Middenlaan, her eyes flew open.

She was surrounded by total darkness and for a few seconds had no idea where she was, or how, as if the whole concept of gravity had been sent reeling and she now, abruptly, found herself trapped in the force field of a magnet's opposing poles. The darkness wasn't an absence of light, but the presence of something heavy and viscous pressing on her airway and threatening to slowly suffocate her. In the distance she heard something squeaking, soft and hesitant. Was that what had woken her up? She had to suppress the urge to scream. Screaming would only make it worse, she knew, not-screaming was the only way to stay in control of the situation. Breathe, she thought, breathe, breathe, breathe. She tried to think of the photographer, his calm hand on her cheek, his smell, which reminded her of his profession. *Developer fluid.* The sound and the rhythm of the words made her come to her senses. She groped for the switch on her bedside lamp, found it and squeezed her eyes shut as a blaze of light made the sticky darkness vanish in one go.

Four numerals lit up in a soft orange glow on her alarm clock, 04:01, but it took her until 04:02 to realize that those numbers represented the time of day; time ticking on, and not some bomb-like gadget counting off the minutes until it went off and her home exploded. The squeaking continued. It wasn't until she held her breath in order to hear it better, and the noise suddenly stopped, that she realized it was her own breathing. Her awareness seemed to be delayed, held back; she was running behind, as in a film where the picture and sound are just a bit out of synch, making it lose all verisimilitude for the viewer.

"Developer fluid." Minnie whispered the word softly to herself, once, twice, three times, until finally that weird cloud was lifted from her mind and the world resumed its steady course around the sun and its own axis. It seemed to her that she'd been gone for years, far away, in a strange land and a strange life, and was now being thrust back into her own life, with no idea what had happened to her in the intervening time or who had been watching her. Watching her? She swung her feet out of bed and took a few unsteady steps, a foal on stilts, opened the window wide and exposed herself to the freezing cold.

Aside from a few stars piercing the dark, there was hardly any light to be discerned. What was it with the street lighting these days?

Was someone manipulating the switches whose internal clock was seriously out of whack? The moon, as far as Minnie could tell, was a no-show too. She wondered if it could be one of the rare eclipses of the moon, and just as she was trying to figure out how the sun, moon and earth would have to align for that to happen, she detected a tiny sliver, yellow and dull like a toenail clipping. New moon, waxing moon, first quarter, constellations. Did people who knew the difference between those things feel less at sea? Of course not. The more you knew, the less you knew; that, tragically, was the trouble with knowledge.

Less than twenty-four hours from now it would be February. Ever since January 3, when they had signed the contract in Specht's office before having sex in a haze of green chartreuse—an event Minnie remembered almost exclusively for the way the wind had squealed through the window, and how she'd tried to decipher that sound—she'd not had any contact with the photographer. Everything she had to know was written in the contract, which she could spell out word for word by now.

> As of a date in February to be advised [by the photographer], he will follow the undersigned, Minnie Panis, for twenty-one consecutive days with his camera. He is to operate with the utmost discretion and under no circumstance interfere, no matter what the situation may be. Neither of the two parties will attempt to contact the other from February 1 through March 21, 2012. The only means of transportation permitted will be by bicycle.
>
> No earlier than the twentieth and no later than the twenty-first of March (15:00 hrs) [the photographer] will deliver some photographs (quantity to be determined by him) at the offices of Specht

> & Vink Notaries, Prinsengracht 997, where undersigned will collect them on the evening of March 21. From the day the contract is signed, i.e. January 3, 2012, until the day undersigned decides to make the project public, but in any case until March 21, 2012, both parties are sworn to secrecy. In the event of breach of contract the fine is €20,000 (twenty thousand).

Aside from Minnie, the photographer and Specht, no one else knew about the project. She had fobbed off her agent with some vague story about "taking some time off for reflection" after all the hoopla of the past few years. She was well aware that he didn't fully believe her, he wasn't born yesterday, but he'd had a box of nasty scented candles delivered ("to aid reflection," it said on the pink card that accompanied it), and then left her alone. You couldn't accuse him of having no sense of humor, anyway, thought Minnie, who'd immediately dumped the cloying, nauseating rubbish in the trash.

Before the summer she had received an invitation to a winter symposium at Leipzig's Hochschule für Grafik und Buchkunst, at the instigation of Neo Rauch, who taught there and whom Minnie considered one of the greatest artists of the twenty-first century—as did Brad Pitt, who had shelled out almost a million dollars for Rauch's painting *Etappe*. Making an exception, she had immediately accepted. Lectures, panel discussions and symposia in general made her uncomfortable, because there always seemed to be something very specific people wanted to know, and Minnie could never work out what, precisely. Besides, there were always at least five different discussions going on at once: theoreticians discussed theory, whereas artists had their own distinct views of reality.

At a conference some years ago, after taking part in a panel discussion about "the future of conceptual art" as an "expert practitioner" and being subjected to a load of hogwash about the artist's craft today being a carefully constructed pose aimed at boosting and glorifying an art market with ridiculously inflated prices that was kept going by a cartel of art czars, mafia bosses and billionaires, Minnie had attended a lecture by AA Bronson, co-founder of the Canadian collective General Idea. From the seventies until the death of two of its three members from AIDS in 1994, the collective had made a big splash with its cheeky and later more serious subversion of popular culture. AA Bronson was literally the last man standing, and his talk was a wistful look back at an era long come and gone, ending with life-sized photo projections of his colleagues as they lay dying; gaunt and wasted human wraiths, robbed of everything but the disease itself. Minnie had felt great sympathy for this man, whose only role now was that of survivor, and who'd been lugging these two dead men around with him for twenty years.

In the evening, at a dinner for the speakers in the rector's office, they'd started talking. He turned out to be a sweet old hippie, who besides being an artist was also a healer. He explained that he gave Tantric massages that could lead to a full-body orgasm, and also practiced a related version that he called "butt massage," a very advanced technique for which both the practitioner and the subject had to be in the right state of mind. He'd fixed her with a long, meaningful stare, his face largely hidden under a full grey beard, the eyes greatly magnified by thick glasses. Just as she was considering accepting his more or less explicit proposal, a (likewise bespectacled) PhD student from New York's New School had butted in, bestowing on AA Bronson *his* ideas on Bronson's idea of life as a radical social construct with all the political implications thereof. AA Bronson had patiently listened to his monologue, which rambled all over the place; it was obvious he was used to this, and Minnie had had to conclude, awed, that this man was not only an artist and a healer, but also a diplomat. The dinner turned into a wild party, someone sent out for more alcohol, which was delivered, already iced, by a kid on a motorbike; the discussions grew more and more boring. Minnie, wandering through the corridors in search of a bathroom, came across AA Bronson and the PhD student squeezed onto a little loveseat, their bodies intertwined, Bronson's hands under the young man's shirt. "Come join us," AA Bronson had said to her without stopping the massage nor even looking up.

Minnie had sworn never again to take part in any gathering of this sort, until that invitation from Leipzig, which, as already noted, she'd received well before the previous summer, when she'd still been scarfing down tubs of Ben & Jerry's ice cream with the photographer, and assumed the affair would be just a brief interlude in his life and her own. She hadn't thought about the invitation for months. It wasn't until a few days ago, when the agency called her to tell her they were mailing her a ticket to Leipzig leaving February 22 plus a hotel booking, that she realized with a start that she wouldn't be able to go, given the fact that she had just signed a contract stipulating she was not to leave Amsterdam between February 1 and March 21. After some hemming and hawing she managed to come up with the excuse that she was suffering from burnout, and that there was nothing for it but to cancel the trip. This was the first time it occurred to her the project might be a flight from something.

She was nervous. She had talked to the photographer in grandiose terms about "a truth proposition," "mutual obligations" and "implications," but the more she thought about it of late, the less she was beginning to understand those words herself. Sometimes they struck her as hollow and meaningless, at other times they seemed as ponderous as rock outcroppings on a mountain face, boulders ready to let go and crush her. When had the idea taken hold of her? That too was difficult to reconstruct. She liked to tell herself it had been a spontaneous inspiration, after that radio broadcast, during her phone conversation with the photographer, something like an epiphany. But even epiphanies had to come from somewhere. "Most things start before they begin," the head of her art school had told a hall full of graduates, tapping the side of his head, "the artist's task to bring what lies there, latent, to the surface of consciousness, and give it shape." Perhaps she'd been pushed in this direction for years, she thought, puffing out little white clouds of breath into the dark night, and the photographer had just provided the last push she needed. It was quite possible. Over the past few months her mind had returned so often to that hot August night that she'd begun to wonder if she really had been that deeply asleep when the photographer had caught her in his lens. Sometimes, as she stared at those photographs in *Vogue,* they seemed like memories.

She shivered. For several nights running they'd had a spectacular freeze, by Dutch standards at least. Temperatures of ten and even fifteen below zero centigrade had been recorded in the north. The entire city was in an uproar: half of the citizens wildly excited at the prospect of the canals freezing over, the other half confounded by the mass hysteria of the rest.

She ought to close the window, go back to bed, but suddenly she had the sense she was being watched, silent eyes in her back, red laser points scanning her. The feeling grew, throttled her, it was an effort not to wheel around. Her breath was still squeaking in her chest, she must have some medicine lying around somewhere, a blue plastic inhaler to puff powder into her airways. Slowly and calmly, trying to ignore the strange paranoia of these past ten minutes, she shut the window.

When she turn around everything was quiet and normal—except for a cat with eyes like laser beams on the floor at her feet.

Minnie let out a scream, a clipped "Oh!" that sounded ridiculous, and which she corrected by adding *"shit!"* to it. The cat cocked its head but otherwise did not budge.

Judging from the blue collar and calico coat, it was Mies, the neighbors' tomcat. He—once, when Minnie had referred to the animal as "she," the neighbors, both architects, had explained it was actually a "he," named for Ludwig Mies van der Rohe—must have jumped onto her balcony and slipped inside through the window. Even though she'd occasionally felt him slinking past her legs upon opening the front door, he had never performed this trick before. Quite a feat, thought Minnie, looking at the minuscule gap between the window and the ledge, and back at the cat. Since the window tilted inward, there was no way for it to get out again. Which didn't seem to bother the cat at all. As far as Minnie could tell, it wasn't a skittish animal, not even a cagey one. It just sat there, stoically awaiting its fate.

Minnie had been allergic to cats for as long as she could remember. When she found herself in the presence of a cat she'd start squeaking like a badly oiled machine; an immune system protest that was not only quite pointless, but also an attack on her own body. How long had that cat been there? She thought of the infinitesimal dander flakes floating in the air, sucked into her lungs, into her body, which was now working itself into a frenzy of histamine production to ward off the invasion.

She would have liked to pick up the animal and hurl it back onto the neighbors' balcony, but she knew that touching it would exacerbate her allergy. To her relief he got up and followed her as she opened her bedroom door, descended the stairs and walked down the corridor. At the front door they both halted. The cat looked up, questioning. "Well, bye, then," said Minnie, half expecting the animal to lift its paw in greeting, like a Japanese good-luck cat, instead of a harbinger of doom answering to the name of a deceased architect.

It was almost five now, and sleep a distant and unreachable destination, even though the night was not yet done. After she'd vacuumed up every cat hair, speck of dander and dribble of spit from her bedroom, taking a shower and putting on a robe, Minnie started pacing restlessly around the house. It was a familiar routine, meant to shrink the distance between herself and the world after it had been stretched out of shape: she'd touch something, pick it up, feel its heft, and put it back again. It had nothing to do with feelings of attachment, it was more a matter of gauging, measuring. If she could gauge what she possessed, then surely she couldn't *not* be there. She believed that even the deepest abyss could be bridged by, for example, a pencil. Or a tube of toothpaste.

In the chest that she pulled out from under her bed an hour later, she found, under a pile of heavy woolen sweaters, mittens and scarves, a black cardboard box. She lifted it onto her lap, and slowly, as if the contents were a surprise, took off the lid. She waited until it was 7:30, then got in her car.

MINNIE WOULD NEVER ADMIT it out loud when there were other people around, but her favorite painting was Picasso's *Les Demoiselles d'Avignon.* She had first seen it as a slide projection. "Here we see five naked prostitutes around a bowl of fruit in a Barcelona brothel," announced the drawing teacher, who had inspired her more than all the instructors she'd had afterwards taken together, "but it wasn't the subject matter that was the most shocking thing about this canvas by far."

According to the teacher, this work, from 1907, marked the start of analytic cubism, which over the next few years would evolve and get radicalized, mainly by Picasso and Braque. Some art historians called this one pre-cubist, but that was nitpicking at best—if you insisted on seeing it that way, then you could call everything all the way back to the Flemish Primitives "pre-cubist."

"Notice the angular, contorted bodies," said the teacher. "The mask-like heads of those two on the right. The harsh lines, the facets, the distortions. Everything happening at once, in the same place. Look at those noses, those knees, those breasts. The background spilling into the foreground!"

Three quarters of her classmates had already completely

checked out, staring outside longingly, where the air quivered with the promise of recess and summer. But Minnie was mesmerized. *Everything happening at once.* The dull, flat image was transformed into something profound and mysterious, an opening to an alternative reality.

The instructor turned to the few students who were still listening.

The modernist avant-garde to which not only Picasso and Braque but also Matisse and Derain belonged, was rebelling against everything that was bourgeois in their eyes: positivism in science, naturalism in painting, the static geometric principles—all overturned and trampled upon in this work. They were living at the right time for it: in 1895 Röntgen had discovered radiation, which made it possible to turn the human body inside out (to test this, Röntgen had taken an x-ray of his wife's hand, who was said to have exclaimed, on seeing the carpals, metacarpals and phalanges, that she was seeing her own death, not an unreasonable response, if you consider the fact that every living body is of course potentially a dead one), and 1899 had seen the publication of the first edition of Freud's *Interpretation of Dreams.* There were all sorts of riddles seething beneath the surface of the visible, and that was precisely what the artists were looking for. They rejected Euclides, whose principles of perspective had for centuries been every artist's touchstone. Down with the illusion of three-dimensionality! Down with the idea that every moment in time has its determined corollary in space! The cubists embraced the philosopher Henri Bergson, who introduced a new concept of time, which he called a *durée*: time was not an objective given, but depended on people's individual experience and intuition. Time, and therefore space, could be kneaded, stretched, and reconstituted.

"Without the cubists," the teacher concluded, on the verge of being cut short by the dictate of the bell for recess, "there would have been no Dadaist photomontages in the 'twenties, no surrealist fantasies in the thirties, no dizzying James Bond film clips, no *Matrix*, that movie you're all so crazy about." He shouted that last bit to be heard over the shrieking of the bell, fingers pointed high in the air, as if trying to lift himself physically above the noise. A few days later, Minnie took her dishwashing salary and bought herself a book about twentieth-century avant-gardism, complete with a large, shiny picture of *Les Demoiselles*, which she would trace with her fingers every night before going to sleep

Shortly after finals she had spent a week in New York, staying with her mother's cousin. She went to MOMA late one Tuesday afternoon, starting in the top floor galleries and then diligently working her way down, a dizzying bounty of art that in her memory all blended together into one great capsule of color, light, form and noise. When she finally stepped into the gallery where the painting was hung, her heart skipped a beat. There it was, not a facsimile but the original, just as Picasso had painted it almost a hundred years ago, huge and clear as a curtain that lets the sun shine through. Time, space, and the bored tourists all ceased to exist. There wasn't any difference between seeing and feeling any more, between being there and not being there. This was the sum of all things, everything was equally grand and equally non-existent, this was ecstasy. Finally (after a few minutes? Quarter of an hour? Three-quarters of an hour?) she forced herself to walk out of the gallery, down the stairs, and into another gallery, but she knew she only left in order to be able to make her way back again, slowly, tormenting herself with circuitous detours.

Ever since then she had never been in New York without going to see the painting. Time and again she was relieved to see that it was still there, silent, majestic, waiting for her to come.

*

Minnie parked the car just outside the village and strode up the high street to the water's edge. The lake was quiet and still. The glistening ice looked black in the morning light, thick and unimaginably smooth. In the summer there was something cloying and excessive about the view, an explosion of primary colors, but now, with just the skeletons of trees and the grey haze of frost on the fields, it was reduced to a pale rudiment of lines and planes. If the summer belonged to Matisse, thought Minnie, the winter belonged to the young Mondrian.

Removing her long-stashed-away Vikings from the black box and unwrapping them from their dishtowels, wiping the skates' greased blades with a cloth, the supple leather, the black-and-white laces, she felt like a child unwrapping a Christmas present.

Everything that happens will happen today—where had she heard that?

She stared at the dark ice and suddenly it occurred to her that the lake was extremely deep, deeper than the deepest ocean trough, a conduit to all the mysteries that had dwelt in the center of the earth since the beginning of time. It was expressing something urgent, which both alarmed and excited her. By tomorrow everything could be totally different, the smooth ice grown pitted and porous, until it cracked, broke up, disappeared, and for at least three seasons wouldn't let on about the awe-inspiring transformation of which it was capable.

"Skaters aren't much different from religious zealots," her ex, the young artist, once told her. "They talk about the condition of the ice as if it's the Holy Scripture, and they glide across the water like reincarnated Christs, single-mindedly convinced of their mission." He would have no part of it; if he'd wanted indoctrination, he'd have joined some kind of sect. Minnie had shrugged and said that still, she'd rather be a zealot than a knee-jerk atheist. The roots of their later breakup were planted right there, of course, but these things are only evident in hindsight.

She put her shoes in the box and stuffed it in her backpack. She looped the laces of her speed skates twice around the instep, the way she'd been taught by a neighbor of theirs, a divorced skating instructor who was trying to make a good impression on her mother. They'd taken Tram Line 9 to the Jaap Edenbaan rink every Sunday for a year—Minnie, the neighbor, and his son, a kid a year older than Minnie who spent the entire outing yelling, running and stomping his feet; the effort made him get so red in the face that Minnie thought his head might explode. The boy was hopeless at skating, which sent him off into impotent rages, spread-eagled on the ice, kicking his skates against the wooden posts.

After the lesson the neighbor always gave them a juice box and a graham cracker, which the boy would smash to bits with his fist and then lick the crumbs off the table, grinning, because he knew it made his dad furious. (It wasn't until much later that Minnie understood it was the father's fault, for humiliating his son with those skating lessons, and that the boy's bad behavior had just been his way of dealing with the mortification.) The neighbor always brought gingerbread in his backpack for himself, which he devoured as if it was a baguette. That was the memory that had stayed with Minnie most: the man tearing at that loaf with his teeth, the idea that you didn't always have to have bread cut into neat slices.

*

It wouldn't be getting crowded until a few hours later, when the starting shot went off for the skating tour that would lead the participants in a wide arc past villages with sturdy names like Zunderdorp, Schellingwoude, Zuiderwoude and Holysloot.

A father holding the hand of a bundled-up toddler cautiously picking his way along the edge of the lake kept yanking the child up by its little arm whenever its feet slid out from under it. A little farther on, a wiry old man glided forward with deliberate strides. His hands were folded around his skate guards behind his back, and his torso was so rigid that it didn't look as if he were being propelled by his own legs, but by a self-driving machine he was simply sitting on. Even the most perfectly formulated thought could never beat a perfectly executed action, thought Minnie, gazing at the languid ease of the man's progress. It made her think of the little Japanese man years ago who'd picked up her drawings off the street, zigzagging from one side to the other; the fear she'd felt that she would never know even a fraction of what he knew.

Minnie made her way cautiously through the rushes until she got to the open ice and was able to start making longer strides. She hadn't skated in years, but her body seemed to have stored away the basic strokes, as if it had just taken a brief break, and was simply picking up where it had left off. Her feet would probably start cramping very soon, not yet used to the weight of an entire body pressing on those two thin blades, but what the hell. The ice was like a mirror, reflecting the golden light of the sun, which at this hour was just emerging above the horizon. What from far away had seemed grey and dull, up close held an entire spectrum of color. The weird events of the previous night suddenly seemed very distant. The wind, cold but not unpleasant, blew on her cheeks, and for the first time in weeks she didn't feel she had to be on her guard.

At the narrow passage separating pond and meadow, she was overtaken by the old man, who gave her a stiff nod that was perfectly in line with his skating technique.

"Watch out for wind craters, Mrs.," he shouted at her as he passed her. "That low-lying sun is capable of blinding you badly. I don't want to have to pull some Sunday skater out of the ditch today."

She watched him go. He had greater speed than she had first thought. "You have to let the ice work for you," the neighbor had told her back in the day. "Ice is slippery because the surface molecules vibrate so hard that they're virtually liquid. The ones underneath are solid. So you won't fall through."

A few kilometers farther on she paused for a rest, leaning against a farmyard fence. Her muscles were already shaky from the effort. As a child, those vibrating molecules had seemed endlessly fascinating. If even the smallest particles in the world could pretend to be something else, wasn't *everything* different than what it was? Every week she would stare at the ice for minutes at a time, squinting, determined not to allow nature to pull the wool over her eyes. But, just as she never managed by pure willpower to make objects fly through the air, so she had never been able to catch the ice vibrating. It was a disappointment, although it did provide her with more food for thought, about the universe and everything in it that couldn't be seen with the naked eye.

While thinking about all of this, Minnie had been staring blankly at a sheep close by, which seemed to be pacing in tight, systematic circles, casting nervous looks over its shoulder. It wasn't until the animal sank to its knees that it occurred to Minnie something was going on.

The sheep sank to the ground in slow motion, gracefully almost, as if it had anticipated its fall and was quite resigned to it. Minnie looked around. There wasn't another sheep to be seen anywhere. The animal was down, and it was all by itself. Without wasting any more thought, she quickly changed out of her skates and put on her shoes before cautiously approaching the sheep, which was running its tongue along its lips and scratching the frozen grass with its forelegs. It seemed uneasy, but not exactly panicked.

Minnie walked around the animal, clueless as to what to do—her knowledge of sheep was pretty much limited to the wool sweaters in her closet. In spite of lying there so helplessly, the animal gave off a vibe of strength, as if it were built to outlive all other species in some post-apocalyptic world. Maybe it was fine for it to lie there like that, she thought to herself, and this scene was perfectly normal. It wasn't until she'd spotted the yellowish fleece protruding from its hindquarters, wet and as round as a water balloon, that she realized there was definitely something going on.

It was the depth of winter, it was so cold the ground creaked underfoot, but this sheep had decided to lamb out in the open air, entrusting itself to whatever clueless city slicker happened to come along. Bad idea, thought Minnie, and began walking toward the farm, in search of a farmer.

*

"I don't know whose ewe this is," said the farmer. "I only keep cows."

They looked down at the animal, still lying on her side, and now anxiously craning its head back, to where it must be feeling all sorts of things moving around.

"She must have walked a long way to end up here. Ewes tend to wander off by themselves when they're about to birth, but this one here looks like she's overdone it a bit. The closest sheep farm is several kilometers from here."

The farmer pointed vaguely in a northwesterly direction. He was young, definitely no older than thirty, with a broad, suntanned face. Wisps of yellow-blond hair escaped from beneath a blue wool hat. He looked more like a surfer than a farmer, thought Minnie. Accidentally tossed onto dry land by a tidal wave. He looked vaguely familiar.

The farmer crouched down by the little yellow balloon.

"Shit," he said. "It's empty."

"There's no lamb?" asked Minnie, and immediately regretted it. There *must* be a lamb; the sheep was in labor.

"Normally you'd see the little head and the legs in the water bag," said the farmer in a surprisingly patient voice. "Then you can just let the sheep do her thing, even outdoors in the freezing cold. But this lamb's stuck, darn it."

He stood up and shut his eyes. After a few seconds he opened them again.

"Listen, girl," he said to the ewe, which made no sign of acknowledging their presence. "We're going to get you up on your feet and take you to that barn over there, so a little cooperation would be appreciated."

Looking at Minnie, he asked what her name was.

"Good. Minnie. This may not be easy. Females in labor tend to ignore men who tell them what to do, especially when they're told to get up for a walk."

Together they crouched behind the ewe and pushed her upon her feet in one swoop. She stood on her legs, befuddled, ready to sink down again. But then, abruptly, she recovered, and without needing further encouragement, tottered after them to the barn.

"Ha," cried the farmer, surprised. "Meek as a lamb, who would have thought?"

It was dark inside the barn, which, from the look of it, was being used to store all sorts of equipment, tools, and disintegrating pieces of furniture. The farmer trotted to the back, returning with a bundle of straw and a bottle with a plastic teat. Meanwhile the ewe, who had started wheeling around again with the water bag dangling out of her rear, was now slowly circling to a stop.

"OK, Winnie," the farmer said to Minnie, "Now I'll have to act fast. The way it's positioned, the umbilical cord could snap."

He took out a long plastic glove that covered the length of his arm. Without further ado he shoved his hand inside the animal, placing his other hand on the animal's belly. For a dairy farmer, he seemed to know his way around sheep pretty well.

"Holy cow," he exclaimed, astonished. "I do believe there's another one in there."

Awestruck, Minnie watched the dexterity with which the farmer grabbed the legs of the first lamb and pulled it out of the ewe. A few seconds later the baby lamb was out on the straw, skinny and elongated, slimy, covered in what remained of the sac. The farmer slapped its side and pushed it in front of the mother, who promptly started licking it. Its little head moved, and then gulped in its first breath of air.

"We should really wait until she starts having contractions again," said the farmer. "But since the first one was breech, I don't trust it."

He started milking the ewe. The udder promptly squirted out a yellow stream of colostrum, which he caught in the bottle. (Minnie was surprised she knew that word, colostrum; a piece of knowledge that must have been gathering dust in some remote corner of her memory since childhood.)

"The milking makes the contractions restart," said the farmer, and indeed, it was obvious from looking at the ewe that she was getting ready for another delivery. Again the farmer's hand disappeared into her hindquarters. It took longer this time, but a few minutes later the second lamb made its appearance. The farmer quickly tore off the membrane covering its mouth, but unlike the firstborn, this one didn't automatically start sputtering for air.

"Complications," he said. "The way the first was stuck in there probably strangled this one's umbilical cord."

Briskly he grabbed the inert lamb by its hind legs and asked Minnie to go to the back of the barn and fill a bucket with water. Grateful for having something to do, she ran in the direction the farmer had indicated.

The barn was larger than she'd thought. In the semi-darkness she saw the outlines of all kinds of machines whose function were a mystery to her. She found the bucket against the back wall, next to a barrel of water. A big wooden door let in the bright sunlight through a narrow crack. The light fell on a still life of stacked flowerpots and a jumbled pile of bark. Minnie looked up, her eyes following the shaft to where it lit up the rafters, which in turn cast dark shadows into the cavities between. She stood rooted to the spot. She had already seen this once, *exactly* this.

A very strong sense of déjà vu may occur.

For a brief instant everything froze in place, but then she shook her head. This wasn't the time for nebulous feelings of foreboding. There was a life to be saved.

With a sloshing bucket she hurried back to the farmer, who dunked the lamb's head into the water several times in quick succession. Then, suddenly gently, he laid it down in the straw. Hooking his fingers into the animal's ribcage, he pulled upward, then pushed the ribs down again with both hands. He repeated this about ten times.

Minnie watched, mesmerized, as the farmer performed this manoeuver, gravely and with dedication. It made her think of the wiry old skater with the measured gait, the barmaid pouring chartreuse into the glasses, the girl with the hennaed hair who kept tentatively touching the top of her own head.

"Too bad," the farmer said suddenly. His hands let go of the little animal, hovering in the air for a moment, like a prayer. "Dead as a doornail. Maybe it was already dead before labor began. Who can tell."

The ewe was still busy licking the first lamb, quite oblivious of the loss she had just suffered. The farmer picked up the dead lamb in one hand. What were you supposed to do with a dead animal? Did they get buried, cremated, tossed in the shredder? Minnie didn't dare ask. She stared at the farmer's big hand around that little body and then at his broad face, which she just couldn't seem to place.

"Yeah, yeah," he said. "You recognize me, don't you. Actually, I was on TV last year, *Farmer Seeks a Wife*. Ever since then, people have been staring at me the way you are now. Most people have no idea where they've seen me before. They think they know me from grade school, or, who knows, the gym. The truth is that they know me from sitting on the sofa, staring at a TV screen. Would you like a cup of coffee?"

THE FIRST FEW days of February passed so unremarkably that Minnie wondered if she hadn't actually wound up in some kind of lull, a pause in time. What was it she'd said to her agent again? *A time for reflection.*

She knew an actress who used that expression. Once a year the actress would travel to a convent in Italy with her group, to meditate in total silence for three weeks under the tutelage of a chemistry teacher who was also a Vipassana meditation master. The students sometimes encountered the nuns who lived in an adjacent wing, gliding through the corridors, mistresses of silence and devotion.

One morning, the actress said, a note was slipped under the door of her cell. It was from the Vipassana teacher, who asked her to come to a certain door on the second floor that afternoon and five minutes before three. When the actress arrived she found the Vipanssana teacher standing there with an old nun. The nun took a key from her pouch, it was like something out of a movie, and opened the door. It was too dark to see anything at first, but once she was accustomed to the gloom, the actress saw something unbelievable. There, lined up against the back wall, were five mummified nuns, traditionally dressed in the black habit with the white scapular and a big silver cross at the chest. The skin on the faces was like parchment, but still completely intact. Four of the five seemed to have fallen asleep peacefully—eyes neatly closed, expression calm—; only the face of the last one held a look of terror. Her mouth was wide open and her cheeks were as hollow as Munch's screamer.

"They looked like some sort of prototype," said the actress. "As if I'd walked into a science fiction movie in which frozen corpses are returned to life or something." The Vipassana teacher had whispered in her ear that the mummified nuns dated back to sixteen hundred something. They had remained plastered inside the wall for centuries, no one knew why, but being entombed in the wall had wound up preserving them for all that time. The old nun, with tears running down her cheeks, mumbled a prayer in Italian, and then the Vipassana master intoned a mantra in Sanskrit. The actress hadn't really felt much, but when a few days later, in the chapel, she had an impulse to kneel next to some of the nuns before a statue of Christ, something inside her had suddenly let go, very weird, as if she were shattering into little pieces, but at the same time held intact by a bright light. "It's all about letting go, in there," she had told Minnie, who had then asked what you were supposed to do once you managed to let go. The actress had shaken her head sadly. (Nobody shakes their head sadly any more, thought Minnie, except in cheap novels and soap operas.)

"Letting go is an activity," the actress said after she'd finished shaking her head. "And a goal in and of itself. You have to keep doing it. Thinking that you'll reach some end point is a very western concept. Just think of it as endlessly going round and round in circles. You can keep track of the number of circles, but only as a ritual. The numbers themselves mean nothing. Hey, wouldn't that be a great idea for an art project? Your work is conceptual, isn't it?" Minnie nodded, because she didn't have the energy to explain that it had already been done once, in 1977 to be exact, during the tenth Paris Biennial, by Marina Abramović and Ulay.

*

She had kept her diary as clear as possible until March 21, as she usually did when working intensively on a project. The problem with this project was that the work consisted of just being there. And being there, Minnie realized, was not only a largely passive affair, but also a prison of sorts: being there meant you couldn't *not* be there. This confirmation of one's existence was in a metaphysical sense reassuring, but in practice, or in this particular case anyway, it was more of a constraint.

"We're building a panopticon for two," Minnie had said to the photographer after they'd signed the contract and were walking out the door of Specht & Vink on January 3, a month—it might as well have been an eternity—ago. "Old-school Foucault. Although it's hard to tell which of us is the jailer and which the prisoner." She had more or less practiced saying it beforehand, and to her chagrin it sounded that way too. "The prohibition against contact of any sort applies to both of us, and that implies imprisonment. And yet—I'll be completely visible to you, naturally, while I'll only be able to suspect your presence. Still, the question is: in this situation, who is disciplining whom?"

"No," the photographer had answered, after they'd strolled along the canal for a while in silence. "It's me, watching you. I have my camera, or as long as we're in panopticon-rhetoric mode: my all-seeing eye, which records everything and forgets nothing. In fact I am God, kid. And you are an insignificant little creature scrambling about this earth under my supervision, until I decide it's enough."

They slalomed around piles of garbage scattered all over the street. On the corner of Prinsengracht and Vijzelstraat, the previous day's tempest had yanked a sapling out of the ground, roots and all, and it was now lying horizontally, swaying in the wind like a baby being rocked in its cradle.

"You are that tree," the photographer had said. He was visibly pleased with the comparison.

"Oh yeah?" said Minnie. "I'm still the one who decides where you go with your 'all-seeing eye'. If, in the course of the three weeks you've chosen to follow me, I decide to, I don't know, tour around Amsterdam on one of those Hop-on-hop-off buses, then that will also be your lot, more or less."

"The only means of transportation you're allowed is a bike."

"I can ride really fast. I might decide to bike in circles for hours. Or bed down on the sidewalk. Walk around for weeks in a ski mask. Rob a bank. You get my point."

They walked into a bar that looked like an iPod and sat down on square white leather stools on thin stainless steel legs. Looking back, thought Minnie, those stools mirrored and presaged the red velvet ones they'd sit on later, in that dark bar on Rembrandt Square, when they had long reconciled themselves to how the evening would end, and the fact that they had insinuated themselves into each other's lives in a most peculiar way.

"Yes, you could," the photographer had said at that earlier juncture, when everything was already set in motion, although they were still pretending there was nothing going on, or not very much, anyway. "But you'd only do it because you were prompted by the thought that I was there, with my lens, to pin you down, to freeze you in the moment. To immortalize you. No matter where you turn or go, kid, you're dependent on my gaze. To be more exact: on the suggestion of me looking at you. What kind of bar is this, anyway?"

Minnie said she had no idea, he was the one who had gone in as if he knew where he was going, upon which the photographer said he had just been following *her*. "In other words, the problems have already begun," he said with that chuckle of his. At the same time two glasses of Prosecco appeared in front of them. The glasses had a square base and a stem with a kink in it. Ridiculous. The kink, especially, was too much. They clinked. Minnie asked herself if the photographer did hold more sway over her than she'd been telling herself, and remembered that she hated Prosecco. Perhaps he was right. Or perhaps no one could be right, because this was all just theoretical, and theorizing was the way strategists and intellectuals passed the time. Ten truths for every theory. Someone must have said that some time or other—there was no way nobody ever had. Sooner or later everything became a one-liner.

"I once saw a play by Beckett, *Happy Days*," said the photographer after gulping down some Prosecco. Yet another pumping Adam's apple, thought Minnie, always the same thing. "A woman is buried up to her waist in a pile of dirt. She's constantly rummaging in her purse and jabbering away. Her husband is lounging behind the hill. He hardly ever says anything, and when he does it's only to read random newspaper headlines or to show his wife she's annoying the hell out of him. In that world there are no days, no nights, just an ocean of light and an earsplitting bell to make them wake up or go to sleep at set times, or what passes for time.

"In the second act the woman is buried up to her neck. She is completely immobile and can only look straight ahead. There's a gun next to her. Something has changed and nothing has changed, don't you see?"

"Where did that gun come from all of a sudden?"

"It was in her handbag. In the first act she could still have taken her own life, in the second act it's too late. It's just her head sticking out of that mountain."

"In Beckett, no one is able to commit suicide," said Minnie. "All those characters live in a timeless universe. Without time, everything is forever."

She didn't exactly know how she'd come by that piece of wisdom, but it sounded true. The photographer nodded slowly.

"There's one scene in which the woman takes a little mirror from her purse and smashes it on a stone. She explains exactly what she's doing as she does it: I pick up this mirror, I smash it on this stone. She announces she's throwing it away and then throws it away, knowing full well that the next day it will be back in her purse as if nothing had happened. She lives in a world in which words, and even deeds, are totally stripped of their consequences. A naked world, peeled down to the nub, which consists only of meaninglessness."

With that, he drained the last drop of Prosecco, then, holding the hideous glass at the kink, balanced it on the tip of his index finger. His shutter-finger, thought Minnie. All ruthlessness wrapped up in one fingertip.

"Anyway," he said, "you'd think it wasn't necessary for that woman to do all that talking, would you, he isn't listening anyway, but the point is that she does have to do it for him. She can only talk because she knows she's being heard, or rather, she can only exist in the knowledge there's still someone sitting behind that hill. 'Someone is still looking at me, still loves me,' she says at one point. 'Eyes on my eyes,' or something like that; what she would do without them? The answer, in short, is that all she'd be able to do is stare straight ahead, lips sealed, neither alive nor dead, but in some ghastly limbo."

"Is it a sad play or a happy play?" asked Minnie.

"Both, probably," said the photographer. "It's happiness teetering on the edge of the abyss. Now that I think of it, I couldn't name another work of art that's as perfect a depiction of human despair. That harsh light, the over-the-top gabfest, the hysterical cheeriness. It's all too clear the woman is going nuts, but she insists on clinging to life until the very end, clinging to a chronology of things that no longer exist chronologically."

"And now you're implying that I'm that woman in that pile of dirt."

"The question is: why the gun, why is it there?"

The photographer jumped off his stool and, digging a ten-euro bill out of his wallet, slipped it under his glass.

"Come," he said. "Let's blow this tacky joint. Let's go grab a bite to eat, then another drink or two, and then I'm taking you back to my place."

Minnie knew it wasn't at all cool to fall for this kind of flagrant macho display, but not everything needs to follow the rules of good taste. She followed him out of the iPod bar into the street, into the evening, the ever deeper and darker night, and it was as if they were already chained to each other then—two guards, two prisoners.

FREEDOM WAS THE working title Minnie had given the project, but in those first days of February she had to wonder if *Bored Stiff* wouldn't have been more appropriate. Other than that strangely emotional lunch with her mother on the first day, nothing out of the ordinary happened. She swam more laps than ever, shopped, took aimless bike rides along the IJ River, read books, and basically felt like a sixty-five-year-old who'd just retired. She often found herself staring from her window to the window across the street for minutes at a time, although she didn't know what she was hoping to see.

On the seventh day she'd had it with the regimen of calm, orderliness and routine. She went shopping in P.C. Hooftstraat and bought a tight little black dress that cost a small fortune. She went to her hairdresser in the Jordaan, whose name was Yrrah, which is Harry spelled backwards because Yrrah's parents had really wanted a son, and would have called him Harry after every male in the family back through the generations. Yrrah gave Minnie a very light trim, she never cut a lot, she was a subtle hair stylist and didn't get influenced by the latest silly trends. "You have to look at the person," she liked to say. "Everyone is an individual."

At eight p.m. Minnie ordered a taxi. She had squeezed herself into the dress and smeared her face with such quantities of makeup that it ended up looking like a mask. She had thought it would make her feel anonymous, safe and camouflaged, but instead it gave her too much face, garishly overdone features vying for attention. It almost looked, she thought, staring into the mirror, like the faces of *Les Demoiselles*. Naked. Grotesque. Wild.

It wasn't until she spotted the cab turning into her street that it occurred to her she would be breaking the contract if she took a taxi. For a moment she hesitated. Even though it didn't in the strictest sense of the word have anything to do with *knowing*, she was quite sure the photographer hadn't yet started following her. No one would be any the wiser, and the transgression would simply be erased, like that tree in the forest falling without anyone hearing it, meaning it hasn't really fallen. On the other hand, you couldn't just turn every moral quandary into an ontological problem—you could justify practically anything that way. So she said she was sorry, paid the driver double what the ride would have cost, and since the dress was incompatible with a bicycle seat, put on a pair of sneakers and, before she could change her mind, quickly pulled the door shut behind her.

The evening was grey, damp and chilly; it was still ten below. There went Minnie, in flimsy ultra-sheer pantyhose, with a mask-like face and a bag holding a snazzy pair of red Manolos. Visible through the stocking was a greenish purple bruise shaped like Australia (every bruise ends up taking on the shape of Australia), which had over the course of the week slid from her hip down to her upper thigh, sediment in a river. If it hadn't been so bitterly cold and such a fucking drag, she'd probably have had a good laugh at her own expense.

After the sheep episode, over a week ago now, Minnie had followed the farmer into his kitchen for a cup of coffee. While waiting for the coffee to drip through the filter, they'd chatted about the TV show that had left the farmer with some fame but no wife. Both were trying not to think about the dead lamb lying on the floor of the tool shed. "It's nature's way," the farmer had said, by way of farewell. "Sometimes they live and sometimes they die, there's not much that can be done about it."

As soon as she was back on the ice, she noticed that the interruption had caused her muscles to stiffen. The skates felt too tight on her feet, the ice seemed less smooth, the headwind stronger. And then, just before she got back to the village, she'd got her right blade caught in a groove. There was nothing she could do, the check was too abrupt, and she was sent flying, like some cartoon character crashing into an invisible wall. Her knee smashed into the ice first, then her hip. She didn't feel a thing, but was intensely conscious of the fact that she'd fallen, that it couldn't be helped and that she'd just have to accept it. She lay sprawled on the ice for ten seconds or more. There was no one in sight, neither man nor even beast. Without the sound of the rasp of metal on ice, there was only silence. It's all gone wrong, I've made a mess of things, thought Minnie, and suddenly she was flooded with a great sense of relief. It had all gone wrong, and there was nothing left that could go wrong. She knew exactly what she had left. Not until she'd hauled herself back to her feet, had skated the last hundred yards, stowed the skates back in their box and hobbled to her car, did she notice the pain, the nagging pain of a stupid bruise, which has nothing to do with all the other kinds of pain, which is why it is so intolerable.

Once back in Amsterdam, the whole outing began to seem

unreal to her, a dream that might hide some kind of meaning, but couldn't really, because its details were too nonsensical for words. Only the color palette spreading across her hip over the next few days was a reminder that something had definitely happened, but the memory remained unwilling, a souvenir of a place she'd never been.

When, after a half hour walk, Minnie arrived at the Stedelijk Museum, or at least the part that was still open during the protracted renovations, she ran into a gaggle of unrepentant smokers outside the door. Tall, skinny models with dangerously low-cut necklines, men who looked like John Travolta (the old, not the new one), designers wearing glasses taking up half their faces. From inside came the pulsing sound of music and the din of voices.

"Minnie!"

One of the smokers disengaged himself from the group and threw his arms around her. Pointy sideburns, satin tie, a hot pink carnation in his breast pocket. It was her coke-sniffing fashion-designer friend. She remembered the last time they'd spoken, the time he'd informed her, shouting into the phone, about the photos in *Vogue*.

"So great to see you! How *are* you!"

He waved his pack of cigarettes in her face, and then a lighter.

"You look terrific," he said. "A bit fuller in the face, or something. That makeup really does something for you."

Using his shoulder to lean on, she swapped the sneakers for the Manolos, took a big drag of the cigarette, and straightened. It was amazing how different the world looked when your eyes were four inches higher up. She knew the heels still didn't make her any taller than the average woman wearing flats, but she had the feeling she was towering over everyone else ("megalomania," the photographer had once said to her with a grin, when, standing next to him in the same heels, she'd claimed she was taller than him).

"*Everbody's* here," said the friend. "You name it. Rufus Wainwright is supposed to put in an appearance and perform a song."

The invitation said that it would be a simple party, an "intimate affair." Maybe, she thought, in the fashion world, "intimate" meant the exact opposite of what was normally understood by the word.

Ever since being featured in *Vogue,* she had been getting quite a few invitations of this sort. The most bizarre one was the invite from Italy a few weeks ago. A former minister in Berlusconi's cabinet had sent her a round-trip ticket to Olbia-Costa Smeralda in Sardinia, for a *grande festa* on his yacht. "Better not accept this one," the accompanying post-it advised, further graced with a trio of exclamation marks and winking smiley-faces, "if you're ever thinking of going into politics."

The cigarette didn't taste good to her. Grinding it out with the tip of her shoe, she couldn't stop herself peering up and down the street. In search of a shadow, perhaps. Someone who could vanish into the night. Suddenly she wasn't so sure anymore that it hadn't already begun. From behind their designer glasses, their hair, their cigarette smoke, she felt the people around her observing her. Which was what everyone had come to this party for—to see and to be seen, brazenly, but with a veneer of decorum.

"What are you working on these days?" she heard the friend asking someone. It wasn't until he'd said it again that she realized the question was meant for her.

"Oh, nothing concrete, really," she said. "A time for reflection."

"That's good, that's great. There are artists who get so totally caught up in their work, know what I mean? Who think their whole life is a work of art. *So* seventies."

"Yes," said Minnie. "Shall we go in?"

She felt like disappearing into the crowd, warm bodies squeezing past one another, fabric, skin, not having to talk.

Standing next to the coat check, a plump girl—who at second glance wasn't a girl but a middle-aged woman who, in a basically hopeless attempt to turn back the clock, had adopted a hairdo consisting of two peroxided braids and a tiara—fumbled with an iPad. Turning the thing impatiently from side to side while busily swiping her finger across the screen, she finally managed to pick Minnie's name out of the guest list. A skinny girl on platform heels offered her a mint-green cocktail that did not by the furthest stretch of the imagination taste of mint. If it tasted of anything, Minnie thought, it was of dry dirt. She was surprised to find that the drink was lukewarm.

"It's Japanese," said her friend, tapping the glass. "A rare brand of *shochu*, I bet it's made in one of those authentic Japanese villages with the unpronounceable names, mixed with green tea. All very select, only a pity it tastes so bad."

He drained his glass in one gulp.

"Apparently," he said in a conspiratorial tone, his face close up to Minnie's, "they're working on a new fashion show that's truly mind blowing."

His breath smelled of something that's been left in a cellar too long.

Following her to the coat check, he started telling her about the fashion show that was to be held the next summer at Paris

Fashion Week. It was still top secret, but he'd heard through the grapevine that the collection—the designer duo's first haute couture collection, after years in ready-wear—was inspired by the Japanese Zen garden of the Ryoan-ji Temple in Kyoto.

"There are fifteen rocks scattered around that garden. No matter where you stand, it's impossible to see all of them at once. The idea is that the view of all fifteen rocks is reserved for those who have reached enlightenment, or whatever they call it in that culture. In the show, the models will be the rocks, see, and the catwalk is the garden. I can't imagine what that's all going to look like, but it sounds great, don't you think? Everyone who's anyone is doing Asia these days."

One of the John Travoltas loomed up behind them and grabbed the friend by the shoulder. A back-slapping exchange ensued, a fascinating, exclusively male ritual exemplifying the entire course of ape-to-human evolution in broad strokes.

"This is Minnie Panis," said the friend, "Google her."

Travolta crushed her hand, and with a loud laugh informed her that his home was airports all over the world. Then he raised his hand, yelled a loud *"Ragazza mia!"* and made for a wrinkle-faced lady in a Chanel suit.

"His name's Lorenzo Lotto," said the friend as they watched him lift the lady off her feet by way of embrace. "Just like the artist from the Renaissance. How crazy is that?"

There was a speech, some kind of award was handed out, a gigantic pink cake with ribbons was sliced up and doled out; more tiaras. All the while the designer duo stood around on the podium looking a bit lost, as if they'd wound up at their own party against their will—which was quite likely, thought Minnie. Finally Rufus Wainwright, seated at a white baby grand, sang a French song in a heavy Quebecois accent about a whore on the streets of Paris, and then, in English, something about a gay Messiah who would one day return to the earth, to be baptized in sperm. The lights were dimmed, with just a single spotlight on Rufus Wainwright. "Better pray for your sins," he sang over and over again in long drawn-out, nasal tones reverberating with both deeply felt pain and a penchant for camp.

Minnie was leaning against a pillar on the periphery, just outside the crowd, and suddenly it touched something in her: this man sitting at that glitzy baby grand, his drawling voice, his pain, the spectators, all wallowing in their own despair. Even though she knew better, she imagined the photographer skulking somewhere in a corner, meticulously recording her every move, and suddenly she understood what it was that was wrong with that prisoner-jailer theory. The point wasn't which of the two had more power over the other, but which one of the two was the focus of the attention.

Minnie stared at the people listening to the concert in the dark, thinking themselves unobserved. They held themselves less erect, their features were less self-consciously taut. They no longer existed exclusively in relation to other people; for a short while, they were there as themselves. In a few minutes the lights would be turned up again, and then everything would go back to the way it was before. "Where were we?" they'd say, referring to a conversation they wanted to pick up again, because there was always some conversation to pick up again, even if there hadn't really been one, and it never occurred to them how apt that phrase really was, because they had in fact been off in some place unlike most of the places they knew, more distant, stranger, darker.

ON THE ELEVENTH DAY everything changed.

MINNIE BLINKED a few times as the sun announced itself through the thin curtains of her bedroom window in filtered whiteness.

It had been overcast for several days, less cold than before and yet colder, or more desolate, anyway. The temperature had been hovering around the freezing mark, and puddles had started forming on the ice in the canals, first just along the edges and under the bridges, but then everywhere, until cracks and holes started appearing in the ice.

Staring at the plane of her window as it grew brighter, Minnie stayed flat on her back, hands resting on the place where her belly met her hips.

Something was different, a change in perspective. Her heart was pounding wildly in her chest, as if she had just made some enormous effort; her T-shirt was stuck to her body, clammy wisps of hair clung to her forehead. Yet she felt luminous, weightless.

She had been dreaming, or pictures had been streaming through her mind, still-lifes she didn't really understand. A typewriter on a wooden table, the grooves of an escalator tread. A black leather wallet. It wasn't until she turned her head to the side to find herself staring at the darkness under her bed that she realized she wasn't in her bed, but on the floor next to it.

It's started, she thought, gazing at the dust bunnies collected in the recesses under the bed. She couldn't be sure, yet she was sure. *Eyes on her eyes.*

When she opened the curtain, the sunlight flooded inside unimpeded, sunbeams of biblical proportions, great searchlights descending upon her from heaven. Through squinting eyelids she peered at the window across the way. She imagined she spotted him, her prison guard, watching, waiting for the right moment, whatever that might be.

Encore une journée divine, she whispered to herself, *a perfect day,* in Jesus Christ Our Lord Amen.

*

Minnie left her house with no clear-cut plan. Once outside, she was bowled over by the milky light tinting everything white. Even the air she inhaled was white, a cloud of cold and light in her lungs. The world shimmered, it looked like a goddamn stage set, a glossy winter-in-the-city travel brochure. She walked until she reached the edge of town, wide avenues lined with low row-houses in the shadow of looming apartment buildings, some made up of large glass loft spaces, others broken up into hundreds of little boxes sheltering at least ten times the number of apartment dwellers.

Arriving at the lake—her destination, apparently—she was met with a serene and still frozen expanse. The thaw hadn't made same the destructive impact here as in the inner city. Less people, thought Minnie, less of all the things people get up to.

She walked into a café with big picture windows overlooking

the frozen pond. The walls were covered in a deep purple wallpaper printed with French lilies. Above her head dangled a gigantic chandelier with blue light bulbs. As always when confronted with an aerial contraption of this sort, she imagined the thing letting go of the ceiling, in a process so drawn-out that it couldn't be detected with the naked eye, but that now, at this exact moment, had reached the critical juncture, the infinitesimal shift from remaining attached to crashing down on her head. It would be an idiotic way to break your neck, naturally, but it did happen.

She ordered a cup of coffee.

Saying the words—a cup of coffee, please—suddenly filled her with excitement. There was nothing more banal you could do, and that was what made it so thrilling: she was someone ordering a cup of coffee, and at the same time she was someone who was only acting as if. She couldn't wait for the coffee to arrive, the way the little spoon would clink against the saucer, the cellophane-wrapped ginger cookie next to it, the way she would sip it. From now on everything was part of the project. The possibilities were endless.

For form's sake (woman reading in café), she took a book out of her bag. It was a thin book she'd picked up at her mother's house years ago because the title had intrigued her: *Slaughterhouse-Five*. She knew it was an American literature classic about the bombing of Dresden, but the title sounded more like a horror-film remake. The cover image was meant to make you think of a tombstone, with the words of the title written in an arc inside it.

Her agent, who was a great lover of literature, had once pulled the book from her bookcase, exclaiming that it was a rare first edition. She'd never gotten around to reading it, something held her back, the subject matter perhaps, but on an impulse, she had grabbed it just before walking out the door that morning. Now she opened it for the first time. There were faint pencil marks on the flyleaf that had been erased by someone, or maybe they had simply faded over time. It looked like her mother's old-fashioned, sloping penmanship, but whatever it said had become illegible.

As Minnie started leafing through the book, a piece of folded paper fell out. She unfolded it carefully. In the top left-hand corner were two words, typed on a typewriter probably: *Read This.* Nothing else, a voice from the ether.

"There are almost no characters in this story," she read on one of the pages from which the piece of paper had fallen, *"and almost no dramatic confrontations, because most of the people in it are so sick and so much listless playthings of enormous forces."*

She wondered if she looked like some ordinary woman in a café reading a book, waiting for her coffee. She wondered if she *was* that. The coffee arrived and everything was going according to plan, at least, until she seized the cup by the ear and brought it up to her mouth.

The disgust was acute and overwhelming. She stared, revolted, at the black slop in the cup, which suddenly looked like sewage to her, filthy, old, putrefying in the sun. The disgust spread throughout her body, it was something existential, a nausea originating in the cup of coffee, but which couldn't be returned there. Before she could get hold of herself, she let go of the cup. It smashed on the floor in two pieces, the coffee spattering out around it in an expanding puddle.

The waitress came running up with a yellow cloth. Minnie could already picture the cloth absorbing the coffee, big brown stains marring the sunny yellow. It was more than she could bear. As if she was taking part in a farce where everyone was running in every direction, opening and closing doors, bumping into one another helter-skelter, Minnie dashed to the ladies' room, where she proceeded to energetically spew the morning's yogurt and toast into the toilet bowl. Still panting, trying to recover from the internal onslaught, she was reminded of the sushi episode of years ago, when she'd had such a yen for sushi in the store, and the way the craving had turned into complete revulsion for no apparent reason.

She stared at her own eyes in the mirror, still watery from the vomiting. Their sickly glimmer fascinated her, just as she was always transfixed by her own pale, puffy face whenever she'd been crying, the clumped-together lashes, the snot dripping from her nose. Maybe, she thought, you could keep vomiting or crying for as long as it took for everything that was wrong to be rinsed from your body, leaving you as clean as a load of white laundry.

Back in the café, where there wasn't a trace left of the shattered cup, but where a fresh cup of coffee was waiting for her on her table as if nothing had happened, and it was all right for her keep dropping crockery on the floor for all eternity, Minnie said she was sorry, but she had to go. She handed the waitress a ten-Euro bill, and without looking back she hurried out of the café, where the chandelier was about to crash to the ground at any moment, these things happen; the world is a place of improbabilities.

AT THE WATER'S EDGE she stood still for a while, feeling the tentative warmth of the sun on the pale, chapped skin on her face and the sour aftertaste of the vomit still vaguely present in her mouth. It was February 11, 2012, the day was clear and cold; it was Saturday. She looked around, but couldn't see him. In the distance, on the far side of the pond, she spotted two hazy clusters of people. Bare winter trees, a car parked on the side of the road. That was all. This was the intention, she told herself. *He will operate with the utmost discretion and under no circumstance interfere, no matter what the situation.* She peered at the ice and wondered just how rapidly the molecules had to move in order to make the ice slippery but solid, and how that speed was measured or recorded.

She took a first step. Then another, then another, then another. She was luminous and weightless. Nothing made any sound.

ALL IS FALLING

On July 9, 1975, the Dutch artist Bas Jan Ader, aged thirty-three, set sail in a Guppy 13 christened *Ocean Wave* from Cape Cod, Massachusetts, for a solo Atlantic Ocean crossing. He had made the sea voyage to the United States fourteen years previously, and this time planned to cross the same ocean back to the land of his birth. The trip was the second part of a triptych called *In Search of the Miraculous*, which began as a show in the Claire Copley Gallery in Los Angeles and was to wrap up with a show at the Groninger Museum when he arrived home. The little sailboat, barely twice Ader's own full length, was one of the smallest pocket yachts ever made. Never before had anyone hazarded an Atlantic crossing in a boat of such dimensions. Not only was it a performance art piece, it was also a stab at breaking a world record.

Three weeks after his departure radio contact was lost. Nine months later the little boat was found by a Spanish fishing vessel off the coast of Ireland—partially submerged, the mast snapped off, the panel ripped away to which the safety cord had been attached. An examination of the algae growth indicated the boat must have been drifting around unmanned for at least half a year.

Bas Jan Ader's last voyage spanned three months. Nobody knew what caused him to be thrown overboard. It could have been a heavy storm, a monster wave, a navigation blunder, a fault in the boat's construction. Neither could it be ruled out that Ader simply jumped—out of despair, depression, disorientation, or whatever other words there are for madness.

For weeks after Ader's boat was found, his friends, fellow artists and fans of his work were convinced it was the artist's ultimate trick, perfectly in line with Ader's enigmatic attitude to life. They thought he would merrily—although merry wasn't exactly a typical mood of his—resurface in Los Angeles someday soon, because though he might be good, he wasn't completely nuts. The only ones who immediately realized it was for real were his wife, Mary Sue Ader-Andersen, and his mother, Johanna Adriana Ader-Appels. They knew him, and knew he was neither a prankster nor a provocateur. What's more, his mother had written a poem hinting at his death in the waves months before he was found. Later on she would claim it had been a vision.

Johanna was the widow of the preacher and resistance fighter Bastiaan Jan Ader, who in 1944, two and a half years after the birth of his eldest son Bas Jan, and just weeks after the birth of his youngest son Erik, was executed by firing squad in reprisal for a Resistance attack on a German soldier—only because the Germans needed to round up a few candidates to prove they'd deal harshly with all resistance, and his Christian name started with "A".

Eight years before his death, early one summer morning in 1936, Bastiaan, a recent theology graduate and married less than six months, had set off from Amsterdam on a three-speed bicycle with drum brakes, bound for Palestine. People who knew him were scandalized by this "crazy undertaking," which couldn't possibly come to a good end. Johanna was the only one who had faith in a good outcome. She knew her spouse was an adventurer, but definitely not a reckless idiot.

Half a year later Bastiaan Ader had crossed Germany, Czechoslovakia, Hungary, Turkey, Syria and Lebanon, arriving one fine morning in Jerusalem. From there he continued on to Cairo, where he boarded a freighter for Greece, returning to the Netherlands by train via France.

On the way he succumbed to typhoid, his bike bit the dust too many times to count, and he kept winding up penniless in places that weren't exactly known to be safe. None of it fazed him, however, and the "crazy undertaking" went down in history as a heroic quest with a triumphant outcome. His execution in the woods at Rhenen eight years later turned his life story into a tragedy in the best Christian tradition: pioneer, servant of

God, martyr.

All in all, Johanna, who after the war lived as an Evangelist preacher in Nieuw-Beerta, Groningen, wasn't unfamiliar with the more mysterious aspects of life: the zigzagging patterns traced by rivers in a landscape, the mirror-images and replicas, the countless indescribable things hidden beneath the surface of the tangible. When she dreamed and then wrote a poem about her son's death at sea, she recognized the dream for what it was: the harbinger of bad news to come.

Bas Jan Ader's body was never found. The body of work he left is meager, if not practically non-existent. It consists of a smattering of performances, installations and short films, a substantial portion of them created over a single weekend. It is tempting, yes, maybe even inevitable, to judge his work in light of his subsequent disappearance.

His death wasn't just a stupid traffic accident (James Dean, Albert Camus, Lady Di, Roland Barthes, Pierre Curie, Antoni Gaudí, Grace Kelly, W.G. Sebald, etc., etc.), or some stupid disease (most of humankind), but the outcome of a very deliberate exercise in detachment. Anyone choosing to play Bas Jan Ader's life backward, right up to the point when his father started out for Palestine on his bike six years before he was born, will see that his disappearance was just as inevitable as the vast ocean defining the periphery of the world.

It's enough, for now, to go back to 1960. We see Bas Jan as a student at Amsterdam's Art Academy, eighteen years old, blond, blue-eyed. A handsome boy. He has a single piece of paper with him, nothing else. Every drawing assignment gets drawn on that piece of paper. Then he'll erase the drawing, make another one, rubs that one out too, makes another one, erases it, erases, erases. By the year's end he has nothing to show but that flimsy sheet of paper, so abraded that you can see right through it.

A year later Bas Jan stops attending art school, or is kicked out, or somewhere in between. He hitchhikes his way to Morocco. He has no real memory of his father, how could he, but he knows him from the stories of his mother, who also wrote a book in the late 1940s about his father's daring resistance struggles. In short, Bas Jan admires his father, the adventurer and resistance hero, and feels the same restless blood coursing through his own veins, so wildly sometimes that his body can barely contain it. In Tangier or Casablanca (or it may have been Rabat; a seaside town, anyway) he embarks as a deck hand on a yacht bound for the United States.

Curiously enough, the yacht is shipwrecked just off the coast of California. That must have been fate, Bas Jan tells himself as he steps ashore in Los Angeles. He enrolls in the Otis College of Art and Design, and falls in love with Mary Sue, the director's daughter, whose clear blue eyes and thick blond hair betray her North-European roots.

They get married a couple of years later in Las Vegas. In the meantime Bas Jan, besides teaching at art schools, has begun studying philosophy. There is a photograph of the wedding day in which we see him, looking remarkably handsome (with a reputation of being something of a skirt-chaser, nicknamed 'Doctor Rock'), leaning on two big wooden crutches at his bride's side. The crutches are symbolic, since there's nothing wrong with his legs. An attempt to be funny? No, he took art and life too seriously for that; ironic, certainly, but always dead serious.

In 1970 Bas Jan Ader starts on his *Fall* series: three short silent films in which the artist, as the title suggests, suffers a number of falls. We see him tumbling, chair and all, from the roof of his house in L.A., we see him riding his bike into one of Amsterdam's canals, we see him hanging from a tree branch above a pond in the Amsterdam Woods for several long minutes until he can't hold on any longer and plunges vertically into the water, like an icicle snapping off a roof.

This last one, *Broken Fall (Organic),* is the most intriguing of the three. There's a man hanging from a tree branch, and the spectator knows that one or the other will eventually let go: either the branch will snap off the trunk, or the man will be torn from the branch. It's that simple. Nothing terrible is going to happen either way, since the man isn't all that high off the ground, and there is water beneath him, which will save him from breaking his neck—for now. Nevertheless, the suspense is worthy of Hitchcock.

Broken Fall (Organic) is a moving piece. The artist has put himself into a situation from which there is only one way out: through the agency of forces of nature greater than himself. The capitulation to those forces has begun the moment he grabs the branch with both hands and lets his feet dangle in space, swaying like laundry on a clothesline. Sometimes he'll try keeping completely still, but then his body will suddenly contort as if trying to give itself the heave-ho, his hands grabbing the branch again in a brave but vain attempt to stave off the inevitable. The body doesn't yet realize what the brain has long comprehended—there is a person hanging from the branch who has made himself transparent, vulnerable as the soft skull of a newborn infant, at the mercy of the mysterious and inexorable laws of gravity.

Does the inevitability of falling render Bas Jan Ader's attempts futile? Yes, of course. Yet there is definitely a point to them: *the value is in the effort.* In hanging from that branch, he is consciously choosing loss of control, and it is that choice that marks the difference between freedom and the lack of it. As absurd a hero as they get: a Sisyphus Camus would have approved of—freedom and futility as two sides of the same coin.[1]

Bas Jan Ader isn't known to be much of a talker, especially not when it comes to his own work. Yet he did have something to say about his *Fall*

[1] Camus died in 1960 at the age of forty-six in a car accident, the year Bas Jan Ader turned his back on the more common beaten track by erasing his own work, and ten years before he began his Fall series. It is plausible that Bas Jan had come across Camus' Mythe de Sisyphe by the year of the author's death, not only because existentialism was at its peak then and Camus had received the Nobel prize three years previously, but also on account of Bas Jan's early interest in philosophy. Furthermore, it certainly isn't unthinkable that reading that book reminded Bas Jan of his own late father riding a bike to the promised land, for no reason and for some reason, the artist who wasn't an artist. Had Camus, for his part—just like his frenemy Sartre—only grown to a respectable old age, he might have heard about Bas Jan Ader's disappearance at sea. It would probably have appealed to him: the lonely struggle and its ultimate failure, because there's no success like failure, and failure's no success at all.

series on the odd occasion. "The artist's body as gravity," he says, probably in English, or else in Dutch with the heavy American accent he'd acquired, "makes itself master over him." Voilà: Albert Camus, in ten words.

When after two long minutes that body falls, it knows at last what Camus knew, as did the Taoists in ancient China, the sadhus of Varanasi, the first rabbis, the Zen Buddhists, the medieval mystics from Cologne to Antwerp: the one who lets go, understands the universe. The body in the air is for a rare second invincible.

In the melodramatic but poignant photo *Farewell to Faraway Friends,* from 1971, the artist stands on the rocky shore of an extensive body of water, which we assume is the sea. The sun is sinking into, or rising from the water; the blood-red color of the sky screams at you in full Kodachrome at its peak.

The lonely silhouette inevitably brings to mind Caspar David Friedrich's epitome of Romanticism, *Der Wanderer über dem Nebelmeer (The Wanderer above the Sea Fog).* Man versus the elements, nature's ferocious beauty, fear and longing compressed together into a single experience. We can't see if Bas Jan Ader is facing us or the water, but there are things that can be conjectured.

See him standing there in that sentimental landscape. He hears the roar of the sea and can taste the salt crystals as he runs his tongue across the back of his hand, undercurrents stronger than what's implied by the rhythmic pounding of the waves. He knows perfectly well that it is just a matter of time before he gives himself over to it. You can say what you want about him, but not that it's a pose, that he's only flirting with pain and loneliness. Whoever and wherever these "faraway friends" may be, the artist is already in all seriousness waving them goodbye.

A year later—it's now 1972, the year Andy Warhol was making endless reproductions of Mao Zedong and Picasso was painting his famous last self-portrait—Bas Jan Ader staged a performance that was documented in sound recordings and photographs.

The Boy Who Fell over Niagara Falls is based on a story in *Reader's Digest* (titled "The Boy Who Went over Niagara Falls," a subtle but important difference). The artist sits in a chair with a lamp next to him and reads the story out loud, sipping at a glass of water and draining the last drop just as the story comes to an end.

The story can be boiled down as follows:

On July 9, 1960, James Honeycutt, fisherman and friend of the Woodward family, living on the banks of the Niagara, invites their seven-year-old son Roger for the first boat ride of his life. Just imagine the little boy's excitement! His older sister Deanne, who is seventeen, gets in too, but reluctantly. She isn't very keen on that rushing Niagara River. Strapping herself into one of the two life vests on board, she sits down, unwilling and sulky as only toddlers and teenagers can be.

The boat, less than thirteen feet long, is made of aluminum and equipped with a 7.5 hp outboard motor. It's when Honeycutt gives the little boy the rudder to steer the boat and isn't paying attention that things start to go wrong: the boat crashes into a rock and the engine cuts out. They've drifted dangerously close to the edge of the falls, which Honeycutt, strangely enough, realizes only at the last moment. Far below them drifts the pleasure boat *Maid of the Mist*, allowing visitors to experience the spectacle of the Falls from as close up as possible. "Look," the guide announces, "that line up there marks the point at which everything is irrevocably sucked into the falls." One of the tourists points at the tiny blue boat suddenly looming up on the rim. "That one too?"

In a last-ditch altruistic deed, Honeycutt tosses the only other life vest at Roger, shouting over the roar of millions of gallons of falling water that he shouldn't be scared. Of course Roger is scared, he's scared stiff, the boat is rudderless, he can't swim, he's going to be swallowed by this terrifying water monster. So this is it, he thinks as the boat capsizes, I'm going to die. The water drags him down, then spits him up again. He screams for help but the alarmed witnesses on shore see only his sister Deanne, who is fished out of the water at the top just in the nick of time. Poor Roger is too little, and his voice too weak; it was never more tragic to be a child. In moments of lucidity he thinks of all the toys he owns, of birthday cake and ice cream, of his parent's grief at his funeral. Then he lets go, it's that simple, it seems: one minute you're in a little boat, the next you're resigned to dying.

Roger remembers nothing about the fall itself. It doesn't feel like falling, anyway, rather like floating down on a cloud, a hard slam against the surface, and then plunging deep down. When he comes back up to the surface he instinctively starts to yell and shout. People on board *The Maid of the Mist* suddenly see a little orange dot in the water, and the unimaginable seems to be true: the little dot is still alive. And so Roger Woodward goes down in history as the first person (other than madcap stuntmen) ever to survive a fall over the Niagara Falls. And not only that: he made it with barely a scratch. If he'd been heavier, he'd surely have smashed to death on the rocks, like the unfortunate James Honeycutt. That's how it goes: the thing that in the first instance puts you in trouble, will finally prove to be your salvation.

It isn't hard to guess why Bas Jan Ader found this story so endlessly fascinating. Here was something miraculous that had taken place, but which fully complied with the laws of physics: gravity had done its work, the little boy had surrendered to it, and the human body had proved itself invincible. It's on another order altogether from falling from a tree branch into a canal; at least a thousand percent more intense. Shit, thought Bas Jan, sipping his glass of water, this is the kind of marvel I've been looking for all my life.

Three years later, and exactly fifteen years after Roger Woodward's

Niagara fall, Bas Jan climbed aboard his own little boat. We can assume that he had taken everything into account, on a practical level anyway. He was an experienced sailor, he knew the North Atlantic ocean as well as it can be known, he knew how the wind blew, where the stars were in the firmament, how much he was allowed to consume daily in order not to run out of food. He slipped a copy of Hegel's *Phenomenology of Mind* into the inside pocket of his life vest. He was as prepared as you can be for a voyage like this. Three months later he drowned at sea.

Was his voyage the ultimate failure, as has been suggested by some? It depends on the way you look at it. In a literal sense, no, he did not succeed in reaching the other shore; but on the other hand, reaching the other shore was never his goal. The goal lay in the very attempt, and that's a crucial difference.

Bas Jan Ader wasn't trying to discover what was on the other side, he knew what was there: the flat lands of the country where he was born, that land below sea level, the small community where his father had served as preacher and where his mother was still spreading the Word of God, in the Ichtus Church that stands in the village square of Nieuw-Beerta. No, his quest was of a mystical, rather than geographic nature, abstract rather than concrete, no matter how prosaic the image of a man in a boat eating a can of beans may be. What he was hoping to find could well be what he'd previously just glimpsed as he fell: complete severance. A long drawn-out, horizontal plummet through time and space. This was no longer an exercise, this was the "real thing," and the commitment was total.

There is a chance he did find it, *The Miraculous,* drifting on that vast ocean, all alone with his own body and the elements. There's also a chance he never found it and was mostly scared, lonely, desperate; human.

Was Bas Jan Ader fully aware he was putting his life on the line for the sake of this art project? The answer, yes, seems all too evident. Without staking his life on it, the quest would ultimately be meaningless, a good gimmick at most, technically advanced, but far from miraculous. Some people even think it was downright suicide: it wasn't just that there was a chance he would die; there was practically no chance he would survive.

Interesting to note: after his death, the book *The Strange Last Voyage of Donald Crowhurst* was discovered in Bas Jan's art school locker—a reconstruction of the bizarre ocean crossing of sailor and businessman Donald Crowhurst.

All kinds of business missteps had landed Crowhurst in such financial straits that on an impulse he signed himself up for the 1968 *Sunday Times* "Singlehanded around the world" Golden Globe Race. He would win, and the prize money would solve his financial woes in one fell swoop.

After a rough crossing from England to the Azores, his trimaran (paid for by mortgaging his home) turned out to be a lot less seaworthy than he'd hoped. He then made a decision that suggests not only desperation but also a deeply-held sense of decorum: he quietly abandoned the race, but continued to send his (fake) daily coordinates to the race organizers, while aimlessly drifting around somewhere in the Atlantic. He kept two logs: one with the real data, and the other a cooked-up account of the journey he was supposed to be on. This went on, practically without a hitch, for several months. Transmitting one far-flung position after another, he never left the Atlantic behind. After a while, knowing he had dug himself in too deep to get away with his lie, his only remaining wish was to "finish the race" without being unmasked.

It isn't difficult to imagine his alarm when suddenly, eight months later, the race committee advised him that he had left all the other vessels way behind, and was pegged to win the race. His lies had been too good! It was a possibility that had never even occurred to him. Added to which, the lonely months at sea, with one foot planted starboard in reality, and the other portside in his fibs, had started making him a bit loopy. Adrift on that ocean, he was the only one in the whole wide world who knew he had utterly failed, and that's a heavy load to carry. *Too* heavy for one person to bear (at least this one), as became clear when the news of his imminent victory turned his mild derangement into blind panic. The tone of his entries grew more and more desperate, degenerating into an unintelligible verbal stew, as wild and senseless as the sea itself.

Still he kept sending out the fake coordinates on a daily basis: the lie had become an integral part of his body, it had grown into a stubborn tic overriding any and all sane thought. When a month later he had lied his way to within reach of the finish line, he broke off all radio contact, and vanished. Twelve days after his last entry in the "genuine" log ("It is finished, it is the mercy"), his boat was found, completely intact, somewhere in the North Atlantic. There was no sign of a shipwreck, but when the two versions of his log were discovered in the cabin, it wasn't hard to reconstruct what had happened.

The fact that Bas Jan Ader had read this strange story before his departure implies he was well aware how his own voyage might end. And yet something doesn't add up. First of all, Donald Crowhurst was a sad case, and his end will go into the history books as a tragic, senseless death. He kept digging himself in deeper, until finally he made such a mess of things that, trapped in a tangle of lies and self-deception, there was nothing left to do but to jump overboard. (Can you blame him? Who can deny it was the only way out of all his problems?)

Second, and this is far more pertinent, life meant something quite different to the two men. To Crowhurst, like most people, life was a succession of more or less haphazard events and ultimatums closing in on him like rising water, ever colder and ever wetter, until it engulfed him and he drowned. Ader, on the other hand, allowed himself to be guided, but not ruled, by the vagaries of the cosmos. His art turned his life into a sophisticated, all-out quest for the mystical. Art *was* his life, in the way breathing is, or one's heartbeat. There was no need to translate one into the other, because to him, the language was one and the same. A language he had taught himself the year he was kicked out of art school, and which he'd perfected when he got married under the neon lights of Las Vegas, leaning on his wooden crutches.

This approach to life is not without danger, naturally. Anyone who makes no distinction between life and art will tend to make radical decisions. For that is what art demands, if it aspires to be more than mere decoration for the walls of mansions that would otherwise get swamped in their own vastness. Also: if one is completely indistinguishable from the other, what, then, becomes of "the other"? The art is swallowed up by the whirlpool that is life, and vice versa, until it gives rise to a hermetically sealed system in which neither any longer really exists. The art is no longer art, and life is no longer life. It's that simple.

So, wasn't it evident that Bas Jan Ader was aware of the fact he was risking his life not only in theory but also in a truly practical sense? If you preserve life in a vacuum-sealed art terrarium, is there any room left for death? I mean *real*, commonplace death, the body shuddering and jerking until all life is crushed out of it, the waves closing overhead as it helplessly succumbs, until it swells up with fluid and bobs back up to the surface, bloated, bloodless, putrid?

Bas Jan Ader wasn't making a sea voyage, he was creating an art piece. He wasn't a stuntman, and he wasn't a prankster. He was an artist, and even if he was risking his life for art, he also felt that art protected him.

Just as that body dangling from the branch didn't realize it was going to fall, the body in the little boat didn't know it might die, even if the mind had considered that thought a thousand times—in reading Crowhurst's story in the breaks between classes, every time he took a shower, or in the middle of the night when Mary Sue was asleep, dreaming of babies. It wasn't until the very last moment, after the fall, the struggle and the stupefaction, that the body must have known that *this was it.* Bas Jan Ader's death only marked his artwork's final gesture, not its ultimate completion. Anyone claiming otherwise is deluded as to the nature of art.

1984

MINNIE'S FIRST noiseless near-disappearance took place on the ninth of July 1984, the day of her birth. She arrived fourteen weeks early, no more than a vague promise of a human being. If she'd been born a week, or even a few days earlier, she would not have been considered viable, according to the medical guidelines of the time.

Before the baby was placed in an incubator for transportation, the doctor briefly held her up to the mother's face. The skull, if you could call it that, was squished into a weird shape, and the limbs were inconceivably skinny. Although she was aware it would be small, Minnie's mother was shocked at the actual dimensions of the infant lying bloody and inert in the doctor's palms. As if he had just yanked out a heart from somewhere and was now presenting it to her.

Minnie's mother, who one year earlier had delivered a baby who was stillborn, wondered what this was supposed to represent, this unformed child that had come into the world without an epidermis, without fat, yes, even without any real bones, or so it seemed. It felt like a punishment and at the same time a blessing, but since Minnie's mother refused to believe in a divine providence, she told herself that it was what it was: a child on the heels of another child, it might live, or it might die, although the doctors had made it clear enough she should prepare herself for the second possibility. It had nothing to do with divine justice.

But Minnie did not die. They kept her in the neonatal intensive care unit for thirteen weeks, hooked up to tubes and catheters. She had three brain hemorrhages and turned yellow from an overproduction of bilirubin, but she was a tough one, said the nurses with names like Chantal or Charmaine, a real fighter. Minnie's mother peered through the incubator's portholes at the translucent infant that didn't look like a fighter, but like a helpless little bird. So tiny and so nakedly on display, like the crown jewels in a heavily guarded museum. Someone is looking at you, she whispered, someone loves you. She stuck her hand through the opening and touched it, carefully, ever so carefully. Is this incubator friendlier than my uterus? she wondered. A ridiculously sentimental thought, for her. As if it had anything to do with friendliness.

At night, at home, she tried picturing what the child looked like again, how tiny it was and the way it lay there in the hospital, in the ICU, in the incubator. The tubes, the skin. The other people in the hospital, hundreds of them, the sick, how they all slept. The more she tried picturing it, the less the child was left behind. The child is a set of circumstances, she thought to herself. An experiment in living instead of a life. She wondered if this signified something about humanity in general.

When they let her take it home, the little thing weighed a good deal less than the average newborn. Two bags of sugar and a few tomatoes. Or eggs, thought Minnie's mother, it felt more like eggs. She had a fantasy that she let it slip out of her hands. Over and over again she pictured it in her mind's eye—the child smashed on the floor, the shell and the yolk. She was surprised how little effort it would take. How noiseless it would be.

The infant's silence was almost absolute. Not only did it never cry, it sometimes simply stopped breathing. Minnie's mother was afraid that that meant it was mentally retarded. That was a risk, they'd said, in the hospital. They could save the kid's life but they weren't responsible for anything more.

Sometimes she'd watch the child for minutes on end, trying to find any sign of defect. She snapped her fingers right next to the little ears; she waved a stuffed animal in front of the little face. With slight movements of the head and a minimal shifting of the eyes, the child showed her that it was neither deaf nor blind. At least that was something, Minnie's mother told herself, even if it wasn't much.

At night too, the child was quiet; it didn't even cry when it was hungry. Sometimes Minnie's mother would deliberately put off nursing it, but that only made it sleep even longer than usual. Her colleagues at the cancer society said she was lucky to have such a good baby. *They* hadn't had a moment's peace and quiet since they'd had kids. Minnie's mother nodded and tried looking at the child as if she was aware how lucky she was, but it did not return her gaze, it just lay there in its cot with its eyes closed, it slept and slept and slept, neither confirming nor denying anything.

Meanwhile Minnie's mother herself hardly slept at all any more. She grew so exhausted that she was past the point of feeling sleep was still possible. If she did manage to fall asleep, she always, almost without exception, dreamt of being engulfed by towering waves, smoldering lava or raging winds. She'd wake up in a sweat, terrified that she'd find the child dead in the little cot beside her. Dead and blue, she pictured it, asphyxiated because it had refused to take another breath.

When one night she discovered the child with its eyes wide open, staring motionless into space, she'd picked it up and, from fear and frustration, shaken it, like those mothers you read about in the papers, crazed, hollow-eyed mothers that shake their babies to death. Hers had just stared at her in surprise, or rather, had stared right through her, as if it wasn't looking at its mother but at something behind her, or within her, or whatever. "*God damn it*," said Minnie's mother, and said it again, and again, louder and louder in the silent night: goddammit.

The next day she brought the child back to the hospital. There she went, her heels clacking *tick-tick-tick* on the linoleum. In the hospital everything was crystal clear, you had to read signs and follow directions, there were information desks, chairs of light-colored wood, and doors, hundreds of doors. The twilight zone Minnie's mother had dwelt in over the past few months suddenly seemed unreal to her, walking along these corridors with her child. Maybe, she thought, life needs to be no more complicated than a hospital. She sniffed the sterile smell of cleaning products and rubber gloves. For the first time in ages her spirits rose a bit. They were going to be a normal twosome, she and the child, and this was the beginning.

"YOUR CHILD IS in great shape by the look of it, Mrs. Panis," said the pediatrician, who had just introduced himself to Minnie's mother with a name that sounded like "James Johnstone," although it could have been Johnston or John Stone—although on second thought, the name James John Stone didn't sound right. Minnie's mother had never seen him on the ward before, in any case, which did surprise her, but only fleetingly.

Doctor Johnstone was a tall redhead with a slight American accent and freckles covering every visible inch of his body. He seemed too young for his role, around thirty at most. Minnie's mother stared at the plethora of freckles speckling his face and had this vague urge to smear cream all over it to make it all uniform.

Standing next to Johnstone was the neonatal ICU's head nurse, who called all the incubator babies "tough ones" and "fighters." She was a woman of unbelievable girth. Every time Minnie's mother used to see her bustling about the ward, she'd been surprised at the contrast between this woman and the preemies, the excess of flesh versus the paucity thereof.

The three of them looked at the child on the exam table. Dr. Johnstone had just finished shining a light in its eyes, sticking a probe in its ears and listening to the heart with a stethoscope.

"She's wonderfully healthy, really, for such an extreme preemie," he said. "A bit small perhaps, but that's normal, completely normal."

The baby stared at the ceiling, the little hands clenched in minuscule fists by its side.

"A real fighter," said the head nurse, with a hearty smile that pressed the fat of her double chin deeper into her neck.

"But it *doesn't* fight," said Minnie's mother, "that's the problem. It doesn't *do* anything."

"Nurslings mostly drink and sleep," replied the head nurse, "you can't really expect any more from them. Parents are often disappointed, but that's because they have unrealistic expectations."

"I don't have unrealistic expectations," said Minnie's mother. "Babies are supposed to cry. This one doesn't."

Now that she had come here, she wasn't going to get fobbed off like that.

"Many parents think their baby should immediately be capable of all sorts of things," the head nurse went on. A strand of minuscule drops of sweat beaded her hairline. "And then they're upset when it turns out they don't really *do* anything except, well, *be* there."

"What my colleague here means," said Johnstone, and he made a circular gesture with his hands, revealing a portion of his forearms, which were freckled even on the underside, "are you concerned that caring for you baby is less interesting than you were expecting?"

"My child never makes a sound," said Minnie's mother, "*that* is what I mean. Look," she said, poking her fingers into the child's ribcage as it went on staring at the ceiling unperturbed, "it just lies there, all day long. There's something objective about it."

"Something objective?"

"It makes me think of an object."

"And can you tell me when this... objectification started?" Johnstone again made a circle with his hands. It reassured Minnie's mother. As if everything of a problematic nature fit inside that circle.

"It's supposed to *do* something," she said. "This isn't normal."

There was a pause, during which all three of them stared at the child as if hoping that the answer would somehow be revealed out of the blue.

"Have you heard the one," said the fat head nurse, "about the little boy of seven who's never spoken a word in his life? His parents think he's retarded. One evening at dinner, they're having soup. Suddenly the boy turns to his parents. *'Die Suppe is kalt!'* he cries. Astonished, his parents ask him why he's never talked before, upon which the boy answers, *'Bis jetzt war alles gut.'*"

"He says it in German?"

"That's the joke. What it's about: maybe your baby is simply content. Babies don't all cry the same, just as all adults don't cry the same. It all depends on the individual."

Johnstone picked up the child, holding it out in front of him with outstretched arms, and started walking it up and down the room.

"I want you to examine it," said Minnie's mother. Her voice sounded tense, the tone overly shrill. She took a deep breath to calm herself down.

"I refuse to take it home with me if it's like this," she said, in her normal voice.

The fatso and Johnstone stared at her; the child stared at nothing. Minnie's mother said it again: "I refuse to take it home like this."

She was amazed at this turn of events, the inexorability of her own words now that they had been uttered twice.

"Mrs. Panis," the head nurse finally sputtered, "this is a hospital, not a department store." A vein throbbed in her neck. 'You can't just return your child and expect us to take it back. It isn't a... microwave!"

Minnie's mother imagined the ward with every incubator holding a microwave instead of a baby, a ridiculous thought that was almost funny enough to make her laugh. She didn't even have a microwave at home, she wouldn't know what to do with one. Johnstone still stood there with the child in his outstretched arms. He was whispering the same three words over and over.

Where are you?

Had she heard him right? Was this huge American really saying that to her pint-sized child? Had he finally understood what she meant? He seemed lost in thought, no longer aware of the two women who were now staring at him in silence—ah, blessed silence, now that that fat bitch had finally shut up.

Then he looked up.

"Don't you worry," he said. "We'll make your child get better."

THE HOSPITAL HAD some time ago opened a special center for babies that cry excessively. It was the first and only such facility in the Netherlands, Johnstone told her; it was unique.

The center, located in an annex of the obstetrics wing, was founded with money from a very wealthy private donor. Legend had it that he had sired nothing but inconsolable crybabies, five in all; it had driven his wife so crazy that she'd wound up being committed to a mental institution.

"The center is nothing less than a revolution in the field of neonatology," said Johnstone. "The babies are reprogrammed there in no time. It's going make us internationally famous before the decade's end, mark my words."

They halted in front of a wide door.

"What do you hear?"

From the corridor beyond came the sound of a nurse's muffled footsteps. She was carrying a vase of flowers. She pushed one shoulder against a swinging door, which closed soundlessly behind her as she slipped through. A life can be measured by the doors that are opened and stepped through, thought Minnie's mother, and for the umpteenth time in the past few months she was amazed at the thoughts coming into her mind that really didn't seem to have anything to do with her.

"Nothing," she said.

"Exactly!" cried Johnstone. "The center is totally sound-proofed." He held the door open for her. Behind it there was another door. "Observe," he said.

There was no way Minnie's mother could have been prepared for the noise on the other side of that door. It completely engulfed her, like the waves in her dreams, more powerful than anything she could possibly have stood up to. It wasn't until she'd been there for some time that she managed to separate out the various sounds that together made up the noise. There was monotone whining, howling, gasping for breath, bawling. Drowning out all the rest was a horrible screeching that seemed to get louder with every shriek. In the midst of the din, it suddenly occurred to Minnie's mother that she'd somehow become used to the unreal silence she'd lived in over the last several months. The formidable reality she was now exposed to made her gasp for breath. Minnie, in her arms, didn't seem bothered by the noise, stoically continuing to stare into space.

"Impressive, isn't it?" Johnstone shouted. "And to think that some of these cases can keep it up for hours! A near-superhuman feat, if you ask me."

The center wasn't at all like the NICU. It was a windowless space with a low ceiling making it seem smaller than it really was. The walls were lined with cube-shaped black sconces that cast a dull yellow light. It was such a great contrast to the brightly lit hospital corridors that Minnie's mother had trouble orienting herself. Not until Johnstone led her farther inside was she able to distinguish certain shapes and features. Much of the floor was covered in a red geometric pattern carpet that looked like an Asian antique. Arranged around it were a long, backless wooden bench and two wooden blocks. A couple of cupboards in a corner, and that was it. Not a stuffed animal or toy anywhere, no colorful pictures on the walls.

Two women Minnie's mother took to be mothers were sitting on the bench, with their screaming babies on their laps. Three other mothers and one father were walking around the room in a circle, rocking their babies to the beat of their footsteps. Some of the babies were swaddled up to their necks, which made them look a bit like giant larvae.

"You're in luck," Johnstone said, "we've had a new batch come in today, so the noise intensity is relatively high. A few days from now, the din will already be drastically reduced. Every child that's admitted here is assigned its own personal, specially trained caregiver."

Minnie's mother didn't see any nurses in the room.

"Do the parents stay the whole time as well?" she inquired.

"Certainly not. It is crucial that they see their child only during fixed visiting times. The people you see here"—he gestured with his arm at the wooden bench and the people pacing in a circle—"are all caregivers. They don't wear lab coats for the simple reason that we want the children to feel at home. Besides, it isn't good for children to be turned into patients from infancy. That becomes a self-fulfilling prophecy, don't you see?"

Johnstone opened a door leading into a smaller, rectangular room. In it ten or a dozen cribs were lined up in a neat row. Some held sleeping babies. Classical music came piped through speakers in the ceiling. Amazingly enough, the noise of the room next door did not penetrate here.

ALL THE FISH NEEDS, was painted in swirly red letters on the long wall across from the cribs, *IS TO GET LOST IN THE WATER*.

"Zhuangzi," said Johnstone. "Are you familiar with the Tao?"

Minnie's mother shook her head. She asked herself what this was all supposed represent, nurses who looked like parents, and babies listening to classical music.

"It's an extremely interesting ideology," Johnstone went on. "I'd almost call myself a Taoist, although of course the Tao that can be expressed in words isn't the real Tao."

He gazed at Minnie's mother with a look of triumph, as if he'd just poked holes in an argument she'd made.

"Help me remember to give you a copy of the handbook, later. We do that for every intake. Let us now get on to the formal part."

Shutting the dormitory door behind them, they walked back through the central space, where the howling was still swelling and ebbing like a continually breaking surf, and into a third room. This was by far the smallest, containing just a simple wooden desk with a typewriter, a filing cabinet and two wooden blocks like the ones in the central hall.

Johnstone invited Minnie's mother to sit down on one of the blocks.

"Care for tea?" he asked, and without waiting for an answer slipped back out the door. Minnie's mother gazed around the austere, windowless room. Minnie was sitting motionless on her lap, staring at the typewriter. What did she see? Minnie's mother tried to imagine seeing a typewriter for the first time without knowing what it was. But the harder she tried, the less she was able to do it. It remained a typewriter.

When Johnstone returned a few minutes later, he was carrying a tray with all kinds of things on it, including a curious clay teapot inscribed with Chinese characters. He put the tray down between them and took a seat on the block across from Minnie's mother.

"So," he said, "we are going to make your baby cry." He took a few rolled-up dark-green leaves from a glass jar, carefully pried open the teapot lid and stuffed the leaves inside. He poured hot water from a thermos into the pot, proceeded to wind up a little egg timer, then replaced the lid on the teapot.

"Ordinary babies," he said, "have a kind of inbuilt filter, which sees to it that external stimuli don't all impinge on them with the same force. Crybabies are missing that filter, which means they can get unsettled by something as minor as the crinkling of a newspaper or a chair scraped across the floor. Add to that the fact they can sense the stress of their parents, who are at their wits' end from all the crying. By the time the parents bring their baby to this center, everyone's exhausted. Nobody's getting a moment's rest, try putting yourself in their shoes!"

Putting herself in their shoes wasn't hard for Minnie's mother, and suddenly, without warning, something wriggled its way out of her stomach and sped upward into her chest, her throat, her nose, and, finally, her eyes. The tears felt hot on her cheeks. Johnstone pushed a box of tissues at her the way they did on TV; a tissue box that, she now saw, was one of the items on the tray. The tissue she dried her eyes with had a vaguely organic scent. She inhaled deeply. Forests, she thought. She calmed down.

Johnstone resumed his story in a quiet voice.

"Once the babies get here, we send the parents home as soon as possible, to break the vicious cycle of stress immediately. In order to make a complete reprogramming of the child possible, we begin by reducing the stimuli. No windows, very little light, no toys, as you just saw. And, God, no mobiles above the cribs, ever! Whoever invented those was a moron. All they do is upset the babies."

Johnstone's sudden agitation seemed to take him aback, and for a moment he was quiet.

"Anyway," he went on, "thus as little stimulation as possible. Seeing that their own limbs may provide the most distraction, we often swaddle the babies so that they can't move. Most effective. Besides that, I have been experimenting with sound. Some babies calm down with Bach, others from the white noise of the television, it all depends on individual preference. For the others it's simply a matter of predictability and regularity. I like to compare it to this age-old tea ceremony—" Johnstone made a wide gesture with his arms that took in the tray and all the implements on it—"*the School of Fragrant Leaves*. Every stage has to be completed with the utmost precision. It's in the repetition of the steps wherein lies perfection."

At the exact moment he'd said the word "perfection," the timer went off.

Minnie's mother looked on as he began deftly fishing the tealeaves out of the water with a wooden skewer. The leaves had swollen to at least three times their size.

"Now we must wait six more minutes, in order to bring the tea to the right strength and, no less important, to the right temperature. That's a very tight window."

Again he set the timer. To her amazement, Minnie's mother noticed that the child on her lap had been moving her head from side to side, following Johnstone's movements closely. Hey, what's this? she thought. In all these months she hadn't once caught the child being truly present in the here and now; it was as if this pretentious tea ceremony had suddenly discovered the "on" switch. Again, and just as abruptly as before, she felt hot tears pressing against the inside of her eyelids. Who did this doctor think he was? A Zen master who used ancient Chinese tricks to bend little babies to his will? A present-day Pied Piper of Hamelin? The spark of anger was shifted to the child on her lap. It's punishing me, she thought, it's been punishing me since birth. Everything in her wanted to storm out of the room, away from this place, from the child, from her whole life as it was now. As if she'd said it out loud (had she said anything out loud?), Johnstone said, "The sense of impotence can lead to fury. If you're turned off by your child, don't be ashamed. Let it come, accept it, and then let it go."

Minnie's mother took a deep breath. The anger had receded, and all she felt now was emptiness, as if she'd suddenly realized that someone had slowly been emptying her out inside. Bones, organs, muscles, everything. She so longed to go to sleep. Just hang on, she thought, hang on just a bit longer. Stay sitting upright on this block. She tried concentrating on the wood pressing into the back of her knees. Like the wood, she was a woman all of one piece.

She tried a smile.

"Very well," said Johnstone, and he was smiling too. "My plan is quite simple. Little..."

"Minnie."

"Little Minnie, obviously, has the opposite problem of the babies we normally take in here. Well then: we'll treat her in the exact opposite way. We'll increase the stimuli. The screaming babies around her provide her with a great example, to start. Next we'll make her life as erratic and unpredictable as possible. We'll keep it up until we find the right balance to get her to start crying. From there we can begin working on normal, desirable crying behavior. You needn't worry that we'll hurt her, or flash strobe lights in her eyes, or anything, she'll be treated with the most tender loving care." Planting his elbows on the table, the doctor brought his face up close to hers. "Now, what do you think?"

Minnie's mother didn't know *what* she thought. It sounded unorthodox and, moreover, not well medically grounded, but what were her alternatives? She couldn't see herself returning home with the child, back to square one. And so she nodded, started filling out the intake form, and, when the egg timer went off for the second time, drank a cup of tea that tasted of what she imagined was a Chinese mountain range.

MINNIE'S MOTHER stopped in daily at the center, which she privately, half joking, half reverently, called the School of Fragrant Leaves. Johnstone and she had agreed that she should never tell the staff ahead of time when to expect her, in order to enhance the unpredictability that was part of the treatment.

At home she expressed her breast milk, so that she'd have to spend as little time at the center as possible. It was hard for her to see Minnie in the arms of the caregivers, their endless patience, the warm understanding, the usurpation lurking beneath the surface. Besides, the collective howling of the other babies was still as torturous to her as ever, so that it sometimes took her a few minutes of dithering outside the double entry doors before she gathered up enough courage to go in.

She'd often find her child surrounded by the screechers, whose existence it did not acknowledge, as far as she could tell. After two days Johnstone had had a separate niche installed for Minnie, with a TV, a stereo system and an infant seat. The alcove was partitioned off with a folding screen, and the child was given a pair of special headphones to wear, so that the music wouldn't over-stimulate the other babies (although they made enough of a racket themselves to drown out an air raid siren, thought Minnie's mother). It was a ludicrous sight, a baby with headphones on, and besides, Minnie's mother had her doubts about how much the tiny, only very recently developed ears of her child, her daughter, could tolerate.

Johnstone assured her, however, that it would do no harm, he had discussed it with a friend of his, an ear-nose-and-throat specialist, who'd confirmed what Johnstone already knew, which was that stimulating the infant's hearing is important for the development of speech and social skills. And so the child sat there for several hours a day listening to all sorts of music, as well as watching *Thunderbirds,* the evening news, and nature shows of lions devouring zebras.

Nurse Ramses, who only worked the morning shift, took the child out for a walk every day. On Dr. Johnstone's orders they visited nursery school playgrounds, railway stations, cafés, shelters for the homeless and addicts, highway overpasses. They even attended a public court hearing once.

Ramses was a scrawny kid from an Egyptian family, whose arms and legs had a mysterious tendency to swing in circular motion. He had a downy little moustache above his lips and deep craters in his cheeks attesting to a serious case of acne in the not too distant past. Of all the nursing staff at the center, Ramses was the only one Minnie's mother had taken a liking to, because he was wholly without the militant ideology of calm and efficient cleanliness that made the rest of them so insufferable.

One morning during the first week of Minnie's admission, Minnie's mother walked into the facility just as Ramses was preparing to take Minnie outside. Together they strolled over to the Bijenkorf department store, which was having a sale; Ramses said it reflected the way a country functions right after a coup. He told

Minnie's mother of his ambition to become head nurse of the pediatric ICU. He loved children more than the elderly, he said, because they were a bit less stinky. A broad grin spread across his face as he said it, showcasing each individual bristle of moustache.

They parked the stroller at the store entrance. Minnie's mother did not protest when Ramses picked up her child and carried her. She admired the way he threaded his way through the jumbled heaps of sale items, talking softly to her daughter all the while. "Look, girlie," he told her, "this is how people spend their Saturday mornings. They work hard all week long, and then they come here. That's how they keep the e-co-no-my going. Those are panties, three for the price of one, and that over there, those tubes and jars in all those colors, that's called cosmetics. Ladies consider it perfectly normal to plaster their faces all over with that stuff, can you imagine? And now—here we go!—we're on an escalator. You've never been on one of these before, have you..."

To her surprise, Minnie's mother saw her daughter's head move up and down, as it had a few days earlier during Dr. Johnstone's tea ceremony.

"Come," she said impulsively to Ramses, "I'll treat you to a piece of cake at Holtkamp's."

It was a bright December day and there they went: a mother, her child, and the scrawny Egyptian with the laughable name. The air seemed more saturated with oxygen than usual, the colors brighter, and Minnie's mother realized the fog of exhaustion was slowly lifting. Suddenly Ramses stopped short. He knelt down on the sidewalk, started prying something out from between two stones, and held it up a couple of seconds later, pinched between his thumb and forefinger. It was a silver coin, round and intact, glittering in the sunlight. Minnie's mother, glancing at her child in the stroller, saw that it was staring at the coin, fascinated. Although it went against all her assumptions, she hoped from the bottom of her heart that it was a good sign. That the secret suspicion she'd had, that her child was never really meant for that little body, would prove unfounded.

*

Twelve days after she was admitted to the center, the log recorded that on Sunday, December 9, 1984, at around 10:45 a.m., in the presence of the department head, Dr. Johnstone, and the nurse on duty, Ramses Fatiqi, Minnie Panis, five months old to the day, had, for the first time in her life, shed tears.

Johnstone was in an extreme state of excitement when he called Minnie's mother. "There's been a breakthrough, Mrs. Panis!" he cried. "Your child has been crying. Rather, your child just started crying again, and it's the third time today. Wait." There was a rustling sound on the other end of the line. Then Minnie's mother heard a very faint wail, like the cry of a tiny animal that's got itself trapped somewhere. She realized she was holding her breath. "Are you still there, Mrs. Panis? Come in as soon as you can, I'll show you something that will blow your mind!"

They were in the central space's screened-off alcove, Johnstone, Ramses and Minnie. Minnie reclined in the infant seat with the headphones on, in her normal state of complete inattention bordering on serenity.

"Watch," said Johnstone, giving Ramses a sign.

"Watch," said Ramses. Limbs swaying around, he pushed the

PLAY button on the stereo.

What Minnie's mother saw happening to the child next was nothing short of a miracle. In barely a few seconds, the little face contorted itself into a grimace she had never seen before. The eyes squeezed shut, the little mouth started trembling; then the hands balled into little fists and the legs began kicking wildly. She opened her mouth (all three leaned in closer to the child in one smooth reaction) and began to cry, weakly, but indisputably. This went on for a few minutes, minutes in which Minnie's mother, despite everything in her resisting it, couldn't suppress the thought that her child was being ushered into the world for a second time. There you are, she thought, and it's about time, too.

The crying stopped just as abruptly as it had begun. Johnstone removed the headphones from Minnie's head and she looked around, a bit dazed.

"We still have to work on the volume," he said. "And the frequency, of course—as long as she can't talk yet, she'll have to use crying to show that she's hungry, or that something hurts."

Ramses pushed EJECT, put the cassette tape into a case, and handed it to Minnie's mother. HILDEGARD VON BINGEN was handwritten on it in ink, nothing else.

"Fascinating," said Johnstone. "I tried out all kinds of things on her, from Rachmaninoff to Pink Floyd. Then I tried a recording of the Pentecost Mass sung by a Gregorian choir. I saw that it affected her a bit, so I started testing out Gregorian chants on her until I got to Hildegard. And off she went! A true connoisseur, that child of yours. These songs are quite a bit different than the traditional chants. Hildegard has, how do you say, a most idiosyncratic signature."

"So Medieval church music makes her cry," said Minnie's mother.

"Precisely. This is music from the twelfth century. Hildegard von Bingen was one of the earliest Christian mystics. She led the Rupertsberg monastery, near Bingen in Germany. She was clairvoyant from an early age. At the age of forty-three she began having visions, which she chronicled in three great tomes. She also wrote medical and botanical texts that are still consulted to this day. She was a celebrity even in her own time. She was an adviser to various eminent clerics, and corresponded with figures such as Bernard van Clairvaux and Emperor Frederick Barbarossa. For a woman of that era, this was all quite unprecedented. You might call her one of the first feminists in history: as early as the year 1150 she spoke up for a woman's sexual pleasure! But OK, I digress. The point is that she also wrote music. She is one of the first composers in the history of music known by name. This cassette features the liturgical chants, inspired by her visions. They seem to evoke a strong emotion in our little Minnie."

"You mean to say my child is moved by this music?"

"That's quite possible, yes."

"That's ridiculous."

"It speaks to a sensory and emotional sensitivity that one doesn't often find in such a young child. It calls for a delicate approach. It's like a rare and precious grand piano: with a worthless pianist sitting at it, it means nothing, but find the right musician to play it… anyway, to make a long story short: your daughter is far from a dummy, but she does need special handling."

"What do you propose?" asked Minnie's mother.

Johnstone again made that embracing gesture with his arms.

"We'll keep her here for a while longer. We'll let her listen to the music just before a feeding, so that she'll start associating crying with hunger, until she doesn't need the music anymore. Since we are now starting an intensive training program, I'll ask you not to visit. The parent often has a counterproductive influence on the process. Once the crying finally reaches a healthy volume and steady frequency, we'll send her home."

On December 15, 1984, Minnie's mother watched on the nightly news an unmanned spaceship from the Soviet Union being sent into space, headed for Venus. It would take half a year, the correspondent said, to get there. As the screen filled with clouds of white smoke, the phone rang.

"She is ready for take-off," Johnstone's voice on the other end announced. "We have reprogrammed her in record time. She could have taught that dog of Pavlov's a thing or two."

2012

THE HAND THAT DRAGGED Minnie out of the water was large and pale and strewn with hundreds of freckles. Later she often thought of that hand, which in her mind took on the mythic proportions of a Manus Dei, come down from heaven itself to save her, as if, good God, she were a character in some Stephen King novel.

THE RESCUE WAS PERFORMED with amazing efficiency: one moment her body was being sucked under water, the next she was lying securely on her side, high and dry on the bank.

"Can you hear me?" the hand asked, slapping her lightly on the cheeks, slaps she couldn't really feel but was somehow aware of.

"You've had an accident," said the hand.

Minnie concentrated on the word, in three syllables, *ac-ci-dent*; and divided down the middle, *acci-dent*; then he spoke again: "You've been lucky."

She allowed herself to be pulled up, felt her back resting against something vertical; this must be sitting. The hand now turned into a person. Everything about this person was large: his limbs, his head, every facial feature. You don't know where to look, thought Minnie, each of the components he's made of demands so much attention. Shocks of orange hair poked out beneath a black woolen hat.

"Am I hurt?" she asked. "I mean, is there anything that should be hurting me?" It sounded idiotic. Either you were hurt, or you weren't hurt.

"How many fingers?" asked the rescuer, squatting in front of her and now holding three enormous fingers in the air.

"Three," said Minnie, but once she'd said it there were no longer three. "Two."

Speaking wasn't easy, something seemed to be delaying her mouth. She'd have to do something about that. Work on it.

"Three or two?"

"Two. I don't know why I said three at first, it's obviously two, I saw it right away. Two. Obviously."

She felt some tingling in her fingertips and looked down. Where her hands should be, there was nothing, or rather, there was something, but it wasn't hands. It was wrapped all around her, she realized, her head was covered in it as well.

"What is this?" asked Minnie.

"A rescue banquet," said the rescuer, as if it was the most normal thing in the world.

"A rescue banquet?"

What were they talking about? She pictured a long table overflowing with sumptuous dishes.

"Blanket. To isolate you against the cold."

"I'm not cold."

"That's right," said the rescuer. "That's just the problem." The next thing she knew his two hands were covering her face.

"Don't be alarmed, Minnie," he said. "Your head makes up ten per cent of your body. I'm using my own body heat to warm you up. The extremities are of crucial importance."

Minnie closed her eyes. The darkness beneath the hands was reassuring. The sound of her own silly name too. She wished the rescuer would say it a few more times. Or that he'd end every sentence with her name, the way some people do after taking a training course. Life coaches and realtors.

"I'm going to lift you up now," said the voice belonging to the hands. "And then I'm going to put you in my car. You can't stay here any longer. Not a good idea, in this cold."

The hands were removed and then she saw herself detaching from the ground, a bundle of glittering golden foil—like a goddamn candy bar wrapper! She wanted to tell him it wasn't necessary, all that lifting, she was an adult and adults never had to be picked up or carried around.

"Standing on your own feet is extremely ill-advised in a situation like this," said the rescuer, as if he could hear what she was thinking. He didn't seem to have any trouble carrying her full weight in his arms. He bounded up the bank with great bouncy strides. From her golden cocoon Minnie stared at the azure sky, the crowns of the gnarled plane trees. Why couldn't people, too, just start out in one spot, grow up to the sky, and stay there forever?

"Have you ever heard of after-drop?" asked the rescuer, not pausing for an answer from the little human heap in his arms. "That can happen if the victim moves before the body is sufficiently warmed. The cold blood from the extremities is suddenly pumped throughout the body, lowering the temperature even further, which can cause sudden cardiac arrest. A good example, I think, of a situation in which good intentions and lack of knowledge make an unhappy marriage, with all its tragic consequences."

If Minnie had had the energy, she'd have pointed out to her savior that his voice would be perfect for a TV documentary or public service announcement, but by the time they reached the car she was utterly exhausted—as if she'd been the one who'd had to carry that huge man in her arms up to the road.

She felt herself being gently lowered onto the back seat. She wanted to object, she wasn't supposed to be in a car, she'd be breaking her contract if she was transported in any other vehicle except a bike. She was shivering.

"Ah," said the rescuer, putting his head in the door, "you're finally feeling the cold. That's excellent. But you must stay awake."

From close up she saw he was older than she'd thought. His face was etched with fine lines, rivers in a landscape.

"Did you know that southern Louisiana is the earth's most rapidly disappearing land mass?" she said. "It loses a piece of land the size of a football field every forty-five minutes. Since the thirties, an area the size of Delaware has been lost to the ocean."

In the car he'd talked to her nonstop, constantly turning his head to look back to make sure she was still awake. Most of what he said went way over her head, but it didn't matter, the point was the sound and the rhythm.

It wasn't until they'd set off that Minnie realized the rescuer wasn't the one at the wheel. He had a driver. Since she was lying with her head behind the driver's seat, she could only see a small section of the back of his head. He wore a grey chauffeur's cap as if it was something you wore in all seriousness, and not just something you wore to a party. And perhaps that was the point. Every profession needs a uniform; only, some uniforms are a bit more caricaturish than others.

She felt dazed and at the same time, in some uncoordinated way, alert. She knew there were important things demanding her attention, but the important things were just beyond her reach. Her brain got itself stuck on that chauffeur's hat instead, the blond curls emerging from it, the minuscule crumbs in the upholstery's creases, the exaggerated realism of it all.

After a while the car stopped. She had managed to work her arms free of the cocoon, strange, pale limbs that didn't seem to have much to do with her. She was surprised to see she was wearing a baggy grey coat, with nothing underneath barring her underwear. Again she was lifted up in the air. A grey parking lot, an elevator, a front door, a threshold, a bride carried across the threshold.

"Welcome to my abode," said the rescuer after carefully lowering her onto a chair. It wasn't clear where the driver had gone. Maybe he didn't even exist outside of the car. A little dog came running up to them, jumping wildly up at the rescuer and then starting fanatically to chase its own tail.

"This is Frank," said the rescuer. "Frank Lloyd Wright, to be exact. I got him from the pound a few years ago. He has an abnormality that makes him spin round and round in circles like this all day long. He reminds me of the Guggenheim."

For the third time that afternoon the rescuer stretched out his formidable hand at her. Even in relation to the man's body, it was completely out of proportion.

"Johnstone. James. How do you do."

Of course, thought Minnie. Of course your are, because—why not? Taken altogether, there was a kind of logic to it. Cats in the night, lambs both dead and alive, fish that lose themselves in the water. Maybe, she thought, it had something to do with *feng shui*.

And then she remembered it again, the important thing at the back of her mind. It pushed its way upward, zeroing in on the place where hazy notions are turned into words.

"I'm pregnant," said Minnie.

THE HAZINESS was gone in a heartbeat. Something was spoken, and now it was real.

"Ah," said Johnstone. "That was to be expected, yes."

He had sat down on a chair across from her. Minnie stared at him.

"How often did you have to vomit in the past few days?"

Minnie thought of the sour chunks of mackerel. The yogurt and the sandwich, earlier that day. She felt a fresh wave of nausea starting.

"And that cup of coffee this morning, naturally. It's practically a cliché, I'd say, pregnant women and their aversion to coffee. And not for nothing, either. The fetus doesn't possess the enzyme to deactivate the caffeine's effect. There's been an experiment on baby rats to show the stuff just accumulates in the brain."

Minnie opened her mouth, but couldn't get the words out.

"But the most obvious thing to me—uh, I hope you won't find it impertinent of me." Johnstone pointed at her breasts. "Definitely bigger than in those photos in *Vogue*. How far gone are you, five, six weeks or so?"

"Six," said Minnie. Her voice sounded hoarse. She felt like a kid who should know the answers to all kinds of math problems, but keeps guessing instead. "Five and a half."

His face was freckled all over. The spots were a very light orange, yellow almost, like faded craft paper. They looked as if you could just scratch them off. His features had still not assumed normal proportion, making his face look a bit grotesque, but also friendly. It had something to do with the bristly ginger beard framing it. All in all, it wouldn't surprise her one bit if he had the complete works of Carl Marx in his bookcase and owned three pairs of Birkenstocks.

"How do you know about the coffee?" she asked.

"It's common knowledge."

"You called me by my name. Out there by the water you said my head was ten per cent of my body, and then you called me by my name. Were you following me?"

"Yes," he said simply. "I was."

Without another word, but raising his hand in a "hold it there" signal, he stepped out of the room.

She looked around. This must be the living room. Its scale was impressive, especially in relation to the furniture in it. She was sitting at a long wooden table, not on a chair, but on a block of wood. There were several of these scattered about the room, seemingly at random. The table faced a glass wall that looked out on a meticulously kept garden, which consisted of grass and bushes clipped into squares similar to the blocks of wood in the room. A giant red carpet took up most of the floor of the room, with a pattern of flowers and circular labyrinths, which Minnie guessed was a Chinese antique. Against the left wall was a narrow wooden bookcase filled, she was surprised to see, with nothing but *Suske & Wiske* comic books. That was it. She wondered where the photographer was. Whether he was around here somewhere; whether he could see her.

She heard a jingling sound, footsteps, muffled voices, and then Johnstone entered carrying a tray, which he put down on the table in front of her. It held a clay teapot, purplish in color and etched with Chinese characters.

"It's a Yixing teapot, post-World War II," he said when he saw her staring at it. "Made by the old Zisha master Gu Jing Zhou, still alive today, who may be compared to the great artists of the Ming dynasty."

He calmly started doing all kinds of things with small wooden pincers, rolled-up tea leaves and an egg timer. He seemed to have grown completely unaware of her presence. Who had he been talking to? The chauffeur?

"I take it you did receive my letter," he said suddenly, without looking up from what he was doing.

The letter, yes, of course, the fucking letter—the CBTH, the Maya, cycles, empirical research, déjà-vu, memories, trauma, treatment, torn snippets in the waste basket. *The only thing the fish has to do is to lose itself in the water.*

"I never had an answer from you; I hadn't expected to receive one either. But I knew that one of these days something would happen, a transition of sorts, it was inevitable. I started following you yesterday. I feel responsible for the consequences, you see. I'd have blamed myself if something terrible had happened to you this afternoon." He handed her a cup of tea and sat down on the block across from her. "What you did was very dangerous."

"I know," she said quietly.

"It was very clear that the ice was no longer safe, and still you stepped out on it. To tell you the truth, I've been racking my brain about that for the past hour or so. I don't see you as having a death wish, or do you?"

She shook her head. She had an urge to tell him everything, from the very beginning: about how she'd met the photographer, the *Vogue* affair, the contract she'd had Specht draw up, the performance piece that was ongoing, an ongoing performance Johnstone was now also a part of, whether he liked it or not. She wanted to tell him about fears both vague and concrete. About sometimes not being sure of the reality of her own existence, no matter how pompous that might sound, but above all she wanted to tell him she didn't know if she had tried hard enough to save herself when her clothes were soaking up more and more icy water and all the light was vanishing from the world and the panic had suddenly turned into acceptance.

"Who are you, anyway?" she asked instead. "Why are you so interested in me?"

"I'm a neonatologist, a hypnotist, Taoist and expert on Maya culture, among other things. I first met you when you were just a few months old," he said bluntly. "Knowing your mother, she probably told you very little about it."

"Nothing," said Minnie.

"In that case we'll start at the beginning."

He raised his hand.

"When you first made your appearance on my examination table, you were just about this big."

MINNIE HAD NO IDEA just how long Johnstone had been speaking, but he had refilled her cup at least five times; the teapot seemed bottomless. Finally he fell silent. She could have asked him a hundred questions, but suddenly she was tired, so very tired. Just as it dawned on her she hadn't even thanked him for saving her, he jumped to his feet.

"Good heavens," he exclaimed. "There you are, still sitting around in nothing but your underwear and my old summer coat! How thoughtless of me, how very thoughtless. Bob!"

When he'd shouted the name "Bob" three times or more at ever-increasing volume, a tall, thin youth with extremely pale eyes, blond curly hair and a blotchy red face came running in.

"This is Bob," said Johnstone. "My personal assistant, chauffeur, cook and general go-fer. He will conduct you to the guest quarters."

Bob raised his right forearm in a brief hello, as Hitler apparently used to do when having to greet a great number of people in a row, although Minnie doubted Bob was aware of this historical fact. He didn't appear to be much older than twenty, anyway.

She followed him up a set of stairs, along a corridor, then another set of stairs—how big was this house?

Finally Bob swung open the door to a room resembling the living room downstairs, but a bit smaller and containing a bed instead of a table. He pointed to a door to the left of the entrance.

"The bathroom."

It had to be eczema of some sort, those patches; it looked fairly severe. There was something else wrong with that face as well, although she couldn't pinpoint what.

"I'm an albino," Bob said. "My parents are both dark as anything. Make yourself comfortable. There are clean clothes for you in the bathroom."

The bathroom, like the rest of the house, smacked of the kind of simplicity that costs bags of money. The sinks (two of them) were hewed out of a single slab of black stone that reminded Minnie of a chunk of meteorite. The floor was wooden duckboards, the showerhead a gigantic square meant to evoke a tropical rainstorm.

Oddly enough the—otherwise tasteful—bathroom was chock-full of Rituals products, a brand that had started out on a humble shelf in the V&D department store, but had grown so successful that Rituals stores had started cropping up in most of the country's large and mid-sized cities. It probably owed its success to the products' exotic names, evoking an atmosphere of Eastern mysticism.

Minnie let her eyes travel over the dozens of tubes, jars and bottles on the sinks and in the shower alcove. Fortune Oil, Happy Hand Lotion, Good Luck Scrub, Touch of Happiness, Happy Buddha, Yogi Flow, Shanti Chakra, Shikakai Secret... Never before, she thought, had Western orientalism been so cleverly marketed. For a few lousy Euros, every hard-working stiff could, after a stir-fry from the prepared foods section or a few pieces of cold supermarket sushi, bask in the authentic Eastern bliss of his shower gel. She was amazed that Johnstone would fall for it—not even counting the sickening perfume unleashed when you opened one of those tubes—but then decided Bob was more likely the one responsible. The idea of Bob shopping at one of those stores moved her, and to her own surprise she burst into tremulous sobs. She took a long, hot shower, and scrubbed herself with the Good Luck Scrub until her skin was on fire and the last dreg of dark ice-water banished from her bones. Then she lay down on the bed, naked skin against clean white sheets.

Someone was still watching her, still loved her.

In the spring of 2010, Minnie had flown to New York for a few days to see a major retrospective of Marina Abramović's work at the MOMA. The high point of the exhibition was a new performance piece by Abramović herself. For two and a half months Abramović sat at a table in the atrium all day long. Visitors waited in endless lines for a chance to sit down across from her. They were allowed to sit there for as long as they liked, as long as there was no interaction with the artist other than eye contact.

The Artist Is Present was an absolute sensation, and one of the best-attended MOMA shows of all time. Like Minnie, people from all over the world traveled to New York to see the artist in person, and were willing to wait for hours, even days sometimes, for that chance.

Early one weekday morning, Minnie joined the waiting throng. She was an admirer of Abramović, and was certain that her own artistic career could never have taken off if it hadn't been for this woman, who had been one of the first artists prepared to offer up her own body to art without conditions nor guarantees; guinea pig and experimenter at the same time. Yet it wasn't a death wish that drove Abramoivić over the years to stage grueling and dangerous performances, but the opposite: anything that didn't scare the bejesus out of her was simply not worth attempting. So she proceeded to stab razor-sharp knives between her outstretched fingers as fast as possible, allowed herself to be threatened and maimed by the public, carved a bloody star into her own stomach, swallowed pills that sent her into uncontrollable spasms for hours. In the early seventies she'd nearly died after leaping into a flaming Communist star and losing consciousness from smoke inhalation. The spectators had pulled her out just in time. Afterward she confessed she was mainly frustrated that she'd come up against a physical limit: if you're unconscious, you can't be present. For a performance—Abramović let no opportunity go by to emphasize this—everything revolved around being present. *Presence.*

While waiting in line, Minnie had struck up a conversation with a make-up artist called Pablo Blancas, who was there for the thirteenth time that month. He was on friendly terms with all the guards by now. It was a transformative experience, he gushed, to sit across from Abramović, to gaze at her, to be gazed at by her. Her eyes gave out some sort of magnetic force, a catalyst for all sorts of emotions. His longest sitting spell so far had been seven hours. A few days ago he'd abruptly burst into tears after just ten minutes. It had something to do with Marina's concentration and energy, and all the other people watching. "She soars above her own fears," he said. "She teaches us that we can go farther than we think we can. She sees you, she really *sees* you."

Minnie had found it fascinating that this little Hispanic man, with his neatly trimmed moustache and black hair slick with gel, genuinely believed that Abramović was much more than a mirror in which to see his own reflection. That was the point, she thought, looking at all the people ahead of her, listening with half an ear to the chatter of the disciple standing next to her: even more than the chance of gazing into the eyes of a celebrity, it was about the chance of being seen by *her*, to experience even a fraction of what she was experiencing, to take part in her performance. Surely Abramović must know every square inch of the face of this man who kept coming back by now, yes, they probably knew each other's faces better than the most passionate lovers do. Maybe, Minnie thought, this Pablo Blancas wasn't really a nutcase but a brilliant performance artist in his own right, showing Marina Abramović what *she* was showing the other visitors, thus creating a hall of mirrors in which the differences between the reflection and the reflected were eventually erased.

Toward the end of the afternoon it was Minnie's own turn (Pablo, who was ahead of her in line, kept his sitting short that day; he liked to vary the length of these sessions, in order to experience different attention spans). Her heart started beating wildly as she took her seat opposite Abramović, who didn't open her eyes until Minnie was settled. The first minute was almost unbearable, but after a while her heart stopped racing, the compulsive urge to scream, laugh, or cry went away, and Marina Abramović's face turned into some abstract thing. Never before had Minnie ever stared at someone so brazenly and for such a long time. And yet, to her surprise, it had very little to do with intimacy. Two people were sitting there staring at each other, but only in order to let go of each other, of themselves, to dissolve into the ten thousand things.

SHE MUST HAVE fallen asleep, because when she opened her eyes and looked out, it was dark. She automatically started groping for her phone, but then realized that it had probably found its last resting place on the bottom of the lake.

She splashed her face with cold water, threw on the clothes Bob had left for her (a pair of red velvet pajamas that, strangely enough, didn't make her look like a complete ass) and went looking for Johnstone, whom she found on a balcony on the second floor with his gyrating dog. He was busily trying to scrape something off a sill by the light of a construction lamp.

He greeted her cheerfully and explained he was waging war on the pigeons that were shitting all over the place night and day, and making a horrible racket as well. Nothing seemed to help—he pointed to the buildup of barbed wire wrapped around the railing. At that very moment, as if directed by someone on high, a pigeon came flying along, landing on the barbed wire without any appreciable difficulty. The pigeon was missing a leg, but that didn't seem to deter it either.

"Damn," said Johnstone, shaking his head. "Those birds can walk around on a stump as if the foot's still there. How does it do it?"

"Maybe it's got a phantom foot," Minnie suggested. "Or maybe it's simply forgotten that there used to be another foot, and now it just thinks the stump *is* its foot."

"Well, be that as it may," said Johnstone, "Bob must have dinner ready by now." He aimed a surprisingly limber karate kick at the bird, whereupon Frank started barking eagerly and the startled pigeon flapped its wings, but refused to budge.

They took their seats on the wooden blocks again. The table was covered in a simple white linen cloth, and there was a menorah between them with a lit candle in each of its seven arms.

Bob came in with two steaming dishes. He'd made a Caribbean goat stew, a recipe of his grandmother's, Johnstone told Minnie; the grandmother had run a restaurant in Curaçao famous for its iguana soup, an Antillean delicacy before the iguana was declared a protected species, and subsequently even more sought after, of course.

Bob poured red wine into a large goblet next to Johnstone's plate. Minnie was offered a glass of water. Apparently, she thought, Bob knew about her condition.

"An unusually quiet young man," said Johnstone when Bob was out of the room. "He was once in treatment with me because he never spoke a word until he was five. His parents thought he was a simpleton, also on account of his appearance, naturally."

"Did you teach him to speak?"

"Actually, no, it turned out he was perfectly able to. I made sure that he'd actually say something once in a while. Fifteen years later he was suddenly back at my door, asking if I needed an assistant. It's been two years now. Until then it had never occurred to me that I needed someone like him, but now I can't even imagine what I would do without him. He's created his own position here, and has made me think he's indispensible. Very clever of him."

Earlier that afternoon, when they were drinking the tea from the purple teapot, Johnstone had given her a recap of his life, in broad strokes. He'd grown up in New York as the son of a Dutch father and an Irish-American mother. After studying medicine and specializing in pediatrics, he got a pediatric residency at Mount Sinai Hospital in Manhattan, where in the nineteenth century the pediatric pioneer Abraham Jacobi had set up the world's first children's clinic. In 1975, in homage to his father, who had just passed away, Johnstone decided to take a short trip to the land of his father's birth. Within one week he'd fallen in love with a girl from Amsterdam. "She only lasted a few months, turned out to be a nasty witch, but I never managed to extricate myself from the Netherlands again."

The goat meat was spicy and so tender it melted in your mouth. Johnstone was a heavy drinker; there was something compulsive about the pace at which he emptied his glass, as if he were aiming to get drunk on purpose.

"In your letter you wrote that our concept of time has become 'neoliberal,'" said Minnie, who without being conscious of it had started addressing him more informally. "And that that's what's making societies sick."

Nodding thoughtfully, he pried out a little bone stuck between his teeth and deposited it carefully on his napkin.

"Let me tell you the story of my father."

He took a big gulp of wine, sloshing it around in his mouth, then started talking about the past, but in the present tense. It sounded as if he were reading from a book, thought Minnie, or dictating to a ghostwriter. Maybe Bob usually sat where she was sitting, typing it up for him. It didn't seem inconceivable to her.

"My father, Simon Lipschits, is born into a large Jewish family of street vendors from Rotterdam. He is twenty-one in 1923 when he enlists as a cabin boy on a Holland-America ocean liner. He has big dreams and isn't interested in spending his life as a market vendor selling bananas. In America, the dockworkers and peddlers tell him, you make your own luck. Anyone prepared to work hard is rewarded with cash and automobiles and cigars as thick as your arm.

Upon his arrival at Ellis Island, my father promptly meets his future wife, my mother, Sally Johnstone. Sally, whose grandparents fled the south of Ireland during the Great Famine and settled in Boston, works as an assistant on the Ellis Island medical team; her job is to shine a light into the eyes of the thousands of recently arrived Europeans to check for trachoma, a disease that leads to blindness, is extremely infectious, and the number one reason for refusing migrants entry into the home of the brave. Simon Lipschits doesn't have trachoma, but he does have something else—call it charm, or the power of persuasion—that makes Sally fall for him head over heels. It's a good thing too, since Simon, who is penniless, is not exactly a great catch.

Within two years he works his way up from clerk to manager at Goldman Sachs. His early years, spent among the craftiest peddlers of the Rotterdam street market, have made him a perfect candidate for a career in the financial sector, as it turns out when he starts bringing in business after business for the firm, doling out loans to private investors who trade those loans in for stock market shares, because of course the economy can only keep going up and up, and nobody's dumb enough to stay on the sidelines while his neighbor gets rich in his sleep.

The newlyweds make their home on the eighteenth floor of a brand-new skyscraper on Fourteenth Street, where Sally gives birth to their first two sons, my brothers Max and Philip. They are relatively well off, members of New York's rich Jewish social set. They see Josephine Baker and her leopard on Broadway, and are among the few guests invited to the 1927 wedding of Charles Robinson and Celia Sachs. This is the American Dream Simon had fantasized about in the ship's galley that brought him here, far, far away from his father's bananas. He never dared dream that he'd be living that life so soon.

As the 1920s came to a close, in partnership with a few of his colleagues, smart, hard-working young men like himself, Simon sets up the Goldman Sachs Trading Corporation, an investment fund that appears to offer a revolutionary investment strategy with extraordinarily high returns and minimal risk. The real story is that a considerable portion of the "dividends" gets paid with money put in by fresh investors. The corporation is basically like a man dragging himself out of a bog by his own hair, but the trusting Americans are dazzled and blind, and so the entire nation rushes headlong toward the sun, onward and upward, like Icarus forgetting that his wings were attached with wax."

Johnstone topped up his glass for the third time. Minnie felt warm and a bit tipsy, oddly enough. Since when was watching someone else drink enough to make you woozy? Maybe it was something that happened to pregnant women, although she shuddered at the thought of being like other pregnant women. The next step was to buy a book that told you about all the wonderful changes happening inside your body from week to week. Be that as it may, she could predict, more or less, what happened next; it was in the history books.

"It happens all in one merciless blow, so that looking back, one can pinpoint the very date: Thursday, October 24, 1929. The Dow Jones Index starts to plummet, seemingly out of the blue. Wall Street holds its breath in alarm until the following Tuesday, when the shit hits the fan. The Index keeps falling, and more than sixteen million shares are traded in a single day. That hasn't happened in forty years. Panic sets in, setting off even more panic, like a ball that, once it's set rolling, keeps picking up speed. The decisive end of something that seemed never-ending is at hand. Banks collapse, savings dry up like land reclaimed from the sea, and my father can only watch as the Goldman Sachs Trading Corporation bubble bursts, and nothing is left but thin air. The bank's reputation is in ruins, there is talk of a huge Ponzi scheme, and dozens of people are given the sack, since black sheep must be found to make the others look snowy white. Simon falls into the first category."

"And you weren't born yet?"

"Not by a long shot. I'm an afterthought, an accident. I suspect I may not even be Simon's son, that my father was a doctor working in my mother's department. I've never tried to find out."

"Is that why your name isn't Lipschits?"

"I was born just after World War II, my father didn't want me to have a victim-name. Besides, my brothers and I aren't Jewish, since our mother was Catholic. When my father returned from registering my birth, it turned out he'd registered me under Johnstone, my mother's name."

At that point Bob came in again. Without a word, and in one efficient, elegant movement, he swept up the empty plates and empty bottle, before exiting as silently as he had entered.

"My brothers are already out of the house, drafted into the army, when I am born," Johnstone went on. His posture had been growing more hunched, and for lack of a chair back, he propped himself up by planting his elbows on the table.

"It's 1946, and my mother, born the first month of the year 1900, is forty-six. After the crash of '29, they moved from Manhattan to the Bronx, because my mother found work there as a nurse. My father has been bouncing from one job to another until, irony of fate, he is able to open his own vendor stall at the Fulton Fish Market on the East River. In some sense the circle is complete; he has followed in his father's footsteps after all, but of course that's what makes it so hard to take.

"When at the end of the nineteen-thirties National Socialism gains a firm foothold in Europe as a result of the reigning economic malaise, with the atmosphere growing more and more anti-Semitic, Simon's own mood grows even blacker than ever. His disillusion is complete when the Second World War breaks out and German troops march across the border into the Netherlands. The letters he receives from time to time from his family back in Rotterdam keep growing more alarming in tone. When he reads about the establishment of a Jewish Council, with which all Dutch Jews are ordered to register, he begs his parents, brothers and sisters to flee. He has no way of knowing that it's already much too late to get out, only the very wealthiest Jews are still able to escape. When after January of 1942 he stops getting any news from them, he persuades himself that they got away, that his family is safe in Spain or Portugal waiting for the end of the war, which surely won't last that much longer. Months after VE Day, he receives a letter from a cousin in Amsterdam shattering this last delusion: his parents and most of his uncles, aunts, brothers and sisters were deported via Westerbork to Auschwitz and Sobibor, where they all vanished into a mass grave."

"Christ," said Minnie. "Your father sure had a hard life."

"You might say that his personal traumas were synchronous with those of world history; I've always found that interesting. And a bit corny too, I must add. As if his life were a three-and-a-half-hour Hollywood blockbuster, with violins and drums and all."

"And a happy ending?" asked Minnie.

Johnstone shook his head. Bob walked in again, this time carrying two impressive ice cream sundae dishes. Johnstone immediately dug his spoon into the concoction, which from the looks of it consisted of great scoops of vanilla ice cream drowning in whipped cream, chocolate sauce and gobs of eggnog.

"A ludicrous dessert, I know," said Johnstone, his mouth full of whipped cream. "This is what I have on Saturdays: *kabritu stobá*, the goat stew, finished with a huge dollop of sugar and fat. It's what keeps me going for the rest of the week, in a sense." He grinned, and spent the next few minutes totally absorbed in gobbling down his monster dessert.

"But anyway," he said, wiping the cream from his beard with his napkin. "No happy ending. No matter how hard Sally tries to reason with him, Simon can't be dissuaded from being sure he has blood on his hands. Had he stayed in the Netherlands, he could have saved his family, that's the crazy conclusion he ends up with after filling half a notepad with schematic scenarios of a hypothetical life—hundreds of crisscrossing lines, arrows and branches interspersed with scribbled notations, swastikas and even mathematical calculations. He stops drinking and starts fanatically reading the Torah, something he'd stopped doing years ago, even way before his time at Goldman

Sachs. Waving his finger in the air, he holds forth about the Israelites' journey to the Promised Land, the six hundred and thirteen commandments of Halacha—six hundred and eleven revealed through Moses, and the remaining two straight from God—, and about the prophet Joshua, who crossed the Jordan and led the conquest of the land of Canaan. He talks about moving to Jerusalem, and about the coming End of Days, when the Jewish diaspora will be reunited, the Messiah will come, and the dead will rise from their graves.

"The year I come into the world, my father declares he won't celebrate another Christmas. The holiday he has embraced since arriving in New York that very first year because it stood for all that was American, is suddenly incompatible with his reawakened religious conviction. My mother, who through her work is not unfamiliar with the strange vagaries of the human mind, is seriously concerned about her husband's fanaticism. His notebooks keep piling up. When she asks to read them, he starts raving about the Chosen People and the end of the world, the Kabbalah, secret messages and number systems. He is in the process of writing his life's work, a book that will render all other books irrelevant. His eyes glitter like a sick man's, and his skin is dry as parchment. Sally tries a few times to suggest that he go see a doctor, but he refuses, and she gives in.

"After an incident at the market, when he slips and falls while carrying a crate of mackerel, seriously injuring his back, my father is forced to give up his stall. He throws himself into a heavy self-study program, sitting from early morning to late at night bent over books to teach himself Hebrew. Besides his visits to the synagogue, he barely leaves the house. When my brothers are home on furlough at Thanksgiving, he informs them of his plan to go to Jerusalem, his preparations for the journey, itineraries, transportation, contingencies. "We must learn to defend ourselves," he says at the end of a long and rambling monologue, then stares out the window for a long time, lost in thought. Max and Philip nod, but then glance worriedly at their mother, who is acting noncommittal, and at me, their little brother, who understands nothing. They realize what Sally has long known: their father is losing his grip on reality. The travel plans are as rational as clutching a straw in a muddy swamp.

"As a teenager, I'm ashamed my father, who is now known in the neighborhood as a nutcase. After school I hang out in the street with my friends as long as I can, smoking cigarettes and kicking a ball around for form's sake. During the freezing New York winters and equally hot summers, I ride the subway into Manhattan, where I spend hours, sometimes entire weekends, in the New York Public Library. I read my way though the medical textbooks, commit the anatomical drawings to memory, and recite lists of diseases and their symptoms to myself. My plan is composed of three clear mantras: get away as soon as I can, become the best physician in the world, and never go to Jerusalem."

Johnstone, out of breath, wiped his forehead with the napkin.

"My father's final demise comes from an unexpected direction. In 1975 he is found to have a rare form of thyroid cancer. The doctor treating him tells him that he probably owes the cancer to the x-rays he got at age seven to treat his tuberculosis. This sends my father into a rage. 'You mean to tell me I've been a walking corpse since I was seven?' he shouts, upon which the doctor replies that everyone is a walking corpse, really, from the moment they're born.

"The disease progresses rapidly, like a videotape on fast forward. My father is transported under protest to Mount Sinai, where I happen to work as a pediatric resident and am able to arrange for a private room for him. My mother watches over him day and night. When he wakes up in a panic, wailing that he'll never complete his life's work, she shushes him, and when the rabbi comes for the Vidui Confession, she discreetly closes the door behind her.

"Less than two weeks after being admitted to the hospital, my father dies in the presence of my mother and the rabbi, who closes his eyelids, says a last prayer and then quickly covers the corpse with a sheet. 'The soul has flown,' he tells my mother. 'We think that looking at the body is disrespectful to the departed. I can make the funeral arrangements for you, if you would like. I can give you a ten per cent discount on the whole business, coffin included.'"

AFTER THE MEAL Johnstone took Minnie into a small room that was completely soundproof, which he called his "studio." He went there every evening to listen to music for half an hour or so. His tastes ranged from classical to pop to everything in between. The only music he detested was experimental jazz—even the raw sound of nineties grunge was preferable to that. He followed closely which new bands were hot, and went to music festivals all over Europe several times a year. Currently he was listening to a lot of hip-hop and R&B. Kanye West, Drake, Kendrick Lamar, 2 Chainz. Bob had downloaded all his music in digital form, then brought the LPs and CDs to a storage facility on the city's outskirts.

"I'd like to perform an experiment," said Johnstone. He pointed to an easy chair in the middle of the room—the only piece of furniture. "I want you to sit down over there and close your eyes. That's all."

Minnie did as he said—and the next moment found herself being blown away by singing spilling from loudspeakers on all sides. A spare female voice uttering long drawn-out sounds in a language she didn't understand. The longer she listened, the less the voice sounded to her like a voice. If she stretched out her hand, she thought, she'd be able to touch the sounds.

She was back in the cathedral of Cologne with her mother; she was little—seven or eight years old. The vastness, the grey chill, made her shudder, the saints casting their eyes up to heaven, the candles, and above all the Christ nailed to the cross looming high above her with his loincloth, his bleeding wounds and his crown of thorns. It gave her creeps, and yet she couldn't look away, and when they stepped back into the daylight, she had this urge to go back inside, to feel it all over again.

Brushing her hand across her cheek, she felt something wet. She was crying, but not just crying: she was bawling, with long drawn-out gasps for breath, balled-up fists, snot streaming from her nose. It was grief and great joy, indiscriminate, absolute.

When the music stopped she opened her eyes, astonished. The feeling was instantly gone. Johnstone smiled.

"Excellent," he said, "excellent."

"What *was* that?" she stammered.

"This afternoon I told you that when you were a baby I had to make you cry because you refused to do so on your own. I didn't tell you *how,* exactly, I did that, and since you didn't ask, I thought it might be worth it to have you experience my method again in person."

"Your method?"

"Babies are sensitive to music, but I had never seen anything like what it seemed to do to you. Can you explain to me what you felt, just now? That's something one can't ask a baby, sadly, so I've been groping in the dark for all these years."

"It's hard to explain," said Minnie. "It isn't something you can put into words."

"Just try," said Johnstone calmly. He made a circle with his hands—a doctor's gesture, probably meant to reassure patients.

She closed her eyes and tried to retrieve the feeling.

"I don't know, when I think or feel, who it is that thinks or feels," she said. *"I'm merely the place where things are thought or felt."*

"Countless lives inhabit us," said Johnstone.

"Yes," she answered, startled by the aptness of that quote. "Maybe that's closest to what I mean." She kept her eyes shut; it was nice sitting there with closed eyes.

For a while neither spoke.

"Minnie," Johnstone finally said. He put his hand on her shoulder. "You really don't remember why you came back seven years later for more treatment, do you?"

1991

MINNIE'S MOTHER WAS about to leave her office for a lunch date with a potential donor who worked at CERN on a project he called the "WWW"—it was difficult to explain but had to do with global connectivity, data streaming and something he called hypertext—when she received a call from a non-work related number.

"There's a bomb threat."

It was Eli's father. He was just above her on the telephone tree set up to allow parents to be informed in an emergency. He had called her only once before, over a year ago, when the kids' previous teacher had had a nervous breakdown. Minnie had told her that everyone in her class thought Eli was disgusting because of the hole in his teeth that smelled of rotten eggs.

"A bomb threat," she repeated.

"They've evacuated the entire school. Everyone's safe, out at the far end of the playing field. They're trying to find the bomb."

"So we just have to wait?"

"The best thing you can do is to go over to the school, that way everyone collects their own kid once it's all over."

Minnie's mother thought about her appointment. It had taken her weeks to get the donor to agree to giving her half an hour of his time. She knew there was money there, and she also knew how to wangle it out of him. There had been an obituary in the papers a few weeks ago. Not long afterward he had called the foundation to announce he was considering making a donation. Same last name, the right age. A simple follow-up confirmed what she'd suspected: he was indeed the son, and his father, a well-known former politician, had succumbed to lung cancer.

She would keep to a businesslike approach, but as soon as an opening presented itself (there was always an opening), she would subtly and quietly bring up his bereavement. "There is nothing that can make up for your loss," she would say. "But with your contribution, we can invest in a future that will be free of this disease." It was of crucial importance not to be the one to say the dire word. Metal scraping on metal, that's what it sounded like, unpleasant and harsh. There was even a chance of a bequest. Nearly half the foundation's income came from legacies. Everyone who had cancer died of it in the end, especially the rich ones. It was an irony, Minnie's mother sometimes thought, that you could make money from a disease you were trying to eradicate. Perhaps some time in the future the foundation would be made redundant, closed down by its own success. She was good at her job, one of the best, there were months when she raked in ten thousand guilders. Her boss had given her an extra reward at the end of last year on top of her end-of-year bonus. It didn't mean that much to her. It was the money she brought in for the cancer that was real: it paid for researchers, laboratories, equipment, all of which was going to result in a future that was better than the present, or one with less illness, anyway. The bonus money was just numbers that would only keep dwindling, to be frittered away eventually on all the trivial little things that made up everyday life.

Things to heat up in a microwave.

No, there was no way she could cancel the date with this globally connected donor. There was a future to be won.

"Is it a hundred per cent safe?" she asked Eli's father, hoping for an answer that would justify her getting there late.

"Well," said Eli's father, who seemed to be giving it some serious thought, "is *anything* ever a hundred per cent safe?"

"OK," said Minnie's mother. The man was starting to annoy her. She felt like telling him his son was getting teased for having decayed teeth. "I can be there in just over an hour."

"Who leaves a bomb at an elementary school?" said Eli's father. "Even if it's supposed to be a joke, it's not funny."

The school was cordoned off with red-and-white police tape. Behind the tape were a throng of parents and a few policemen. The parents spoke to one another in stage whispers, saying "bomb disposal squad" as if it was the secret password of a club to which they now belonged.

Minnie's mother, making her way through the crowd, caught a glimpse of the school building and behind it the wide open playing field, which didn't strictly belong to the school but was loaned to it by the borough. At the far end, where a row of trees marked the edge of the field, she could make out the children, dots of red, blue, blond against the green.

She overheard a mother next to her whispering to another mother that Miss Mieke of Group Three had insisted that her goldfish be evacuated. One of the bomb squad had just come outside with the goldfish bowl in his hands. "An explosives expert specially trained to hunt for bombs," they scoffed, "made to go rescue a few crappy goldfish!"

Minnie's mother asked the mothers what was happening. The mothers, happy to be able to share what they knew with a newcomer, filled her in with loud whispers. The threat had come in two hours ago, and the police had reason to take it seriously. So the staff was immediately instructed to evacuate the school. Why the field? Simple: they keep them all together until the bomb squad declared the building safe again. They had to make sure nobody was missing. The two moms had rushed over as soon as they'd received the call, and so they'd been waiting here for nearly an hour and a half. Every now and then you'd see someone going in or out, but other than that, there wasn't much happening. A policeman had told them it was probably a false alarm. Nine out of ten bomb threats are made by teenage boys, he'd told them, you should see those punks hoping for an explosion. The mothers laughed nervously. Someone waved at a dot in the distance. The gesture made it only about halfway across the field.

As time went on, the excited whispering started petering out. Everything they knew had been said in every way possible. Now they stood there in a silent huddle. The wait, and the chance that they might have to witness a cataclysmic and shocking event, created a bond. No one was really hoping they'd actually discover a bomb, and yet if the climax never came, every one of them would feel a touch of disappointment, which they would camouflage by loudly vaunting their relief.

*

The small blue-and-white striped bus drove up just as nobody was expecting anything to happen anymore, and so it took a few seconds for the crowd to part in order to let it through. On the side of the bus were the letters EOD. Someone whispered, "Explosive Ordnance Disposal," a mantra that were taken up by the other parents, as if the mere utterance of the words would turn them into legitimate participants in the goings-on. If the military were getting involved, said a father in a David Bowie t-shirt, it meant they must have found something. The bus came to a halt in the middle of the schoolyard, and they could just make out a man in a bomb disposal suit climbing out with a number of indefinable objects in his arms and walking toward the building. Slowly, in slow motion, a man on the moon.

Take your protein pills, thought Minnie's mother. *And put your helmet on.*

She stared at the brightly colored spots in the distance. One of them must be her daughter. A little girl in a white linen dress, light as a feather, spine a bit twisted, bare ankles in grass warmed by the springtime sun. A painting by John Singer Sargent briefly flashed through her mind, and then there was a long stint of anxious waiting, for something about which she had only the foggiest notion. A bomb blast, naturally. Although there were many other ways something could explode.

WHEN THE BOMB SQUAD located the suspicious object, it immediately called in the military explosives team, which arrived on the scene in less than an hour. The suspicious object was in a corridor on the second floor, inside a scruffy backpack hanging in one of the bulging cubbies. It was a rather small rectangular parcel, all wrapped up in black duct tape. The backpack in question further contained: an apple, a drinking mug, a box of raisins, an inhaler and a ball of rubber bands. The explosives expert dismantled the little packet in twenty minutes. He took off his helmet, handed the backpack over to the police and declared the building safe, then strode back to the bus with his helmet clamped under his arm. He couldn't suppress the urge to raise his hand at the people behind the police tape. He knew how he looked in that suit.

MINNIE'S MOTHER WAS in the kitchen when the phone rang. She stopped cutting the onions and listened for Minnie's little footsteps scuttling to the telephone. When after three rings she still heard nothing, she wiped the tears from her eyes with the back of her hand and went into the living room.

Minnie's iron-on beads set was laid out on the table: a plastic tray divided into compartments for every color of bead, a workbook of examples, and a variety of pegboards. Minnie was kneeling on the chair, the earphones of her My First Sony over her ears, her back bowed over the table. She was busy copying what looked like an extremely complicated blue-and-white pattern onto a hexagonal form. She counted the rows with her finger, muttering the number and color combinations under her breath.

"Mrs. Panis. Anneke Bot here. Miss Anneke."

She heard the teacher hesitate on the other end of the line. In a while Minnie's mother would lay a piece of tissue paper over the beads, and then, ever so carefully, turn the whole thing over onto the ironing board. Next she would run the iron over it until it started smelling of melting plastic and the beads began to stick together. The smallest mistake could wreck the entire project. Even though the whole idea of ironing beads together was pretty ludicrous, she couldn't deny that the risk of it going wrong was what appealed to her, and she knew the same went for Minnie, who worked with endless patience to get the thing ready for melting, and then invariably lost all interest in the result.

"This afternoon," said Miss Anneke. "It's about this afternoon."

Miss Anneke was a tall, slim woman in her early thirties who wore her hair in a straight, bleached bowl-cut just halfway down her ears, which were always dangling with big silver earrings. The hairdo and the earrings suited her. She was a stylish woman, and no airhead either, unlike most of the other teachers at that school.

"As you know it was a false alarm, but they did find something."

"Oh," said Minnie's mother, "that isn't what I heard." She glanced at the table. The tip of Minnie's tongue was now sticking out between her lips. God, she thought, the kid is just like her father.

"That's right, that was the story we put out. It wasn't a bomb, so it wasn't deemed relevant." Again the hesitation. Minnie's mother wondered what Miss Anneke was trying to get at.

"Well, OK, so it was something that was found in Minnie's backpack. Something I'd like to discuss with you. I could perhaps stop by this evening."

It wasn't a question, and the urgency in Anneke's voice was such that Minnie's mother had no option but to say yes, of course. It wasn't until she'd hung up the phone that she realized she hadn't even asked what they had found in Minnie's backpack.

The backpack was still on the floor in the hall, unopened. There was a label attached to the loop at the top. Minnie Panis, it said in red marker, Grade 4. Minnie's mother always washed the mug and the lunchbox after dinner, with the rest of the dishes. Cautiously, as if she might yet find a bomb in there, she zipped the bag open. She immediately saw what was missing. Slowly she took out the mug, the inhaler, the empty box of raisins, the uneaten apple and the ball of rubber bands, carried them into the kitchen and lined them up on the counter. What was going on, for heaven's sake? Had her daughter put something in the lunchbox resembling a bomb? Had they searched all the kids' lunchboxes? It seemed most unlikely.

She stared at the objects for a while as if they were pieces of evidence. But of what? What could these stupid things tell her? A familiar feeling of nausea started spreading from her stomach to her chest and limbs. The feeling was accompanied with the thought that was always vaguely with her, but which she was usually able to censor: that there was something hidden inside her child. Something lurking just beneath the surface, like a big fish under the ice. Sometimes clearly visible, other times hazy, but never completely gone. What if the ice gets too thin, she thought, and the fish too strong? She picked up the rubber ball and bounced it on the counter. The cutlery rattled in the drying rack.

When she walked back into the living room, she found Minnie still in the same position, on her knees on the chair, bent over the design, her chin in her hands. There's a special kind of concentration that you see only in children. It is, thought Minnie's mother, the gift of totally immersing yourself in an activity without caring if it's a useful activity. She decided not to say anything about the missing lunchbox until she'd spoken with Miss Anneke. She decided she wouldn't allow herself to get distracted by irrational thoughts. She gazed at the pattern taking shape on the hexagon. A blue sea of rough, white-capped waves with a little boat balanced on top. And what was that, underneath the little boat?

"Funny, isn't it." said Minnie, looking up from her work for the first time, "that the boat doesn't know about the whale, and the whale doesn't know about the boat. That they're strangers to each other."

She was fucking unbelievable, really, this kid.

IF MINNIE WAS AT ALL surprised to see her teacher standing in the living room, she didn't show it. "Hiya, Miss," she said, and turned back to the TV.

Minnie's mother shut the sliding doors between the front and back rooms, and poured Miss Anneke and herself a cup of coffee. Miss Anneke. She realized she couldn't even just say the name to herself without the "Miss."

The first thing Miss Anneke did was to deposit the Winnie the Pooh lunchbox on the table. Piglet and Pooh, with above them a quote that had faded through intensive use. " 'WHAT DAY IS IT?' 'IT'S TODAY,' SQUEAKED PIGLET. 'MY FAVORITE DAY,' SAID POOH."

There were little bits of white thread stuck to the lid. Duct tape, thought Minnie's mother, that's what it looks like when you pull duct tape off something. She had a roll of the stuff down in the basement.

"It had black tape wrapped all around it," said Miss Anneke, "which is why, given the circumstances, it was taken for an improvised bomb. The Iraq situation is uppermost in the mind of the military, of course." She smiled, then immediately grew serious again. "Maybe you'd like to open it."

Minnie's mother picked up the lunchbox. It felt quite heavy and solid. Nothing moved inside. Pictures of rotting, mutilated animals flashed through her mind. Birds, mice. A pile of drawings with gruesome depictions of the Apocalypse. Photos of classmates with their eyes crossed out.

What was actually in the tin was as unambiguous as it was baffling: four black leather wallets, in two neat stacks, wedged in such a way that they filled the space exactly. They lay there cool and shiny, parts of a whole, everyday objects that were unspeakably strange. Depraved sandwiches, Minnie's mother thought to herself.

Cautiously—she couldn't help feeling she was upsetting a certain balance—she took the wallets out of the tin. They were all almost the exact same classical model, slightly dented from months, years of sitting in and being taken out of back pockets. Men's wallets. Three of the four were worn at the edges; the last one seemed relatively new. She opened one. Bank cards, a change compartment, bills. Two passport photos of teenaged boys.

"There was a sandwich in there this morning," she said. "I don't understand how. I don't get it. How this is even possible." Even if it's a joke, she thought, it isn't funny.

Through the sliding doors she heard the muffled sound of the television. Boink, boink, Bugs Bunny hammering Elmer Fudd into the ground.

"Someone else could have put them in her lunchbox," she said.

"Yes," said Miss Anneke. "That's possible."

"Why would anyone want to do that?"

"Have you ever caught Minnie stealing, little things? A piece of candy, loose change lying on the table?"

"How can something go from a sandwich to no sandwich, I

mean, within the space of one day it turns into a bomb and then into four wallets but what happened in between, something must have happened in between, something someone else must have done with it."

She was talking too fast, she knew it, but the words just came, *had* to come. She tried to understand it, her own thoughts, the situation. She scalded her mouth on the coffee and thought, yes, there might well be a fish under the surface, but no, her kid was no goddamn thief. She was seven! That made her feel calmer. It was a good, clear starting point. No.

"Minnie has never stolen anything," she said, composed again now. "Besides, I can't see how a child of seven could pick the pockets of four adult men. Do you?"

"No," said Miss Anneke, "not exactly." She fumbled with the blue silk scarf around her neck, delicate and expensive looking.

"So there must be another explanation," said Minnie's mother. "Two possibilities. One: someone put the wallets in Minnie's lunchbox on purpose, or, two: someone was looking for a place to hide the wallets, and happened to find Minnie's lunchbox."

Miss Anneke was staring into her coffee cup, the circlet of blond hair falling over her forehead. A perfect cut, thought Minnie's mother. She squared her shoulders. She wanted her words to land on Miss Anneke, to drive out other possible words.

"Plus: Minnie is scared of the basement. She thinks there's something down there that will swallow her up. That's where I keep the roll of duct tape, under the stairs, in my tool box, in the basement. The darkest spot. I doubt she even knows that tool box exists. But it doesn't matter anyway, since she'd never dare go down there in the first place. I think she believes it's the place she'll fall into and disappear one day. A black hole. As in outer space, black holes."

She didn't know if she was deliberately lying. So many thoughts were swimming through her head that it could easily have been unintended. Besides, lying was too big a word for it; at most, maybe she wasn't explicitly telling the truth because it wasn't relevant. *I doubt she even knows that toolbox exists.*

A few days ago she had to put up a shelf in the kitchen. She'd come up out of the basement carrying the toolbox. Minnie had watched from a safe place at the far end of the corridor as her mother emerged again, first her head, disgorged by the basement, returned to the world. While she'd been busy with the shelf, Minnie had crouched down beside the open box, cautiously running her fingers along the compartments of nails, nuts and bolts, screws and wall plugs. She had handed her mother a screwdriver, had held the vacuum hose under the boreholes in the wall to catch the dust. In the end Minnie's mother had carried the chest back downstairs, and that was it.

"It simply doesn't make sense," she concluded. "There's something wrong somewhere, something doesn't add up."

A silence followed, during which Minnie's mother waited for some kind of confirmation from Miss Anneke. An affirmation of her arguments. Something didn't add up.

Miss Anneke finally looked up from her cup. She was getting ready to say something, Minnie's mother could tell from the way she moved her hands from her lap to the table, her fingers resting on the edge.

"I have been worried about Minnie the past few weeks. I didn't know whether to come and talk to you. It didn't seem... concrete enough, I think."

Minnie's mother could feel her heart pumping the blood through her body, waves of blood, heavy and thick. Inundation. Was that a word?

"She's always been a rather dreamy child, but lately... Sometimes she doesn't really seem to be all there. Not that she isn't physically there, in the classroom, I mean, but in herself. She'll sit staring into space for a long time, staring at nothing in particular, as if—looking without seeing. I've tried different things. I'll say, 'Minnie!' Or I'll shake her by the shoulder. Then she'll look at me as if she's just landed on earth. Or, not landed, I don't know. In space. It happened again recently, on a Monday, in the circle. Her classmate Sibyl had had her birthday that weekend and was telling us about it, when I saw her go. I saw it happen. One moment she was still there, the next moment—nothing. Click, outer space. Her eyes were closed but her eyelids were flickering restlessly, like someone in REM sleep. Her breathing was labored. I saw her classmates looking at her; they saw it too. It upset them. Her classmate Sibyl had had a birthday, but the kids were nudging one another, looking at Minnie sitting there, and they'd stopped listening to the birthday story. I asked, 'Minnie, hello, are you with us?' I said it in an amused voice, so that the children wouldn't think there was anything wrong, but there *was* something wrong, and the children knew it too. After that they started avoiding her, not literally of course, but they kept a respectful distance, something about her... As if it might infect them. It sounds ridiculous, but that's how children tend to experience a thing like that. Classmates. They kept their distance.

"And then this morning. Everything began perfectly normally, we'd had our circle meeting, we were doing arithmetic. Then, less than half an hour before the bomb scare, Minnie asked to go to the bathroom. Ten minutes later I realized she hadn't come back yet. I walked to the girls' bathroom, she wasn't in there, then I checked the boys' bathroom, just to make sure. I was just walking back to the classroom, thinking that maybe she'd returned in the interim, when I heard a sound coming from the cubbies. A very faint squeaking, no, not squeaking exactly, more something lower. Humming."

Minnie's mother knew that sound: some high squeaky notes, and underneath, that creepy hum. She had witnessed it a few days earlier. She'd hoped that it was a one-off thing, an accidental short-circuit, something that could happen to any child. One in every so many thousand.

"Minnie was sitting on the floor in her own cubby; only her legs stuck out from beneath the coats. I bent down to see her. Her head was lowered, her body leaning forward a bit, legs stretched out in front. It made me think of one of those wind-up dolls, I thought, I have to figure out how to wind her up again, or, how would you say that, crank her up again. I crouched down beside her. Wanted to put an arm around her, but the sound... It's hard to explain. Not easy to put into words. But the sound alarmed me, and I just stayed there on my haunches, and I couldn't make myself touch her. She wasn't crying. I don't think she realized I was there, she sat there all alone, those little legs stretched out. I should call the school doctor, is what I was thinking. I must get back to the other children. And then, suddenly, the humming stopped. The squeaking, or, what to call it, the moaning, kept going a little longer, but without the hum underneath. She looked up, and I saw that she saw me. Now she was completely quiet. 'Do you know who I am?' I asked her. I suddenly thought, maybe she'd hit her head very hard on something. A concussion. 'Miss Anneke,' she said. I asked her if she knew who *she* was. She didn't say anything, and I thought... But then she told me who she was. She said, 'Minnie Panis, Group Four.' Then she asked me what she was doing there. I helped her to stand up, but she was unsteady on her feet, as if those legs of hers might buckle at any moment. 'Put your hands on your hips,' I said, 'those are nice and sturdy, they won't let you down.' That helped. I examined her head, but there was nothing to see. She began talking to me in a normal, bright voice. Something about a building she'd been in, a building with Corinthian columns, she said that word, Corinthian columns. I thought, I'll just bring her back to the classroom for now. I'll leave the door open and ask Mr. Johan to keep an eye on them. I'll call the school doctor. But when I got back to the classroom, when we got back, we all had to leave, to get out as quickly as possible. The whole school had to get out. We had to leave everything behind. I thought: Fire. It wasn't until much later that I heard about the bomb. It was chaos, hundreds of children needing to be led outside, all the little toddlers too, we had to make sure no one was left behind. It wasn't until we were all safely at the far end of the playing field that I remembered Minnie and the school doctor. If something happens to her, it's my responsibility, I thought. But she seemed so normal again. Was playing in the grass. The craft teacher had brought out a stack of paper tissue and rolls of wire, they'd started making lanterns."

Minnie's mother tried to follow Miss Anneke's story. It seemed to have an excessive amount of detail, yet also a total lack of it. She felt the old fear once more, the fear of the first weeks of Minnie's life. Fear that took the form of tubes, IVs and monitors. Of sick people attached to their catheters shuffling along hospital corridors. Red signs, green signs. Blue fluorescent light shining on the yellow child to counteract the bilirubin. The smell of sterile cloth, the sound of the word "prognosis." It can all still go terribly wrong, she'd fretted, night after night on the sofa, staring at the moving pictures on the television. It can still go wrong.

"You should have told me this before," she said, and even before she'd said it, she knew it wasn't fair, that it wasn't Miss Anneke's fault. But that only made her more insistent. She needed someone to blame it on. "At home she's normal. There's no way for me to know how she behaves at school."

She said it and again she knew it wasn't true. She had definitely noticed something strange about Minnie recently, and it was sinking in now. Little things she had noticed without attaching any importance to them, the way you might pass a new store dozens of times without noticing it's new, until someone else points it out to you. Minnie, who had come home from school several times these past few weeks exhausted. Minnie, who had gone upstairs of her own volition at night. Minnie, who in the middle of the night had suddenly appeared next to her bed, sleepwalking, mumbling the same words over and over. Minnie, who the week before, during a game of hide-and-seek with the kids in the neighborhood, had suddenly gone missing. The children had shouted her name, had looked behind every car. She'd had no idea anything was wrong until the woman across the street had brought her daughter home. Happened to have found her standing outside the supermarket's sliding doors. In a bit of a muddle, the neighbor had whispered, I think she's in a bit of a muddle.

"I'm sorry," said Miss Anneke. "I didn't handle it properly. Until today I thought it would resolve itself. Children. It's hard to tell sometimes."

She has the moral high ground, thought Minnie's mother, staring at the big silver earrings pulling Miss Anneke's earlobes down a fraction. She knows it, and she knows I know it.

"I'll take her to the doctor," she said.

Right after Minnie's birth they'd taken a scan of her brain. All you could see on the photo was a grey blob, the folds hadn't developed yet. The neurologist had pointed out traces of some small hemorrhages, here and there and there. It didn't necessarily mean anything, he'd said, it happens in lots of babies, but not every baby gets a brain scan. It didn't necessarily mean anything. The wallets didn't necessarily mean anything either.

"And I'll have a talk with her tomorrow. There must be an explanation."

Miss Anneke thought she was a bad mother. It was simple, and therefore true: Miss Anneke thought she was a bad mother; she was a bad mother.

"Minnie's health is what's important," said Miss Anneke, "from a psychological standpoint, too. Maybe something's troubling her. You think they're still so little, but there is a lot going on in the mind of a seven-year-old. Minnie is a smart little girl. One of the brightest in the class, in arithmetic. Remarkable ability to think outside the box."

"What do you suppose is troubling her, then?" Minnie's mother could hear the way her voice sounded, shrill, like someone trying to keep her balance on a narrow ledge. *From a psychological standpoint.*

"There's a lot going on inside those little heads," said Miss Anneke, "that's all."

Her earrings swung forward as she pushed her chair back and

stood up. Forward and sideways. If you looked closely, Minnie's mother thought, it was a funny sight, actually. Rings dangling from a person's ears.

SHE'D BEEN STARING at the wallets, lined up black and silent before her on the table, for quite some time. Miss Anneke had said that it might help when they talked, the physical presence of the objects. Tomorrow they would be returned to their rightful owners, whom the school had identified from their wallets' contents, and who'd already been informed. Three of them, anyway; the fourth was a foreigner, probably here on business or on vacation.

She wished Miss Anneke had taken the wallets back with her. They did not belong in her house. Her child was no thief. That was her bottom line, the starting point of her thinking: my child is no thief. But the more tightly she clung to that thought, the wider grew the opening for a different version.

In the front room Minnie was still watching TV. She was crazy about television, and hardly selective when it came to the programs: she watched the endless stream of cartoons on the Children's Network with the same intensity as the hellish bombing scenes in Francis Ford Coppola's *Apocalypse Now*, a movie she'd seen at least ten times by now, but which never seemed to bore her.

On Dr. Johnstone's advice, back in the day, Minnie's mother had parked her in the baby seat in front of the television for an hour every day. It would stimulate brain activity, Johnstone had said, it would make her more alert and present. She hadn't found it easy to follow his advice. The constant flickering of the screen struck her as an assault on the tender brain of the baby, who'd be lolling in her infant seat in a hypnotized state after just three minutes of it. After she happened to read a scientific article titled "Shocking Ways in Which TV Rewires Your Brain," she'd phoned Johnstone (she could call him any time, he'd said, day or night. He was connected to the car-phone network, so that in theory he was even able to receive calls on his bike). She read the article to him, which said brain scans showed that only the most primitive part of the brain, the brain stem, was still active when the subject was watching TV. The rest was switched off. The brain stem was also sometimes called the reptilian brain, the article said, because it had come down to us from prehistoric reptiles. This reptile brain was in fact the "asocial" part of the brain, purely intent on survival. "It says here," said Minnie's mother, who was growing more and more agitated as she read, "that reptiles eat their young when they are hungry."

Johnstone calmly waited for her to finish and then exclaimed, "Exactly!"

In most cases, he said, it is not a good idea to allow very young children to watch TV, but Minnie's case was the exception. Every sign pointed to the fact that her brain stem was still underdeveloped, even at the end of her time in the incubator. The inability to cry, the abstracted staring, the shallow breathing, the low body temperature... in other words: her survival mechanism. Television, he explained, could he quite simply help her to become a better survivor, precisely because it would stimulate this supposedly asocial part of the brain.

Shit, Minnie's mother had thought to herself, the man sure knows how to swat away every objection.

She'd consequently suppressed her intuitive dislike of the television, and had installed the baby in front of the set for an hour each day. But now, faced with those wallets, she wondered whether it was just another bad decision she'd made over the past seven years.

She knew she had to have a talk with Minnie, but picked up one of the wallets instead, furtively, as if doing something underhanded. Which was in fact what she was doing. It was the one she'd opened before. First she extracted the coins (four guilders and one quarter), then the bills (eighty), then the credit cards, a few train tickets, a business card, faded coupons, a shopping list (*tortellini!!*), passport photos of two teenage boys. She spread it all neatly on the table. L. FRANSSEN was the name on the bankcard. The business card disclosed some more information. DR. L. (LUC) FRANSSEN, MEDIA EXPERT & COMMUNICATIONS COUNSELLOR. She tried to form a picture in her mind of Dr. L. (Luc) Franssen. A man who subscribes to three different newspapers, she thought, a divorced man with two teenage sons he cooks tortellini for on the weekends, which they grudgingly spend with him.

She opened two more wallets. Mark Malevic, sports enthusiast (memberships to a cycling club and a gym in West Amsterdam; an Ajax season ticket; a bill from a sports store for *fl.* 136.50-worth of outdoor equipment) and owner of a boxer named Terry (rabies vaccination certificate). And J.S. Hardus, HARDUS INC. OFFICE SUPPLIES AMSTERDAM-HONG KONG; hardworking businessman with a penchant for horror flicks (movie stubs for *Night of the Living Dead* and *Arachnophobia)*.

There was something moving about it, these lives reduced

to a more or less haphazard collection of banalities. There was a kind of intimacy about it, thought Minnie's mother. As if she now knew something about these people that they didn't know about themselves.

Suddenly embarrassed, for herself and these people she didn't even know and didn't want to know either, she pushed her chair back. *She must go have that talk with her daughter.* She glanced at her watch. It was past nine o'clock. When she slid open the doors to the front room, she found Minnie lying curled up on the rug. From the calm up-and-down movement of her chest it was clear she'd fallen asleep. Minnie's mother stood in the doorway and studied the child. She was at least half a head shorter than most of the kids in her class. "Low percentile," the school physician had called it, a term that infuriated Minnie's mother, but which Minnie herself had promptly adopted as a proud nickname. "I'm low-percentile," she'd once heard Minnie confide in a conspiratorial whisper to an old lady on the bus. "Are you?"

As a result of her small and frail stature, her daughter had the ability to disappear and reappear without anyone noticing her move. This had started the moment she'd learned to crawl, and she used to wedge her tiny body inside cabinets, under beds, in the crack between two loose floorboards. It drove her mother nuts, but she didn't seem to be doing it on purpose. Maybe it was just a bodily function, Minnie's mother sometimes thought, as natural as breathing, or the circulation of the blood.

Because she was younger than her age, technically speaking, Minnie's mother had wanted to keep her back another year in nursery school, but the teacher had advised against it. "She's done with nursery activities," she'd said, whereupon Minnie's mother had asked her what that involved, nursery activities, and the teacher had answered that Minnie was a quick learner and "just wasn't into playing that much." She'd rather sit in a corner with a book than socialize with the other kids, that was all.

Rolled into a little ball, the child looked like a hibernating hedgehog. "We must learn to defend ourselves," a woman was saying on the television. She was seated at a desk, hands folded together. "There are definitely precautions you can take. Think of rope. Think of extra pockets. Of water purification tablets, vitamin pills, canned goods."

Minnie's mother switched off the TV and picked the child up from the floor, which required very little effort. The child felt light as a feather in her arms, or not exactly light, but rather as if she were less subject to the laws of gravity than the rest of the world. Although of course that might be the very definition of "light."

The little girl muttered something incoherent, somewhere in the twilight zone between wakefulness and sleep, but then opting decisively for the latter as her body hit the bed. The glow-in-the-dark stars attached to her ceiling with putty gave off a faint light.

Minnie's mother thought of the night, over two weeks ago now, when she'd found the child standing next to her bed. She'd seemed awake, her eyes wide open. "What's the matter, Minnie?" she'd asked, but the child was muttering softly to herself, her gaze fixed on something that only she could see. Minnie's mother knew that expression by now. The sleepwalking, on the other hand, was new. It had amazed her that the condition seemed more like extreme wakefulness than sleep, the dream more real than anything that could take place in reality. The sentences Minnie had uttered were clear, nothing like the half-mumbled word-snippets of just now. Always the same phrases, over and over again. On an impulse, Minnie's mother had jotted them down on the flyleaf of the book on her bedside table. Then she had carefully led the child back to bed. The next day she hadn't mentioned it, and Minnie didn't seem to remember a thing. She hadn't thought about the episode until tonight.

Softly she shut Minnie's bedroom door behind her. She went to her own room and picked up the book on her night table. It was a first edition of a novel—*Slaughterhouse-Five*. The title was drawn in an upside-down U on the cover. On the inside of the U was a subtitle: *Or the Children's Crusade*. Minnie's mother didn't know if it was meant to be deliberate, but the effect was of tombstone. She had received the book as a gift from a wealthy donor, a developer who had made millions in the early eighties from a chain of fitness centers in the U.S., and who was now using his money mainly to advance medical research and literature. He had sent the book to her office address. Inserted between the pages was a folded piece of paper with the typewritten instruction: *Read this*. She wasn't so naïve not to suspect that he was interested in her in a way that neither involved cancer nor books, but she had no idea how this gift—the title and the tombstone letters—were supposed to express that interest. Besides, she wasn't a big reader, and this book, which seemed to be about World War II and time travel, didn't appeal to her at all.

A week later he had phoned to ask if she would like to accompany him on a business-slash-pleasure trip to Leningrad. It had flashed through her mind that she *could* say yes to his offer, and long after she'd turned it down for obvious reasons, the possibility kept buzzing inside her head, like a refrigerator whose noise you hear only when you're in the kitchen making yourself a sandwich in silence.

Now she opened it to the flyleaf. Three lines, written in pencil in her own slanted script:

> I see the stack of flowerpots.
> The jumble of the tree bark.
> The dark shadows between the roof rafters.

Rafters? It seemed unlikely to her that the child knew that word. She doubted she'd ever said it herself—she couldn't imagine in what context she'd have said it. Could you dream about something you'd never heard of? She read the phrases over again a few times, but they only struck her as even less comprehensible than before. Uprooted words, cut off from... well, from what? She started rubbing her finger across the words, and then kept doing it more and more aggressively, until all that remained was a greyish blot. Not everything had to exist.

Downstairs she turned the TV back on. The woman who was on before had been replaced by a large church choir. She started zapping through the channels. Every one of them featured people saying or doing something. A man holding up a big fish. Two identical-looking old ladies, hunched-hunched-hunched in their threadbare armchairs. Overwrought black-and-white images with a corny voiceover: "*They come from another world, spawned from the light years of space, unleashed to take over the bodies and souls of the people of our planet!*" President Bush mouthing the tired words "*May God bless the United States of America.*" She thought about the flowerpots, the tree bark, the roof rafters. She thought about the word "context." And then she thought about the last wallet still lying unopened on the table.

THE WALLET'S LEATHER was softer than that of the other three. There was a logo stamp at the bottom right; twin triangles on their sides, as on a CD player, fast forward. Other than that it was just as nondescript as the other wallets.

How interchangeable was a life? Minnie's mother had often wondered at how frequently the course of her life was driven by coincidence. How easily things cancelled themselves out. Homes, jobs, friendships, men—they were all replaced by new homes, jobs, friendships, men. A dead child, a living child. She didn't know if it was just a feature of her own life, but suspected it was a far more widespread phenomenon. The only difference between her and most other people was that she was less sentimental, and could not stand the word "destiny."

And yet, when she opened the wallet and realized whose it was, she felt her heart, which she had always considered immune to the shadowy digressions of predestination and melodrama, jump into her throat. A sensation of cold water up to her neck, something dragging her body down from within. *A sinking feeling.*

She shut her eyes until the lurching feeling started to go away. Then she made herself read the name again, and again, until the letters detached themselves and turned into a picture: sign and significance all at once.

She didn't know when he had last been actively in her thoughts. Perhaps he was too closely woven into her very system to allow for any meaningful reflection. In the beginning, sure, she had thought about him constantly, endless circles of what if. What if she hadn't, what if he had? When, at what moment, had everything irrevocably changed? There must have been a turning point, that was a given, but the more she tried to pinpoint it, the more turning points popped into her memory, until they all melded together into one great slippery slope.

Once she'd realized that replaying the memories only made the whole thing more vague and confused, she decided to teach herself to give those thoughts a wide berth. Considering the kind of woman she was, it had worked pretty well, although there'd been moments when even this closed circuit of her inner life had showed a crack or two. Small openings that, annoyingly enough, would for an instant present themselves as possibilities. It had happened more than once that she'd thought she spotted him somewhere. *Click,* urged the mechanisms in her brain, *go up to him,* whereupon her body had refused, thank God.

This was of a different order. This wasn't some vague apparition that might or might not be a figment of her imagination, this was real, more real than she'd ever have imagined it. This was his name, in embossed letters poking up through the plastic of his credit card. *His* credit card. It made no sense. He hadn't lived in the Netherlands for years. It occurred to her that it could just be a coincidence, someone with the same name, but when she kept looking, she saw his driving license, with his passport photo. Her heart skipped a beat (God, she thought, so that cliché is true as well!). Older, but hardly, really, maybe shaved a little more neatly, dressed a bit more conservatively, a bit more successful. Among some currency bills—pounds, but also guilders—she found the card of a rather fashionable hotel in central Amsterdam. The number 106 was scribbled in ballpoint pen on the back.

Running her index finger across the embossed credit card letters, she felt ashamed, ashamed because she was imagining touching something that was truly *him*. The shame spread from the tip of her finger to the rest of her body, the wallet, the room, her sleeping child. She picked up the credit card from the table and pressed the letters, hard, into her cheek.

The shame she felt was at least ten times stronger than she had felt on opening the other wallets. At the same time, she no longer cared. Maybe you could reach an upper limit of shame, she thought, after which it didn't matter any more. The card scorched her cheek, and to her astonishment, the shame was replaced by something else. A sensation of ownership, and something else as well, explicit, urgent and unmistakable. Lust.

Quickly she squeezed her free hand between her legs, her fingers crammed as one against her crotch. The fingers pressed and released, pressed and released, and it was terribly, terribly unsatisfying. She tugged at the zipper of her pants, brought the hand with the credit card down and pushed the slick, cool surface against her pubic bone. She could still feel the imprint of the card hot on her cheek. Numbers, letters, a promise of money and goods. The contrast between the glowing heat and the coolness between her legs felt good. It had something to do with sex, sex and credit. She pressed harder, the card's edges sharp against her labia.

Squeezing her eyes shut, she tried to visualize things that long banished to the back of her mind. The way he had touched her, all over, licked her nipples, belly to belly. The things he'd whispered in her ear. His hand putting his signature to some note or other, the credit card on a silver platter. It was going great, it had been ages, in fact, since she had been so aroused, and then, just as she was having that thought, Miss Anneke's face pushed itself between all the pictures she had so carefully built up in her mind. *The Iraq situation is uppermost in the mind of the military, of course,* said Miss Anneke's mouth, *from a psychological standpoint.* Then the face exploded back to front, blood, bone, brains flying all over the place. What remained was a sticky blond hairball and two large silver earrings, completely intact.

Minnie's mother sighed, opened her eyes and pulled the hand with the credit card out of her panties. It was a bit moist and tasted—she couldn't resist running the tip of her tongue along it—salty, with the tang of bitter plastic underneath. The aftertaste stayed on the back of her tongue, with an intensity way out of proportion to the quick lick she'd taken. She had the childish urge to scrape her tongue with her fingers to get rid of the taste. At the same time she was longing to lick the credit card again.

Just as she was bringing the card up to her lips for the second time, thinking there was nothing that could make this day end more crazily, she heard her daughter's voice.

"Mama?"

Startled, she let the thing fall from her hand.

"Shit," she said.

Turning around, she saw the child standing in the doorway, sleepy but awake, no doubt about that. How long had she been standing there?

"What is it, sweetie?" she asked. She tried to keep her voice neutral, but by her own guess, wasn't too successful. She was grateful, *grateful*, that the chair she was sitting on had its back to the door.

"I keep thinking about the bomb."

Minnie's mother got up from her chair, only then realizing that the zipper of her pants was still open. She pulled it up as if was the most normal thing in the world. Her panties felt damp, it felt as if she'd wet her pants, all she wanted was to take everything off, take a shower, go to sleep.

"There's no need to think about that bomb," she said. "Because there wasn't any bomb. It was just a prank."

It occurred to her for the first time what a strange coincidence it was for some moronic prankster to have chosen that very day to call the school with his bomb threat. If that hadn't happened, they might never have found those wallets. What had Minnie intended to do with them, anyway?

She crouched down beside her daughter in the doorway and stroked the shiny, recently washed hair.

"But maybe they didn't look hard enough."

"They did look hard enough."

"But maybe not *every*where."

"They looked everywhere."

"What were you doing?"

"What?"

"Just now."

"Oh," said Minnie's mother. "You know."

Minnie walked past her toward the table, leaned down and picked up the credit card from the floor. She ran her fingers across the letters.

"Oh," she said.

"Yes," said Minnie's mother. She held her breath, but the child didn't seem to be grasping what it was. The way he used to stroke the underside of her breasts with one finger.

"What were you doing?"

"Minnie." She had no other choice. "Do you see what's on the table?"

Minnie, frowning, looked at the table, then at her mother, then back at the table, as if following an invisible ball bouncing back and forth between them. It wasn't hard to see the little cogs in her head turning as fast as they could.

"Two coffee cups," she answered finally. "My Winnie the Pooh lunchbox. Four wallets and a light blue scarf Miss Anneke probably left here by accident."

Minnie's mother hadn't noticed the scarf until now. When had Miss Anneke taken it off?

"You'll have to give it back to her tomorrow," she said, "I'll put it in a special little bag in your backpack. Will you remember to give it to her?"

"Very probably," said Minnie. "You have a dent in your cheek."

"Yes," said Minnie's mother. "I fell asleep with my head on the table."

"Why was Miss Anneke here?"

"I thought you 'very probably' might have figured that out."

Minnie stared down at her feet.

"Yeah," she said, "probably."

"Well?"

"I *found* them." Minnie was now concentrating on a spot over her mother's shoulder. "They were just left lying somewhere, where I *found* them. She shows me things."

"Who is 'she', Minnie?"

There was a brief silence.

"Hildegard?" Minnie finally said, so softly that it was barely audible.

Hildegard. Minnie's mother had never given that name another thought since stashing away the cassette tape up in the attic years ago. Minnie had been less than a year and a half old. What in heaven's name was going on here?

Minnie patted her own hair with the palms of both hands flat against her cheeks. She gave a deep sigh. Then she looked at her mother.

"I'm a bit confused, I think."

So am I, thought Minnie's mother, I'm very confused.

For the first time in ages, she found herself longing for a cigarette. Poison in her lungs, deep gulps. Back then, holding her breath next to the incubator every time the baby stopped breathing, she had told herself that after this, nothing would ever upset her again.

She cast about for a word to steady herself, and found it.

"To recapitulate," she said, "there are four wallets in our house that don't belong to us. At school they thought your lunchbox was a bomb because it was wrapped in black tape, we haven't even talked about that yet, and then there's some Hildegard who 'tells' you things."

"Yes," said Minnie. "To recapitulate."

The girl seemed calm now. Relieved. This wasn't at all how Minnie's mother had expected the conversation to go. The child ought to have started crying, bawling. She ought to be showing remorse. Shit, she should be protesting, denying the allegations. Instead she was keeping quiet in that way she had, somewhere between resignation and deep contemplation. Minnie started counting to herself, in French, to ten, twenty, thirty, an old trick that helped her not to start screaming, or worse.

She was at *vingt-sept* when Minnie finally began to speak.

SHE WAS TOO EARLY, of course she was too early. She glanced at her watch: more than a half hour to go. The prospect of sitting down, nervously waiting for his arrival while glancing at her watch every ten seconds, jumping every time someone came in, was unbearable. That wasn't the kind of woman she was, not even in abnormal circumstances, especially not in abnormal circumstances.

She lit a cigarette and started walking, leaving the hotel lobby, crossing the busy street, chockfull of merchandise, which was only shifted to other spaces, repositories of stuff that people called houses, or, worse still: home. She grew despondent at the thought of all that overabundance. A person really didn't need much more than a roof over her head, running water, a bed, and some clean clothes. She sometimes fantasized about it: to detach herself from everything she owned, to be left with only the barest necessities to roam around the world. Maybe that was coming close to freedom, although she didn't know if freedom was something to chase after. Freedom was for the birds and the fish. People took vacations, at most.

She walked into a shopping mall with grubby white tiles and warm air that had nothing to do with the temperature outside, but was a wholly self-sustained climate that smelled of plastic and off-the-rack clothing. This time, however, the artificiality of the consumer biosphere had a reassuring effect on her. Without having to buy anything, she could distract herself from thinking about anything she didn't want to think about. She stepped on the escalator, and as she slowly levitated upward with other shoppers above and below her, it occurred to her that they all probably came here in order not to have to think about something.

Recently she had happened on a TV show about a woman who had literally stuffed her house from floor to ceiling with her purchases. There were the narrowest of paths allowing her (and the camera crew) to move from room to room. In her bed a small space was reserved for herself, the rest was piled high with junk. Special offers had become a special obsession for her. She couldn't bear the thought she might be missing a deal, and so she was the proud owner of not one, but three washing machines, and fifteen CD players. Buying, she maintained, was her hobby, that was all. The woman was pale and puffy-looking, and there was no sign that her hobby was making her at all happy. The reporter must have been thinking the same thing, since he was trying his best to expose a trauma of some sort. But the only trauma, thought Minnie's mother, watching the frumpy hoarder, was that there *was* no real trauma, just life itself, and the ability to pause it briefly through the acquisition of more stuff was its own accomplishment.

On the second floor, across from the escalator, there was a store selling cosmetics. It was strange to walk around a cosmetics store in the middle of an ordinary weekday. Normally she'd be at the office, busy with telephone calls and meetings about the future of the fight against cancer. It had been difficult for her to call in sick that morning, not only because it was a lie, but because she was in the habit of going to work even when running a fever. The last time she'd taken a sick leave was more than eight years ago, after the miscarriage.

She had stayed home for three whole days, but only because her boss insisted on it. She found it unbearable, hanging around at home, staring glassily into space, giving grief enough room to run riot. When she was allowed to return to work, she dove back in with such zeal that she brought in a record amount of funds that very week, and her boss treated her to a fancy lunch of little balls of rice rolled in seaweed, and raw fish, on the top floor of a Japanese hotel. "Very exclusive," he'd said, tapping his chopsticks against a purple piece of fish that in some light glistened in all the colors of the rainbow, "the chef here apparently thinks nothing of blowing thousands of guilders on a bluefin." Minnie's mother had tried to think of peanut butter sandwiches and tried to inhale through her nose as little as possible. When her boss had finally mentioned "the loss" in a sympathetic voice, she had looked him straight in the eye and uttered the sentence she had practiced that morning in the bathroom mirror. After that, to her great relief, everything had gone back to normal.

Now she stared at a display of all sorts of jars of white cream, and just as she was asking herself what difference there could be between all those creams, a salesgirl came up to her whose color hair was probably meant to be eggplant, but was actually as purple as that Barney character her daughter liked to watch all day long.

"You're looking for something," said the salesgirl. The sentence didn't end in a question mark. "Can I be of help."

"Well..." said Minnie's mother.

"You would like to have a glowing complexion. May I ask you to take a seat on this stool. Then I can analyze your skin type and recommend something. If you would like."

It was just about the last thing she would like, but in the face of such brute force, she hadn't the wherewithal to resist. Obediently she followed the salesgirl to a stool in the middle of the floor. She glanced at her watch: fifteen minutes to go. What was she doing here, for God's sake?

The saleslady brazenly brought her face up close to hers.

"You have extremely dry skin," she said. "It's alarming how dry it is. It looks painful." It sounded like an accusation. "You need a great deal of help."

Minnie's mother looked at the saleslady's face. She tried to see what her skin was like, but it was hidden under gobs of skin products. Her eyelids were daubed with the same color purple as her hair. Her eyelashes were implausibly full and long; they looked like brushes. Minnie's mother wanted to run out of the store, she wished fervently that she could, which, she knew, was exactly why she couldn't walk away. She had gotten herself into this situation, and now she'd just have to see it to the end.

The saleslady walked away and then returned loaded with products, which she began smearing one by one on her victim's face.

"Shall I give you a bit of mascara as well. I use this kind myself, people sometimes ask me if I'm wearing false eyelashes. Some people simply can't believe that you can get this effect with something as simple as mascara."

The mascara was on her lashes before she could object. The saleslady held up a mirror.

"It looks great on you," she said. "I bet you never thought your face had this much potential."

Minnie's mother stared in the mirror. She looked like a doll in a horror movie. The lashes were downright terrifying, spider legs creeping out of her eye sockets and all across her face.

"So," said the saleslady. "What do you think."

"Yes," said Minnie's mother. She nodded her head, a spineless bobble-head, saluting of its own accord.

At the checkout she paid for all the stuff the saleslady had smeared on her face. She glanced at her watch. She was going to be late.

ONCE MINNIE HAD STARTED talking that evening, there had been no stopping her. The words came tumbling out helter-skelter, as if trying to find a way to be heard all at the same time. That was exactly a week ago. It had taken some effort, but in the end Minnie's mother had managed to reconstruct a more or less consistent story out of it (to be fleshed out later in remarkably precise detail, in therapy reports and tape recordings), which could be summed up, more or less, as follows:

One afternoon in early spring, her daughter had been up in the attic rummaging through boxes filled with old stuff basically waiting to be tossed. Remnants of her own childhood in the sixties, school notebooks filled with essays and math problems, the sort of personal stuff an adult saves because throwing it out would feel like infanticide. At the bottom of one of those boxes, Minnie had come across the cassette tape of Hildegard von Bingen's songs.

Minnie's mother must have stowed it away when Minnie was a year and a half or so, together with the book of Tao that Johnstone had given her but she had never read. Why hadn't she just thrown those things in the trash? Whatever the reason, Minnie had fished the cassette out of the box and read the strange name on the case. Since the little girl was drawn to strange objects, and since she had recently become the proud owner of a rainbow-hued My First Sony, she inserted the tape in her Walkman and pressed PLAY. That's how it had started.

In remarkably precise words, her daughter had revealed the effect of the music had had on her state of mind. "At first I was scared," she told her mother, suddenly calmer after that first flood of words. "And then I felt as if I missed someone terribly, only without *any*one."

The music had made her head tingle, and it had made her cry a lot too. The next few days she kept going back to the attic, to repeat the same ritual. Sometimes, she confessed in a whisper, hanging her head, she'd gone to bed early on purpose, so that she could secretly slip out again.

The sounds began to grow familiar; she felt them throughout her entire body. When she opened her mouth, it looked as if she were the one singing. At the end of the A-side (the B-side was blank), the music stopped abruptly, giving the dramatic sense that Hildegard von Bingen had suddenly keeled over and died. Every time Minnie heard that loud click, it was as if she'd been startled awake, even though she didn't remember ever falling asleep.

Instead of fading, the mystery kept growing day by day. After a while the girl began seeing things, on the inside of her eyelids. Clear, concrete pictures that were different from her usual dreams. The reflection of gold letters in the water (that was literally the way she'd said it: the *reflection* of gold letters in the water), two little soldiers, hands spotted with dots of red blood, white sheets. An "extra layer"—where did the child *get* these ideas?—where she understood things better, and didn't understand them at all.

It happened on a Monday morning, during the morning circle. Minnie's classmate Sibyl had had a birthday that weekend and started describing her party. Almost none of the kids in the class had been invited to it because Sibyl was only allowed to invite seven guests, four of whom were her cousins. Like most of the children in Minnie's class, Sibyl wasn't a great storyteller, and soon became tangled up in an interminable description of the rules of a game involving four flags, two teams and some kind of risk. Minnie's thoughts had strayed to the box in the attic, the voice she could now even play in her head without needing to literally hear the music.

Spiritus sanctus
Moh-oh-ven-sneeah
Almia aahahaaha-est see-anohee
Sooz spiriiii-I omnia

She had shut her eyes, for just a second, and then it happened: the layer slid across the normal layer, and without the tape, without the attic with the books and the dust and the smell of old things, she was suddenly *there*. She saw things that existed somewhere far away, but also things she recognized: the sliding doors of the supermarket down the street, the bicycle rack in front of the bakery, the roundabout at the end of the street, a coat draped over the back of a chair.

When she opened her eyes again, Sibyl had stopped speaking. The children in the circle were now staring at Minnie, but why, she wondered; she'd closed her eyes for only a second. The teacher asked if she was having trouble breathing, but she wasn't having trouble breathing, she was breathing fine, everything was bright and light.

After that one time in the classroom, it kept happening. The pictures in her head kept getting clearer, and although she didn't understand the language the voice was speaking, it always seemed to be pushing her in some direction. Sometimes when she opened her eyes she'd suddenly find herself in an unfamiliar street, when she'd been in her own street just a few minutes earlier, playing hide-and-seek with the other kids in the neighborhood. She'd find little things in her backpack that weren't hers: pencils, erasers, a classmate's autograph book. She was so ashamed that she didn't have the nerve to return them; she just threw them all into the neighbors' trash can instead.

She didn't know exactly when the wallet thing had started. She'd found the first one in the drawer of her nightstand one morning. The next one she discovered in the pocket of her jacket after the class trip to the planetarium. It went on like that until she had four in her possession. She knew it was serious. The wallets felt heavy and real, like all the things that belonged exclusively to the adults' world. If she shook them, she could hear the coins rattling.

She kept them in the attic, in the box with the cassette tape. Every night in bed she'd think about the wallets, they pressed down on her from the attic, crushing her, she couldn't get to sleep.

The solution presented itself one afternoon when she saw her mom come from the basement with the toolbox, and spotted a thick roll of shiny black tape under the compartments of nails and screws. While her mother was occupied with the drill, Minnie took the tape out of the box and hid it under her waistband.

Very early the next morning she finally dared to retrieve the wallets from the attic. At school, during math, she'd gone to the bathroom. Once there, she threw her sandwiches into the trash can, and replaced them with the wallets. Next she wound tape around and around the lunchbox. She intended to go out to the field at lunchtime, to the far end, where the trees began. She was going to bury the package out there.

But the next thing she knew, she was suddenly sitting in her cubby, with Miss Anneke crouching beside her, and soon after that, the alarm bells went off and everyone had to leave the building.

Minnie gazed at her mother, defeated. She looked like a deflated balloon, pale and vulnerable and small, so very small. Her mother didn't exactly know if she should believe the story, or, rather: *how* to believe it. The things her daughter was telling her by fits and starts seemed logical somehow, but it was a logic that horrified her. What did this child *see* when she looked at the world?

"It's going to be OK, darling," she said, saying it over and over again, so that she began to believe it herself. "Everything will be OK."

For the second time that night she picked up Minnie and tucked her into her bed. Long after her daughter had fallen back to sleep and one by one the glow-in-the-dark stars had stopped glowing, Minnie's mother was still sitting on the edge of the bed. This was her child. She had been an enigma from the day she was born, but still this was her child.

The next day she called Johnstone, who had this way of sounding vague in some very specific way. He told her he had set up a new center for specialized therapy and hypnosis. The traditional medical setting had proved too restricting for him, and the center for crying babies could get along without him by now. These past few years he had been exploring alternative therapies for psychological problems and traumas in children.

As he went along he had become drawn to hypnotherapy. He'd enrolled in a year-long intensive training course in hypnosis in northern India, a skill for which he seemed to have considerable talent. Next he had traveled to Guatemala, where he'd spent several months in a house with no walls on the outskirts of the ancient Maya capitals of Tikal and Palenque. He had grown interested in the civilization of the Maya after reading an article in an old copy of *Archaeology*. His trip to Central America had been an impulse, a lucky shot: there, among the monkeys and the ruins, the wisdom of that nearly four-thousand-year-old civilization had settled on him as a radiant beam of light. It was almost unfathomable, how detailed the ancient Maya's knowledge of mathematics and astronomy was, not to mention their sophisticated script and the architectural wonders they erect for the worship of their gods.

He returned to the Netherlands with the building blocks of a treatment method based on hypnosis and the Maya calendar, as well as on his years of experience, let's not forget, in pediatrics and the Tao. A unique combination, it must be said; he had already seen spectacular results in the space of just one year. He gave the children being treated a totally new sense of time, one that wasn't linear—here he fulminated for a while against the politics of Thatcher and Reagan—but circular in nature. You wouldn't be able to see the true impact of the treatment right away—it would take a decade or two—but all the signs were extremely encouraging.

"But I expect you're not calling just for a chat. How is our little Minnie? How old is she now, about seven?"

"That's what I was calling about," said Minnie's mother. "I need your help."

She gave him a quick rundown of what had happened, but skipped telling him whom the fourth wallet belonged to. Not everything that might seem relevant was necessarily so.

"Remarkable," muttered Johnstone when she'd finished. She heard the sound of his pen furiously jotting something down. "Right on the eve of the year of the new K'atun. Most interesting."

"Catoon?"

"The longest cycle in a human life spans roughly twenty years," Johnstone explained. "Even in the Long Count of the Maya calendar, this cycle, so-called K'atun, was considered an important unit of time. Now, by coincidence, the coming year, according to the Maya calendar, is the year of a very unusual K'atun: the last of the thirteenth and last B'akt'un, which, composed of twenty K'atun, is the longest time unit in the Long Count. That's as far as the Maya calendar goes. Some people are therefore of the opinion that in a little over twenty years from now, in 2012, the world will end. Nonsense, obviously."

Minnie's mother was growing more confused by the second, and somehow she suspected that was his intention.

"What do you propose?" she asked, unable to suppress a deep sigh.

"She'll come to me for treatment," Johnstone promptly said. "I knew from the start that she's a special case, that child of yours, quite unique in fact, in my judgment. I won't cure her in the normal sense of the word, but then, your daughter isn't sick, either. Unusual behaviors are immediately pathologized these days, but that's quite unnecessary, if not a great pity. Every brain is unique, some brainfolds a few more crinkles than others, that's the way to look at it. The trick is just not to let the crinkles go off the rails, don't you see? Your daughter isn't necessarily going to turn into a professional pickpocket, or worse—naturally."

Minnie's mother pictured him making that characteristic gesture of his, and in spite of herself, just the thought of it seemed to reassure her. She made a date for an intake interview that same week. Right, she thought as she hung up the phone, here we go again. Then she took a deep breath and dialed the number of the hotel on the card she'd found in the fourth wallet. "Room number 106," she said. "Please put me through to room number 106."

When the receptionist asked whom she was looking for, she said his name out loud for the first time in eight years. The phone rang through. In the hotel room his arm stretched to pick up the receiver.

SHE STROLLED TO the hotel as calmly as she could. She wasn't about to make herself ridiculous by bursting in out of breath. To her chagrin she was already sweating. It was twenty-five degrees Celsius out, for Pete's sake; why had she felt the need to put on black pants and a matching black jacket? He'd probably take her for one of the hotel staff.

The door was opened for her by a person whose job it was. The reception desk and toilets were to her left, on the right was the way in to the lobby. The receptionist gave her an amiable nod. "Hospitality," they called that, a word that, strangely enough, sounded very like "hostility." She had read somewhere that the earliest human languages hadn't drawn a distinction between things and their opposites: negation and confirmation denoted by the same word. Only later, with the arrival of religion, had man begun to view the world as a place of conflicting values. It must have had something to do with the expulsion of Adam and Eve from paradise; everything seemed to go back to that.

She realized just in time that she still had all that junk on her face. In the ladies' room she repaired the worst of damage with water and toilet paper—thank God the Super Feminine XX Lashes

Waterproof Mascara turned out to be not in the least bit waterproof, despite what the package promised. She stared in the mirror. The scrubbing had left red blotches around her eyes, but otherwise she looked fairly normal. It would have to do. Tossing the mascara into the trash, she squared her shoulders and walked out of the bathroom as her own self. The door fell shut behind her with a discreet sigh. In this sort of hotel, everything had to be hushed. That's what the guest paid for.

It was quiet in the lounge. Everyone was outdoors in this weather; when the sun was out, people felt obliged to go outside too, whether they felt like it or not. The contrast with the bright light of the lobby was so glaring that for the first couple of seconds it was hard to see anything but the vague contours of armchairs and tables. She recognized him immediately nonetheless, and he her, because he got up from his chair at once.

They stood facing each other for a while smiling rather sheepishly without showing their teeth—a sign that they weren't going to fly at each other's throats. He looked more or less like his passport photo, but only the way everyone looks more or less like their own passport photo: the features were recognizable, yet in three-dimensional space looked very different from that flattened two-inch square. His hair was still brown and straight, his eyes dark, his figure slender. He looked neater, on the whole, than he used to, although he would never pass for a respectable citizen, if that was his ambition, which she very much doubted. There was something wild about him, and the child had it too. Such things could be channeled at best.

"You haven't changed," he said, which was of course ludicrous.

They hadn't seen each other or spoken in eight years. Still, she had to admit, observing him, that it was striking how much living a person can do without it having any appreciable effect on his appearance. It made you think people basically remained the same at their core, even though you could also argue that appearance is a terribly misleading factor.

She had this urge to throw herself into his arms, to undo all detours and the roads not taken, to believe it was still possible. Hastily she stretched out her hand, an idiotic gesture she immediately regretted, but the hand was already hovering in the air, she couldn't just let it drop. From the slight nervous twitch in his left eyelid she realized at once that he was startled by the gesture—if you know someone, you know him forever, apparently—but he recovered within a fraction of a second. He stuck out his hand, as if it was the most normal thing in the world. A tattoo she hadn't seen before emerged from the cuff of his linen shirt. A two-headed dragon in red and green, spewing fire all across his wrist. His hand was firm, and he shook hers the way you do when closing a deal.

*

He ordered a beer, she a cup of tea (and kicked herself, she didn't want any tea, she was already too hot), they exchanged a few banalities about the weather and the Europa Cup and the Lauda Air Boeing 767 that had exploded the day before above a jungle in Thailand. She had told him about the wallet over the phone, but only in the vaguest terms, which she'd written down on a piece of paper to prevent herself from saying other things. When she'd offered to bring it to him, there had been a short pause on the other end of the line.

"Jesus," he'd finally blurted out, "I don't understand what's happening at all, but yes, of course, yes."

Now she slapped the wallet down in front of him, just as Miss Anneke had done a few days ago.

"It's a strange story," she began. "Or a weird coincidence, anyway."

He picked up the wallet, seemed to weigh it in his hand, but did not open it.

"A little girl in the neighborhood brought it over. She'd found it a few blocks up the street. I happened to be walking out the door."

He looked at her expectantly.

"That's it, really," she said. She felt herself start to blush. Of course he could see right through her, she was a terrible liar, surely he remembered that.

She had met him in the fall of 1981, on a long weekend trip to London, dragged along by a girlfriend who had recently become involved with the punk movement and was set on going to London to experience it "inside out." Minnie's mother had no idea why the friend had decided to invite her of all people, she didn't belong to any movement, least of all punk, but on an impulse she'd said yes. The week before she had kicked out her then-boyfriend—a worthless sort who had been studying law for ten years and still considered himself "a great catch"—, and after all the grief and misery, any kind of distraction was welcome.

They had spent long nights roaming the streets of London, mostly in the pouring rain. Her friend was indefatigable, and had drawn up a whole laundry list of punk clubs, cellars and all sorts of grubby dives they "absolutely could not miss." They went to see obscure bands answering to names like Fuck The C.I.A., Porno

Squad, and The Sucks (and they sounded it too). When this assault on the senses was over, they'd wind up going home with people squatting in big drafty lofts in dicey parts of town—lefty-anarchist types, although surprisingly many of them were actually completely apolitical.

She'd met him in one of those squats. It was the last night of their exhausting four-day trip, she was looking forward to the ferry home, to sleeping, to silence. It turned out later that he had interpreted her aloofness and eccentric (because it was so ordinary) dress as a statement. In any case they'd started talking. He told her he was from Manchester originally, and that he was a musician but wasn't into the whole punk scene. Punk was largely over, anyway. His music was more along the lines of what Siouxsie and the Banshees were doing now, much more eclectic, melodious, less hard-line. He was currently working on his first studio album, all very low budget, but if she was interested he'd let her listen to some of it. When, in the early hours of the morning, the two of them wound up on a sagging, dubiously stained mattress, she was in love.

For several months she went to London every few weeks to be with him. It coincided with when she started working at the cancer foundation, as the receptionist. The weekends in London were a parallel universe, which was what made them so addictive. He introduced her to his circle of friends—musicians, writers and artists who talked about their work as if it was their whole life, a higher calling. It amazed her that these people seemed to read something mysterious and exotic in her own quiet, and relatively unremarkable, self. She waited with trepidation for the moment she'd be exposed, when he would realize how ordinary she was, how little she knew, how little they had in common.

One afternoon they visited an old artist who had a studio in the city and was more or less on his last legs, but was actually a great, famous painter. The crowded space was a god-awful mess. Thousands of paint jars were scattered higgledy-piggledy around the room, with a large round mirror, paintbrushes, pages torn out of books, magazines, LPs, items of clothing, a plaster bust of some dead poet—there wasn't one square inch that wasn't spattered with paint or buried under a layer of junk. The artist, who from the looks of him had begun his morning with at least one bottle of wine, seemed to have no problem with it. She gazed at the strange, obscure canvases propped up on easels or leaning against the walls. Most were unfinished, some were partly ripped up, they made her think of dead bodies, and gave her the creeps. She was relieved when they were standing outside again, and on the way home she confessed in a rare moment of truthfulness that she just didn't *get* that this was art; she didn't understand art in general, and she didn't get his artist friends in particular. He blew up at her, accused her of being a superficial bitch, and even though he later apologized, she knew even then that it was the beginning of the end.

Back in the Netherlands she'd felt tired and irritable, had vague, nebulous complaints, until her doctor looked up from the test results and congratulated her on being pregnant.

*

He took a sip of his second beer, she of her first glass of wine. The alcohol had made them a bit more relaxed. He'd laughed, amazed, at the unbelievable coincidence of the wallet, and said he was happy to be given this reason to see her again.

He told her that he'd been making music under the pseudonym "Fast Forward" for some time. His music was still quite underground, not mainstream, but he had built up an international following of loyal fans, and was able to make a living at it. He came to the Netherlands on a regular basis to perform; he was just halfway through a low-key tour of the country to promote his new album. He had gotten married five years ago to a children's book author. They had a two-year-old daughter.

"I hope you don't mind," he said, "but we named her Minnie."

At the time, in 1982, she hadn't wanted to tell him about the pregnancy. She didn't even know if she wanted a child herself, having never imagined herself a mother. But a few days later, as if he'd had some kind of premonition, he showed up at her door. To conceal the truth with a sea separating them was one thing; lying to his face was something else, and she hadn't been able to keep it from him. To her surprise he'd welcomed the news, and over the next few weeks, infected by his enthusiasm, she slowly started getting used to the idea that they'd be a family, that she'd been wrong in thinking it wasn't going to last. A few months later he moved in with her. Music, he said, was something he could do anywhere. The child was going to be a girl, and he wanted to call her Minnie, after an artistic great-aunt of his, and she agreed because she couldn't think of any valid argument against it, and couldn't think of anything better anyway. In the eighth month the baby suddenly stopped moving. In the hospital they found that the umbilical cord had wrapped itself around one of the little feet, cutting off the food supply. The labor was induced, and a few hours later she'd given birth to a perfect but lifeless child.

“And you?” he asked carefully. “Do you have a husband, kids?”

For an instant she hesitated. She could tell him here, now. But how, where to begin?

After the stillbirth, their relationship had rapidly gone downhill. Neither of them understood the other’s grief, which should have been the same, but wasn’t. Three months later he had packed his bags and taken the ferry back to England. It wasn’t until a few weeks later that she discovered she was pregnant again. “You’ve been given another chance, Mrs. Pauls,” her doctor said. “Take it.” She tottered home on foot, pushing her bike. When she came to a phone booth, she stopped. She had to tell him, she had to tell him *now*, it couldn’t wait until she was home. Tossing every coin she had on her into the phone, she dialed his number and waited. The phone rang three times, five times, ten times; she realized he wasn’t home. Replacing the receiver, she knew the moment had flown, and wouldn’t come back.

How could you tell someone something like that anyway? How could she tell him she hadn’t wanted this child? That if she’d held the tiny embryo in her hand, she’d surely have squished it to death? And how could she explain that she had ended up keeping it anyway, not because she’d wanted it, but because she didn’t believe in either fairness or unfairness. Or that he had yet another daughter somewhere named Minnie (what a laugh), who was seven years old now, physically his mirror image, and wild inside like him? That that daughter had found *his* wallet and that it must mean something, even though she refused to believe in stuff like that—how was she supposed to find words for that?

She shook her head. “No,” she said, “no husband, no children, just me.”

A fat long-haired cat jumped up beside them on the windowsill. She suddenly noticed that there was soft music playing from a speaker somewhere. Not a classical piano concerto, as you might expect of a hotel lobby where a cup of tea cost five guilders, but pop music.

Dance, dance, dance, dance, dance to the radio.

He pushed the cat away and blew his nose into a cotton handkerchief he pulled out of his pants pocket.

"Allergic," he said. They were both silent for a while.

"I would have been happy for you to have it," he finally said. "You would have been a good mother."

"I doubt it," she said, taking a big gulp of the Chardonnay, which tasted sour and not at all "fresh and fruity" as the waiter had promised.

You'd have been a good mother. The memory she'd been so carefully suppressing the past few weeks pushed its way up to the surface.

It had been a bright, hot Saturday. For days Minnie had been whining about the outdoor pool all the kids in her class went to with their parents. That girl was just crazy about the water. She'd passed a whole slew of swimming tests in a very short space of time; the diplomas decorated the wall above her bed in green, blue and red. She had no trouble swimming a considerable length under water. For her last diploma, she'd even had to swim fully clothed under a mock sheet of ice, which she had bravely accomplished, coming up for air sputtering proudly.

It was a mob scene at the swimming pool. There wasn't a square inch of space left that wasn't already staked out with towels, umbrellas, coolers, boom boxes. Children ran around screaming, splashing, slip-sliding and bumping into one another. Clouds of oily smoke billowed out of the French-fries stand, swirls of pink strawberry ice cream could be seen floating in the chlorinated pool water, kids were peeing in the bushes, against the fence and, without a doubt, in the pool itself, since the toilets were clogged with big wet wads of toilet paper. Minnie's mother despised this kind of mayhem, but the child—and in this she was no different from the other kids—was in no way put off by it.

They'd found an empty spot at the very edge of the lawn to leave their belongings. Minnie, exploding with impatience, was already in her bathing suit, practicing her diving moves, as her mother quickly took a snapshot. Her daughter always froze and looked wooden when she had to pose for a picture. That was why Minnie's mother had begun trying to capture her as unobtrusively and "spontaneously" as possible.

"Go ahead," she told her daughter, who hadn't needed to be told twice, and darted off like a tadpole, nimbly zigzagging past the people and towels. Her red and green Speedo suit made her easy to spot, even diving from the springboard into the water. She sat watching her child playing in the water for a while; though small and frail, there was something fearless about her. Then the mother let herself fall back on her towel, closing her eyes to shut out her surroundings and feel nothing but the caress of the warm sun on her skin.

She must have dozed off, because she was suddenly startled awake when the exuberant background sounds gave way to yells of alarm. She sat up and saw two lifeguards standing at the edge of the pool, surrounded by dozens of children and adults. Feverishly she tried to find her daughter's green and red bathing suit, but it was nowhere to be seen.

They got to her just in the nick of time, the lifeguards told her afterward in the staff room, as she sat there with the child tightly wrapped in two towels. She felt the little body shivering right through the towels. She tried not to pay attention to the squeaking sound the girl was making, with a monotone hum underneath.

"People expect drowning children to make a lot of noise," said one of the lifeguards, the oldest of the two. "They think there'd be thrashing and screaming, but it's actually the opposite. They go all quiet and still, so a kid can drown even in an overcrowded pool. All it takes is a couple of minutes. Luckily my colleague suddenly saw something floating down there."

"It was the bright colors of her bathing suit that saved her, Ma'am," said the other one.

"I don't get it," was the only thing Minnie's mother was able to say. "She has four swimming diplomas."

The lifeguards shrugged their shoulders simultaneously.

"Even very good swimmers can drown. There are all kinds of reasons for it. Maybe she'd been in the water too long, got exhausted or became hypothermic. Maybe she got a cramp. Maybe she was accidentally dunked by some of the bigger kids; who can say."

Whereupon all three stared at the child for a while, but just like seven years earlier on Dr. Johnstone's examination table, she showed not the slightest reaction, and again Minnie's mother had to fight the urge to shake her, to scream at her, anything to make her return to being present and alert.

"You should really try to keep an eye on your kid in this situation," said the oldest of the two. "A dead child isn't fun for anyone, is it now."

What he really meant to say came dribbling out of his words on all sides, sticky as ice cream melting in the sun: what kind of mother lets her child drown?

*

She finished her wine quickly. There was nothing more to say; they both knew it had been a mistake to meet again.

"It was really great to see you," he said for the third time, and held out his hand.

"Yes," she said to the dragon tattoo on his forearm.

"Maybe we'll see each other again some time."

Then she walked out of the hotel, back into the sunlight. It was a time to weep, but nothing came—tears, alas, being a product that had been taken off the market.

2012

AFTER BEING FISHED out of the water by Johnstone, Minnie stayed in his guestroom for two more nights. Bob stocked the bathroom with clean towels twice a day for some reason, and she tried out a number of Rituals products until she found one that wasn't too nauseating: Lao Tze Foot Cream.

Lao Tze, or Lao Tse, of Laozi, Johnstone told her, was a Chinese philosopher from the sixth century AD "Spring and Autumn Period," and is generally considered the founder of Taoism. According to legend, Lao Tze roamed around the country giving the people wise advice, which none of them particularly wanted to hear. Disappointed, he decided to withdraw from the civilized world. At China's western border he was stopped by a sentry who convinced him to commit his ideas to paper. That book became the *Tao Te Ching*, or *The Book of the Tao and Inner Strength.*

"Cool, isn't it, that there's a foot ointment named after him," said Johnstone. "I bet he'd never have predicted that, eight thousand years ago."

On the second morning, Johnstone told her about her treatment. From June 1991 until February 1992, she had come to the center for an hour once a week. Johnstone had dug her progress reports out of the archives; she leafed through them cursorily. "Minnie says she is still afraid of a bomb at her school," she read somewhere, and, "Minnie doesn't feel like talking today. Instead she's making a drawing of my face, signed with the words 'shit doctor.'"

There were also tape recordings of her hypnosis session, digitized by Bob. Johnstone persuaded her to listen to them, making her sit down in the armchair in the studio again.

Through the speakers came her own voice as a seven-year-old, clear, untouched by time. The younger version of herself described in the most minute detail the process of going into a trance and being guided by the voice on the tape. She described scenes she could see in the distance, which didn't seem any less real than if they were real life, but real in a different way. She also meticulously depicted the places where she had found the four wallets. In all four cases, it seemed, they'd been left lying somewhere unattended, probably in a moment of inattention on the part of their owners, so that the girl was able to snatch them without any trouble.

"Why do you think I did it?" she asked him the second night. They were strolling through a park lit with green LED-lights, taking a wheeling and tail-wagging Frank Lloyd Wright for a walk. "Snatching those wallets, I mean. There seems to be a certain logic to all of it, but this I don't get."

"No," said Johnstone. "To be honest, I never managed to figure it out either. You yourself never opened any of the wallets. I went and had a talk with your teacher. She told me that three of the four wallets were returned to their owners by the school. After some insistence on my part she agreed to give me their names. None of them had anything to do with you or one another. The last wallet belonged to a foreigner. Your mother returned that one on her own initiative to the hotel where he was staying; she'd found the hotel's business card in the wallet. It was on her way to work, she'd told the teacher, it was no trouble. But it *is* strange, yes. I've always thought it didn't all add up."

Minnie didn't know if she should be mad at her mother, who had never told her any of this. Not about the months in the incubator, not about Minnie's alarming muteness when she was a baby, nor about the bomb scare or the stolen wallets seven years later. There must be even more she didn't know, but she didn't really care. It was too long ago, it made no difference now. She had her own life, and her mother had hers, nobody needed to be rescued, they were the kind of people who knew how to take care of themselves.

Johnstone tossed a tennis ball in the air; Frank showed not the slightest interest.

"Dumb dog," said Johnstone. "Although he's also smart, in a certain way. For instance, when he twists around, he doesn't always do it in the same direction, but alternates left and right, so in the end it comes out even."

"Do you really believe in those cycles?" asked Minnie.

He stared at her, astonished.

"Do you think I've spent more than twenty years pursuing something I don't even believe in?"

*

Her house felt chilly when Minnie returned to it after those days at Johnstone's. As if it had turned its back on her, she thought, picking up some things and putting them back, although that did nothing to heal the rift. Her life suddenly seemed split into before her fall through the ice and after.

She was tied to her project for at least another month. She spent a great deal of time at the window, peering at the window across the way, where she sometimes thought she could see something move. Every so often she'd feel the excitement of that first day again when she'd felt his presence in that café along the waterfront, where she'd ordered a cup of coffee and pretended to be a woman reading a book, but for the most part it started to feel routine. That waitress-performance artist in New York was right: at some point, if you played a certain role long enough, it became part of who you were. Maybe this was the very opposite of a performance, she thought: *not* to be present as a performer, to fade out against the background of your own life.

She had bought a book called *Pregnancy from Week to Week*, possibly in the hope the photographer would see it. The book showed her how the undifferentiated little lump of life was transformed at an exponential rate into a creature with human features. In the eighth week, she read, it was two centimeters long. It was still just cartilage, but a skeleton was starting to form. Even the sex organs were beginning to develop, and inside the relatively large head, the first intimation of a brain was becoming visible.

The bouts of nausea were growing less, only to be replaced by chronic exhaustion, which almost made her long for the vomiting sessions over the toilet bowl. She napped whole afternoons away on the couch, only to wake up in a daze as the sun sank below the horizon. Then she'd lie restlessly awake all night, finally passing out in the early morning hours, upon which the whole ordeal started all over again. More than once she was on the point of crossing the street and ringing the bell until the photographer answered the door. He was the father, for fuck's sake, she didn't have to be the only one going through hell here.

A week after the rescue, Bob rang her doorbell. Johnstone had sent him over to invite her to a dinner at his house, that same evening. It was the start of a weekly ritual: by the light of the menorah (the only heirloom he had inherited from his father) they ate goat stew and vanilla ice cream sundaes. Afterward they'd take Frank out for a walk through deserted streets and parks, which brought out in Minnie an urge to talk. She told him about the déjà-vus she'd had these past few weeks, the episode of the two lambs, the strange still-life of flowerpots and tree bark in the barn, and the way the shadows fell precisely in between the roof rafters. Johnstone would nod at set intervals, but other than that said very little. So this is what therapists do, thought Minnie; they keep quiet and just nod, for as long as it takes for their patients to start understanding themselves, or at least until they begin to feel less like strangers to themselves.

After their walk, Bob would carry a tea tray into the studio, where Minnie and Johnstone would sit and listen to obscure bands, ending with a few tracks from Beyoncé, for whom Johnstone confessed to have a huge soft spot.

"Did you know that Beyoncé has everything she does recorded for posterity?" he said at the end of one of these sessions. "Every photo, literally every single photo that exists of her is stored in a huge archive. You could call her a control freak, but I prefer to regard it as an artwork; the construction of a life that's almost larger than life itself."

It reminded Minnie of Francis Bacon's studio, which she had once visited in Dublin. Originally located in London, it was moved lock, stock and barrel to the land of his birth some years after his death. The studio's landscape, because it *was* a landscape, one that had over the course of time evolved in a more or less natural way, had been reconstructed down to the last detail. A whole team of restorers and archaeologists had worked on it. Even the dust had been labeled, packed into boxes and shipped. Everything you saw was searchable and described in a gigantic database. A mammoth job, especially once you realized that the studio's every square centimeter was spattered in paint or buried in junk. Minnie didn't know which was more absurd: the studio's post-apocalyptic condition, or the fact that this unspeakable chaos was a literal recreation of the original. Was it an ironic commentary on the preoccupation with documenting and authenticity? The last word in artificiality? Or a serious attempt to build the most comprehensive artist's catalog in the world? The great Bacon, sitting on his throne in the underworld, must find it hilarious.

"The thing about Beyoncé's archive is absurd, of course," said Johnstone, "but it does say something about the world we live in."

He told her he was currently obsessed with surveillance and privacy, which he considered *the* philosophical conundrums of our era.

"We're all being watched," he said, "or rather: we are all *allowing* ourselves to be watched. Practically none of us seem to have a problem with putting our entire private lives up on the internet, and no one's particularly bothered about the surveillance cameras everywhere either. There doesn't seem to be any real alarm about this, which is something most science fiction authors of the past completely failed to foresee. I'm waiting for the day, and it's bound to come soon, when the great revelation comes that we've been spied on, tapped, documented by our own governments all this time. Oddly enough, I don't think people will be really worried even then. Something even more dire has to happen first, something that affects every individual citizen, I've been racking my brain over what it could be."

Minnie was tempted to tell him about her project. She was sure he'd have appreciated it: an artist being stalked by a photographer who didn't know he was the father of the child in her belly, and was recording its existence well before its entry into the world.

*

March 21 was both the first day of spring and the last day of the project. Heavy grey clouds hung low over the city, the day was dark as night, or maybe it was just the weather modeling itself after her mood. She was counting the minutes until her meeting with Specht. For the hundredth time she went over in her mind what might await her there. Maybe the photographer had dropped off reams of photographs; maybe he hadn't delivered a single one ("a number to be determined by himself" was how she had had it worded in the contract. It had only occurred to her later that it could also mean none.)

At eight p.m. she rang the brass bell of Prinsengracht 997.

"Come in," said Specht, opening the door so quickly that she suspected he'd been standing there waiting for her to arrive. She followed the little dachshund-man into his office, which to her surprise had been almost stripped bare. Where there had been a heavy oak desk, there was now a stark white designer contraption with two ditto chairs. The many filing cabinets were nowhere in sight.

"My new girlfriend is an interior designer," said Specht. Minnie almost fell off her chair at what he'd confided; not only was it personal, but it was expressed in the first person. That girlfriend must be doing him some good, she thought, looking at Specht, who did indeed seem a lot more relaxed.

"Anyway," he said, squaring his shoulders, visibly embarrassed by his all-too spontaneous outburst, "I was supposed to have a meeting with the photographer yesterday morning, but he never showed up. Later in the day I did find this envelope in my mailbox."

He pushed an A3 envelope across the table after pulling it right out of the wall. It took a second look for Minnie to realize that the entire wall was made up of invisible file drawers. Whoever that girlfriend of his was, she sure knew her stuff.

"I shall now leave the room," said Specht, "so that you may peruse the contents at your leisure."

Inside the envelope there was a smaller envelope containing a handwritten letter, which she unfolded, smoothing the creases by running her hand a few times over it on the desktop, as if to rid the contents, whatever they might be, of any snags or hitches.

Amsterdam, March 20, 2012

Dear Minnie,

First, I must apologize. I haven't fulfilled my part of the bargain. I did not follow you with my camera for three weeks, only for a few hours. The sum you paid me, your portion of the *Vogue* shoot in fact, as well as the sum due to you for breach of contract, will be paid into your bank account this afternoon. What follows is a report on what happened, not an attempt to justify it.

On Saturday, February 11, when you left your house in the late morning, I started following you, slowly, in a car, with all my lenses on the back seat. When I realized you were heading for that big pond, I parked the car around the corner. From that point on I continued following you on foot.

Through my telephoto lens I saw you ordering a coffee in that café, and then opening a book. When, with a sense for drama, you dropped your coffee cup and it smashed on the floor, I felt I was watching a Hitchcockian mystery. Who is that woman, I thought, and what's the matter with her? As I said: it was just as if I were watching a movie. There had to be a plot, I imagined, a conspiracy of some sort. You ran out of view, I saw the waitress shake her head as she began sweeping up the shards as if it was something she was used to. She left you a fresh cup of coffee on your table, which you stared at in alarm—my telephoto lens is very good—as if you believed that cup had reincarnated itself. You had a short exchange with the waitress, and then I saw you storming out of there as if the devil were on your heels.

You walked away from the café and headed straight for the water's edge. You stood there for a while, a lone silhouette against that huge expanse, one human against the elements. With my mega lens I could get up so close that I saw you frown, as if a multitude of thoughts were clashing inside your head. It occurred to me suddenly that I loved you, although it was hard to say who you were just then, separate from the actress playing a role in the movie playing before me.

I wasn't too alarmed at first when you took your first step onto the ice. I had distanced myself too much from the scene to worry. But then you took some more steps, and you kept going until you were at least three yards from shore. That's weird, I thought to myself, that ice is obviously much too thin. Only then did it occur to me that you might actually fall through.

I thought of calling out to you, but I couldn't, I was, like you, playing a part in the script. I couldn't just step out of my role: the only way this was going to work was if we both kept our side of the bargain—not for nothing had we spelled it out meticulously in a contract. It also occurred to me you were doing it on purpose, to test me. Even when the ice broke and I saw you fall in, I didn't really believe it was real. I went on gazing through my lens compulsively, clicking, zooming, a photographer's reflexes.

When you didn't come back up after ten seconds or so, the truth bored its way into my consciousness. This wasn't a movie; you were drowning. I stood there paralyzed, and then, instead of rushing to your rescue, I turned and ran.

Robotically I drove back to the apartment opposite yours, where I'd been camping out for two days. Once there I collapsed. My whole body began shivering uncontrollably, and all I could think was: Oh my God, oh my God, I've let her drown.

I paced up and down by the window for hours, in the hope that the light in your living room would come on and you'd walk in. I stayed up all night long, but my hope that you'd come home began to seem increasingly unrealistic, and by morning I was sure you were dead. Dead and blue and frozen, your body discovered by some jogger. I stayed in the apartment the next day and following night, scouring the Internet for any reports of an accident.

The day after that, in the late morning, you came home. I hadn't slept and was frazzled and drained, but there you were. You were wearing a strange red outfit, but you looked good, healthy, more robust than I remembered. More...present, somehow.

And now for the weirdest thing: I just wouldn't buy it. I had convinced myself that you were gone, and not even your manifest return could convince me otherwise. On a certain level I did buy it, naturally, rationally I knew you still existed, but that didn't much matter.

I gathered my things and returned home. Three days later I received a phone call from Italian *Vogue*. Could I jump on a plane immediately for a photo shoot in Rome? Their photographer was out with acute appendicitis. I didn't hesitate. After a three-day whirl of sets, models and production assistants running every which way, I stayed in Rome for another two weeks on my own. I wandered through the old city in a daze, going into every church, every palace, every museum I happened to pass. I read every brochure, I stuffed my head with information about every king, emperor, revolt, pope and artist the city had ever known. I visited the Sistine Chapel six times, gazing up at the ceiling until my neck hurt while slowly getting crushed by my fellow tourists, who like me were in search of an experience they could add to their other experiences, so that they wouldn't die without first having *lived*.

I left you to die that afternoon. I am a person who is capable of letting another person die. That is something I shall have to learn to live with, just as most people sooner or later discover something about themselves they have to learn to live with.

Good luck and be well, kiddo.

THE LINE AT THE CHECK-IN COUNTER was long and consisted of a mix of Dutch, Russians and Chinese travelers. After a flight via Moscow and Beijing lasting over thirty-five hours, Minnie would land in Ürümqi, the capital of the autonomous region of Xinjian in Northwest China. There she was to board a train that would take her farther west. On Google Maps she had seen that the part of China between Ürümqi and the Kazakhstan border was desolate, and this was confirmed by travel blogs written in Comic Sans describing an endless, arid plateau with the odd deserted village scattered about, which the traveler was advised to leave behind as quickly as possible on her way to more exciting destinations.

Minnie had tried to find a tube of the Lao Tze Foot Cream in the Rituals store at Schiphol Airport.

"We *must* have it somewhere," the store manager said in a voice betraying some panic. "Turning the daily routine into a lovely ritual is our mission."

He disappeared into the stockroom, returning ten minutes later defeated. "No Lao Tze," he said. "I am so terribly sorry. Could I perhaps steer you to another luxury product?"

Mainly to save him from his mortification, she'd bought a bottle of Wu Wei Bath Foam, which he insisted on gift-wrapping for her.

"An excellent choice," he said as he handed it to her. "In the Tao, Wu Wei means something along the lines of 'doing by not-doing.'"

"A semantic paradox," said Minnie.

"A feeling of pure relaxation," said the manager.

She had the photo with her in her carry-on luggage. It was taken at the moment that the ice gave way, the brief splinter of time that had turned everything upside down. She was standing with her back to the photographer, her arms spread like wings, as if at the very last second she'd been trying to take off, to escape what was already inexorably set into motion.

It is a common storyline in books and films: people who leave their entire life behind, disappear without a trace, start anew. It's an attractive idea: a life on *Rewind*, everything in reverse order, so that it starts erasing itself, until you're back to being a brand-new baby again, or even less than that, a fetus, without an epidermis, without fat, without a skeleton, without brain folds. A creature that hasn't yet made any choices, hasn't left anything behind, has never yet had to deal with dumb luck, nor any silly moments of pure joy. To start afresh from that point forward. Without parents to screw you up, without childish fears, without navigation blunders. To choose your own name, and instead of slowly developing into who you are, to already *be* it, a do-it-yourself kit without missing parts, miscalculations or construction errors. No arbitrariness. No obligations. To be nobody, to be nowhere. *All the fish needs is to get lost in the water.*

The line hadn't moved in ten minutes. The people around her were growing restless, they wanted to move forward, to get on with it, but the only place left to go was sideways. Arms and legs spilled outside the queue, suitcases, backpacks, little kids. They sought the confines of their cage and rammed at it, harder and harder until they were finally free, deluding themselves that it was due to their efforts.

ACKNOWLEDGMENTS

I am—both directly and less so—indebted to a great many authors and songwriters. Echoes of their work can be heard reverberating throughout this book, and the reader may spot these herself. There are two, however, whose influence I want to acknowledge here. Scattered throughout the book are quotes from Samuel Beckett's *Happy Days*. I have also taken quotes from the poem *"Countless lives inhabit us"* by Fernando Pessoa/Ricardo Reis [in Richard Zenith's translation].

AUTHOR BIOGRAPHY

NIÑA WEIJERS (b. 1987) studied literary theory in Amsterdam and Dublin. She has published short stories, essays and articles in various literary magazines, such as *Das Magazin, De Gids* and *De Revisor*. She is a regular contributor to the weekly magazine *De Groene Amsterdammer*, and an editor of *De Gids*.

The Consequences (De consequenties) was first published in Dutch by Atlas Contact in May 2014. It won the Anton Wachter Prize 2014 for best debut novel, the Opzij Feminist Literature Prize, the Lucy B. & C.W. van der Hoogt Prize for a debut, and was shortlisted for the Libris Prize and the Golden Boekenuil, the two most important Dutch and Flemish literary prizes. For the latter, she took home the coveted Reader's Choice Award.

The book has now been translated into German (Suhrkamp), French (Actes Sud), English, and Czech (Kniha Zlín).

HESTER VELMANS is a translator specializing in contemporary Dutch and French literature. Her translation of Renate Dorrestein's *A Heart of Stone* won the Vondel Prize in 2001; in early 2014 she was awarded an NEA Translation Fellowship to translate the neglected novelist Herman Franke. She is also the author of the popular children's books *Isabel of the Whales* and *Jessaloup's Song*.